24.95

NIGHTCRAWLERS

"NAMELESS DETECTIVE" MYSTERIES BY BILL PRONZINI

NIGHTCRAWLERS

A Nameless Detective Novel

Bill Pronzini

A Tom Doherty Associates Book
New York

NIGHTCRAWLERS

Copyright © 2005 by Bill Pronzini

This book is printed on acid-free paper.

Book design by Jane Adele Regina

A Forge Book
Published by Tom Doherty Associates, LLC
175 Fifth Avenue
New York, NY 10010

www.tor.com

Forge® is a registered trademark of Tom Doherty Associates, LLC.

Library of Congress Cataloging-in-Publication Data

Pronzini, Bill.
    Nightcrawlers / Bill Pronzini. — 1st ed.
        p. cm
    "A Tom Doherty Associates book."
    ISBN 0-765-30931-9 (acid-free paper)
    EAN 978-0765-30931-0
    1. Nameless Detective (Fictitious character) — Fiction. 2. Private Investigators — California — San Francisco — Fiction. 3. Gay men — Crimes against — Fiction. 4. San Francisco (Calif.) — Fiction. I. Title.

PS3566.R67N45 2005
813'.54 — dc22

                                                                            2004056323

First Edition: March 2005

Printed in the United States of America

0   9   8   7   6   5   4   3   2   1

*For the better half
of the Mulzinis*

ACKNOWLEDGMENTS

With thanks to Michael Seidman for his usual astute editorial comments, and to all the faithful readers who have helped to keep the "Nameless" series alive and well for more than thirty-five years.

NIGHTCRAWLERS

PROLOGUE

FRIDAY NIGHT—SAN FRANCISCO

"**T**here he is," Tommy said.

Bix squinted past him through the passenger-side window. "Yeah. Our meat, all right. Lookit that fag coat, fag mustache, the way he walks."

"Nobody else around."

"Perfect, man."

"You ready?"

Bix giggled the way he always did when he was high, pulled his Giants cap down low on his forehead. "Hot to trot."

"Okay. Let's do it."

They rolled on past, slow. Downhill a ways, the headlights picked out an alleyway between a couple of the big old houses, both of them dark. Bix wheeled the pickup over to the curb in front of the alley. Before it came to a full stop, Tommy was out and moving with the Little League bat under his coat. Bix had to yank on the emergency brake, cut the lights and the engine before he jumped out, and then he got his big feet tangled and almost fell down in the street. Christ. Slow and clumsy and stupid, stoned or sober.

Tommy moved up on the sidewalk, taking it easy, letting Bix catch up. "Hey, pretty boy," he called, not too loud.

The faggot stopped. Tommy moved over when Bix got there, one on either side, facing him, not crowding him yet. Pretty boy, yeah. But not for much longer. Excitement began to run inside Tommy, drying his mouth, putting sweat on his palms. Oh man, oh baby!

"What's your hurry, sweet thing?" Bix asked the queer.

"It's late and I'm going home."

"Pretty late, all right. Where you been?"

"Working. Tending bar."

"Yeah. Fruit drinks for Castro fruits, right?"

"What do you want?" Cool, a little pissed, but not scared. Not yet.

"What you think we want?" Tommy said.

"All I have on me is five dollars—"

"Hey, you got us wrong. We're not after your money."

"That's right," Bix said. "Something else we want."

". . . Oh, so that's it. Well, you've got the wrong person."

"Uh-uh. We don't think so."

"I don't do that kind of thing."

Bix giggled.

"I mean it, I'm not a street hustler. I happen to be in a stable relationship—"

"Stable?" Bix giggled again. "You live in a stable? You and your boyfriend bugger each other in a stable?"

"Shut up," Tommy snapped at him. He said to Pretty Boy, "Lying queer bastard."

Pretty Boy made a disgusted noise and started to push ahead. They blocked him, crowding him a little now.

"What's the idea? I want to go home."

Bix said, "Not yet, sweet thing."

"Come on, just leave me alone."

"We got other plans."

"If you don't get out of my way—"

"What'll you do? Pee in your panties?"

"I'm not afraid of you."

"No? You oughta be, boyfucker."

"I'll yell. I'll wake up the whole neighborhood."

"Uh-uh. No, you won't."

Pretty Boy opened his mouth, but they were all set for him. It was just what they were waiting for, just like the other times. Bix got him in a bear hug from behind and Tommy jammed the greasy rag into his mouth, all the way in. He started grunting and choking, flailing around, trying to kick them with his twinkle toes. Tommy put a stop to that with a punch in the gut, a knee in the crotch. Pretty Boy doubled up, sagged; a moan slid out of him sweet as music.

They dragged him into the alleyway, threw him down, watched him crawl around in a little circle like a dog that'd just been run over. Then Bix started giving him the boot, one two three kick, one two three kick. "Hey," Tommy said, "you don't get all the fun," and he hauled out the Little League bat and went to work himself.

Oh man, oh baby!

The crack of bone breaking damn near gave him a hard-on.

SATURDAY NIGHT—VALLEJO

There she is, he thought.

He knew it as soon as he saw her. The right age, no older than six. Slim, her hair straight and parted in the middle and braided into pigtails. Mostly white skin like cream with a little coffee mixed in. Sweet little smile. Pretty.

Just like Angie.

The woman with her was past fifty, heavyset, slow-moving. And black, all black, not mixed blood like the girl. Probably not her mother. Grandmother, aunt, maybe a babysitter. Not too careful, either. Didn't hold the girl's hand, let her run ahead or veer off or lag behind as they crossed the parking lot. Kept looking straight ahead—worrying on something, not paying much attention to her surroundings. He might be able to take the kid right here, tonight, when they came out. If not, he'd follow them home. There'd be another opportunity soon enough. The hard part was finding her. Now that he had, he could afford to relax and be patient.

He watched them enter the supermarket. Might as well go in himself. He was out of bottled water, almost out of cigarettes; might be enough time to stock up. He was tired of sitting, too, muscles all cramped up. He'd been in the Suburban five hours straight tonight, since four o'clock. Long hours every night after work, longer hours on the weekends, for three weeks now. Driving around, driving around—San Francisco, the Peninsula, San Jose, East Bay, North Bay. Shopping centers, strip malls, parks, day-care centers, anywhere he could think of looking. Two or three that'd seemed right from a distance, but weren't when he got up close. Too skinny, too young, too old, too dark, too light. He knew he'd find her sooner or later, so he hadn't been frustrated or anything. But all the driving and looking had taken their toll. The headaches were back and getting worse again. Not as bad as when he got angry, not so bad that he couldn't think clearly, but bad enough so the Percodan didn't help anymore. Right behind his eyes, so much pressure that sometimes it felt like they'd pop right out of their sockets. He wondered if he needed glasses. Maybe he'd go see an eye doctor later on.

He swung out of the SUV. He'd parked in a shadowed space off to one side, where he had a clear view of the entrance. He pinched his eyes with thumb and forefinger, flexed his back and shoulders, got his legs moving and went inside.

The bright fluorescent glare made him squint and blink. The woman and the little girl weren't at any of the checkout stands or in any of the nearby aisles. Soft drinks and bottled water to his left; he went that way, picked up two quarts of Crystal Geyser, and then moved back and sideways in front of the dairy cases. Still no sign of them until he reached the produce section.

He saw the woman first. Basket looped over one arm, feeling up tomatoes and paying no mind to the little girl. She was running circles around a bin of corn, pigtails flying, playing some kind of game like Angie used to do. He walked by, slow and close. She looked up and saw him. Put on the brakes, gave him a gap-toothed smile that lit up that sweet face like a jack-o'-lantern, then started running again. His throat tightened, his mouth tasted brassy.

Angie, he thought.

He went on up to the express checkout, bought a couple of packs of Marlboros and the bottled water. Outside, the cold air hit him with a rush and made him realize he was sweating.

He opened one of the bottles, took a long swig. Once the brassy taste was gone and the sweat quit oozing out, he was all right again. The ache behind his eyes was starting to ease some, too. That was a good sign. He might be able to sleep tonight, might not even dream.

In the Suburban he lit a cigarette, sipped water between drags. Waiting the way a cat waits—waiting for the good thing to happen. Who was it had said that to him about the way cats waited? Mia? He couldn't stand cats, but Mia'd always liked them. He remembered one time when the three of them . . . when he and Angie and Mia . . .

It was another five minutes before they came out, the woman carrying two plastic grocery sacks, the little girl running and skipping ahead. Their car, some kind of old four-door sedan, was in the first row. The woman hesitated when they got there, as if maybe she'd forgotten something. "Go back inside," he said out loud, "leave Angie in the car."

But she didn't. It wasn't going to be that easy. She was just fumbling for the keys. She found them, unlocked the car, and both of them got in and stayed in. The sedan's engine started, the lights came on. He had the Suburban clear of the space and easing forward before she finished backing up, and he was right behind her when she pulled out of the lot.

No problem following the sedan. She drove as slow as she moved. And it wasn't far to go—less than half a mile through a bunch of residential streets to a single-family home within spitting distance of a neighborhood park. The sedan stopped in the driveway, the woman and the little girl got out and went into the house. He didn't need the number; he'd recognize the place when he came back, couldn't miss that tree with the tree-house in it over in the side yard. All he'd need was the name of this street and the cross street up ahead where the park was.

Tomorrow he'd come back, daytime and after dark both. And as many days and nights after that as it took to find out who else lived in the house, how often the girl was alone in the yard or in the park or on her way to and from school. Pick his spot, wait for just the right time. He had a feeling it wouldn't take long.

When the time came, he hoped she wouldn't make too much of a fuss.

1

I couldn't seem to get used to the location of the new offices. The first week after we moved in, I found myself twice on successive mornings heading toward O'Farrell Street instead of south of Market. Automatic pilot. I'd occupied the old space for a lot of years, dating back to my partnership with Eberhardt. A lot of years and a lot of memories, some bad—like the events of last Christmas that had been the catalyst for the move—but most of them fairly good. Funny, but I was having more difficulty letting go of the musty, crusty O'Farrell loft than I'd had giving up the Pacific Heights flat I'd leased for three decades. No regrets or backward looks there, after I handed over the key on January first.

There was nothing wrong with the new digs. They were at least a couple of steps upscale, in fact. Larger than the loft by half, three good-sized, newly renovated, partly furnished rooms plus private bathroom on the second floor of an old, three-storied, salmon-colored building on South Park. Above us we had an art studio, below us we had a firm of architects, and outside the front windows we had a view of the little tree-shaded park and the architectural mixed bag that housed private residences, cafés, and small businesses like ours. We also had a five-year lease at a surprisingly reasonable monthly nut. Ever since the dot-com industry collapse, prime office space in the city had gone begging and real estate firms and holding companies were only too glad to cut a deal in order to fill a vacancy long-term. An even better deal had been offered to us in Multimedia Gulch, the section between Potrero Hill and the Mission that had been a dot-com haven during the short-lived boom and was now something of a business ghost town, but neither Tamara nor I had much cared for the location. Too far from downtown, for one thing; and there was a small but persistent stigma attached to the area that extended to new firms moving in, as if a Gulch address were a brand of eventual failure.

South Park, on the other hand, was a well-regarded, ellipzoidal chunk of Bohemian-era San Francisco tucked between Second and Third, Brannan and Bryant. In the 1860s it had been the center of the Rincon Hill residential district, home of the city's wealthiest families. After the seat of wealth and fashion shifted to Nob Hill, South Park had had an up-and-down history—mostly down until the 1970s, when urban renewal created SoMa and South Beach and turned South Park back into a desirable high spot. From a business point of view it had a couple of downsides: It was near the Bay Bridge approach and inclined to be noisy, and street parking was at a premium and garage facilities neither in close proximity nor reasonably priced. But those were minor compared to the upsides of location, size, and cheap rent. The new offices were only half a dozen blocks from the financial district, another half dozen from the Ferry Building and the waterfront and the bridge.

Tamara was the one who had orchestrated the move. Haggled with the real estate agent, arranged the transfer of the few furnishings and other equipment worth salvaging from O'Farrell Street, set up the new offices. All Jake Runyon, the agency's new field operative, and I did was some donkey work and arranging of personal space. That was fine with me. Tamara was good at handling details, and she had a long-range vision as to what the agency could and should be if it was going to continue to grow. South Park had been her idea; so had an aggressive advertising campaign to go along with the usual change-of-address notification sent out to our client list.

I suppose that was the underlying reason why, after three months, I still couldn't quite adapt to the new digs. On O'Farrell Street and in the offices prior, the agency had been mine alone—I was the sole proprietor for most of the thirty-plus years I'd been in the detective business. Here on South Park, the agency was Tamara's. New surroundings, new direction. The passing of the baton, the old and settled giving way to the young and ambitious. Fundamentally I had no problem with that; hell, if I had I wouldn't have decided to semiretire and make her a full partner. I was still one of the bosses, nothing of importance was done without my input, and yet I couldn't help a certain feeling of displacement, of being left behind. Made me feel sad now and then. Maybe it was just a function of incipient old age and a lifelong resistance to change. Kerry thought so, and she's a lot smarter than I am.

In any event, there was no question that Tamara knew what she was doing. At the ripe old age of twenty-six she's also smarter than I am. The move and the advertising had paid off much more quickly than I'd expected. Now, in early April, business was booming to the point where we were probably going to have to hire yet another operative to help handle the caseload. As it was, I was working four days and sometimes a full week—nearly twice the number of hours I'd promised Kerry, Emily, and myself when I semiretired. Runyon was putting in sixty-hour weeks, but he was a recent widower, estranged from his son by his also-deceased first wife, and a workaholic. Tamara logged in even more time than that. Now that her cellist boyfriend, Horace, had moved to Philadelphia, and she was living alone, she'd taken to compensating in the same workaholic fashion as Runyon. She'd even begun to do a little of the fieldwork, after hours, ostensibly because she wanted to learn more about that end of the business, but mainly, I suspected, because it helped keep loneliness at bay.

So here I was at South Park bright and early on Monday morning, ready to tackle another full day's workload. The desk in the big anteroom was empty; that was the one Runyon used when he was in, which wasn't often. Right now he was in L.A., on a skip trace connected to a homicide trial for a prominent local defense attorney. The room was big, sunny on sunny days like this one, the walls dove-gray with what Kerry called "black accents," the new furniture stylish black leather-and-chrome. One of these days, if Tamara had her way, there'd be another desk and a secretary/receptionist behind it. I had no doubt that it would happen in the foreseeable future. Nor any doubt that under her guidance the agency would one day be as large or larger than McCone Investigations, down on the Embarcadero—maybe spawn a couple of satellites in other cities.

She was not only a smart businesswoman, she had ambition and an entrepreneurial turn of mind.

The two private offices at the rear were side by side, the one on the west a little larger—the bathroom had been added on to the east-side office—and with the better view. She'd insisted I take the larger one; I insisted she have it. We'd wrangled a little, but as the senior partner I had the final say. When I walked into the east office this morning, I could see her at her desk through the connecting door, which we kept open unless one of us was with a client. She was in her usual pose, hunched over her computer keyboard, a study today in dark brown and spring yellow. There'd been a time when she dressed like a character in a bad street movie, but that was long past. Now she wore suits and blouses and shoes with designer labels and had her hair done by professionals instead of self-styling it with an eggbeater or whatever she'd used.

She'd changed, Ms. Corbin had, in the five years since she'd first come to work for me. And considerably in the four months since the holiday ordeal in our old offices on O'Farrell Street—a hostage situation in which she and Runyon and I had come close to dying at the hands of a madman armed with an arsenal of weapons. That experience seemed to have had a profound effect on her. She was less prickly now, less inclined to grumble and to sudden mood swings, more coolly professional in her dealings with clients. More self-assured, as if she understood herself better and was more comfortable in her own skin. Even her speech was less peppered with the Ebonic and slang phrases she'd sometimes wielded like tools of self-defense. She still had her sense of humor, but it didn't have the edge it once had and she didn't put me on quite as often as she once did. In a way I missed the old Tamara, but I had even greater admiration and affection for the new one.

She was wrapped up in what she was doing and didn't notice me at first. I shed my coat, thumped my briefcase down on the desk, and then entered her office.

"Morning, kiddo."

"Morning," she said without looking up. "I heard you come in."

"Sure you did. Ever vigilant."

"Uh-huh."

"How's that for an agency motto? 'Ever Vigilant.'"

"Retro. Like 'We Never Sleep.'"

"Don't let anybody who works for Pinkerton hear you say that. How was your weekend?"

She said, "Quiet," and then amended it to "Busy. Worked most of Saturday."

"Now you're picking up my bad habits. What happened to your social life?"

"Club scene? Guys with booze on their breath hitting on me? Who needs it?"

"There are other things to do with your friends."

"Not when they've all got love lives."

"Maybe you should take a few days off, fly to Philadelphia."

"Too much work to do here."

"Can't Horace get away?"

"Symphony season's already started back there. He's got no time for anything except that cello of his."

That sounded a little ominous. I wanted to ask her if everything was okay with her and Horace, but I didn't do it. She'd been reticent about their relationship lately, and prodding her would not have gotten me anywhere. Three and a half months apart is a long time; biweekly phone conversations just aren't enough to keep a long-distance romance burning hot. It had to be a strain on both of them. In fact . . .

"Can I ask you a personal question, Tamara?"

"Long as it's not about Horace."

"It's not. I'm just curious . . . have you been on a diet?"

"How come you asking that?"

"Well, you're looking pretty svelte these days."

"Didn't think you'd noticed."

"Trained professionals notice everything. Ever vigilant."

"Uh-huh. Well, I've lost twelve pounds so far."

"By choice?"

"What, you think I quit eating 'cause I'm pining away for Horace?"

"No, no . . ."

"Well, don't worry. I'm losing weight for me, nobody else. Just got tired of looking at myself naked in the mirror. Love handles are okay, but I had bulges big enough for a couple of 49ers' linemen to hold on to."

I let that pass. "What kind of diet are you on?"

"Slim•Fast and rabbit food. Yummy. But I'm used to it, now."

"How much more are you planning to lose?"

"Eight or ten pounds. Until I can wear a size eight without looking like a sack of cookie dough."

"Hot stuff."

"Yeah, well, there's still my big booty and my face. Can't do much about either of those."

"What's wrong with your face?"

"Hah. No competition for Halle Berry, that's for sure."

"Who's Halle Berry?"

"You're kidding, right?"

"I'm not kidding. Who's Halle Berry?"

"Where you been lately? First African-American woman to win a best actress Oscar. *Real* hot stuff."

I said, "Oh," because I see maybe one new film a year that Kerry recommends, avoid newspapers and the TV news, and pay no attention to actors or the Oscars.

"Lot of modern film critics think Louise Beavers should've won one way back in the 1930s," Tamara said, "but you know how blacks were treated in those days. In and out of Hollywood."

"Who's Louise Beavers?"

"Come on now. Don't tell me you never saw *Imitation of Life*. As many old movies as you scope on TV?"

"That tearjerker with Claudette Colbert?"

"*And* Louise Beavers. Delilah. Everydamnbody overlooks her and she stole the picture."

"I've seen it, but not in a long time. Since when do *you* watch old movies?"

"Since I was about ten, if they have black folks in 'em. Don't know me as well as you think you do, huh?"

"Evidently not. Sorry."

"For what?" She gave me one of her looks. "Beavers," she said.

"Right, Louise Beavers."

"I'm thinking other beavers now. You know who Beaver Cleaver was?"

"No. Who?"

"*Leave It to Beaver*. 'Oh, Ward, we just have to do something about the Beaver.'"

"Huh?"

"Take that two ways," she said.

"Take what two ways?"

"Beaver."

"I don't get what you mean."

"Don't you know what a beaver is?"

"Of course I know."

"Well?"

"Fur-bearing mammal. Buck teeth, flat tail, and dam-building skills."

"I mean the other kind."

"There isn't any other kind."

"That's what you think."

"What're you talking about?"

"Beaver. Slang term."

"Slang term for what?"

"You really don't know, huh?"

"I really don't know."

"I'll bet Kerry knows." Mischievous old-Tamara grin. "Why don't you ask her tonight when you get home?"

"I'll do that," I lied. If I did, judging from that grin, I would regret it. Sometimes ignorance really is bliss. "So what's on the agenda for today? Any new business?"

"Nothing so far," Tamara said. "But I turned up a possible lead on the deadbeat dad case."

"Which case is that? Oh, the split-fee from the Ballard Agency?"

"Yup. Turns out George DeBrissac has a cousin who lives in Antioch and owns a second house in San Leandro. Rental property. Five months since the last tenants left, but it was taken off the market three months ago and there's no record of it being rented at that time or since."

"How long since DeBrissac skipped Portland?"

"Just about three months."

"Could be coincidence."

"Hah," she said.

Right. In our business, the old "if it looks like a duck and quacks like a duck, it's probably a duck" axiom usually applies. This was particularly true in deadbeat dad cases. They tend to be the easiest skips we're called on to find, since the individuals are generally middle-class types with little or no criminal history and some traceable source of steady income. George De-Brissac was a well-paid freelance accountant with Bay Area ties; it stood to reason that when he ran out on his ex-wife and two kids in Portland, he would head straight for northern California. The Ballard Detective Agency up there, hired by the ex-wife, had figured the same thing; so they'd called us and farmed out the hard part of the job for half the fee, one of those cooperative deals that become necessary when the client isn't wealthy enough and the fee isn't large enough for the primary agency to send one of its own operatives out of state. The case was Tamara's, for the most part. She hadn't had any luck yet in finding out where DeBrissac was working, if he was working, but now maybe it didn't matter. The relative's house in San Leandro looked like a strong lead—just the sort of place a not-too-imaginative skip would pick to hole up.

I hoped so. The quicker we wrapped this up, the better. Split-fee cases can be unprofitable as hell for the subcontractor if they drag on for any length of time. I've never liked them, but they're unavoidable sometimes in a back-scratching business like ours. Paul Ballard had done a favor for me once, so I couldn't say no when he called on us. Quid pro quo.

I said to Tamara, "You want me to go over to San Leandro, check out the house?"

"Have to be after hours. If DeBrissac's living there, he's liable to be working during the day."

"I don't mind."

"Uh-uh," she said. "You work too hard as it is. Supposed to be semiretired, putting in almost as many hours as I am."

"I still don't mind. Unless you want to wait a day and send Jake over tomorrow night. He won't mind, either."

"Nope. I'll do it myself."

"Now who's the workaholic."

"Yeah, well. Besides, I kinda like fieldwork. No reason you and Runyon should have all the fun."

The voice on the phone was male, young, and hesitant. Its tone held something else that I couldn't quite identify—some kind of emotional upset. "Runyon . . . Jake Runyon, please."

"He's not in. May I take a message?"

"When will he be back?"

"Tomorrow morning," I said. "He's out of town, not due back until after close of business."

"So he'll be home tonight?"

"Probably. Is this a business or personal call?"

Dead air.

"Let me have your name and number, and I'll—"

He said, "No, I'll call him at home," and the line hummed in my ear.

Tamara had just come out of the bathroom and was standing there watching me. As I lowered the receiver, she asked, "What was that about?"

"Call for Jake."

"From?"

"Wouldn't give his name. But I think it might've been his son."

"His son? I thought Jason, Joshua, whatever his name is—"

"Joshua."

"—didn't want anything to do with him. No contact since before Christmas."

"That's right."

"Second thoughts about a reconciliation, maybe?"

"I don't think so," I said. "Didn't sound like that at all."

I had one more nonbusiness call that day, just before five o'clock. This one was personal for me—a little surprising, a little disturbing.

The caller said his name was Buck Trail. And he was elderly and not entirely sober, judging from his cracked and thickened baritone. "You don't know me," he said. "Pal asked me to call for him because he can't."

"What pal is that?"

"Russ Dancer."

It took a couple of seconds for the name to register. My God, Russell Dancer. A name out of the past, a man I hadn't seen in six or seven years or thought about more than a couple of times in passing since.

"He wants to see you," Trail said.

"Is that right? He still living in Redwood City?"

"Not for much longer."

"I don't understand."

"You will."

"What does he want to see me about?"

"Didn't tell me that. Just asked me to call you up, give you the message. I was you, I'd come on down right away. Tonight."

"Why tonight?"

"He's dying," Trail said. "Croakers at Kaiser Hospital give him another day, two at the outside."

2

JAKE RUNYON

His flight from L.A. landed at SFO at 5:05, which put him smack into the middle of rush-hour traffic heading into the city. Not that the stop-and-crawl bothered him. There was a time when it had, in Seattle during the evening rush when he was on his way home to Colleen. Now he had no one waiting, no reason for hurry. Rattling around his San Francisco apartment or creeping along the 280 freeway—one place was the same as another. Her death had taught him patience, if nothing else. Or maybe patience was nothing but a prettied-up name for apathy.

Work was the only thing that mattered to him anymore, the only relief for the disinterest he felt during his nonworking hours. Colleen was gone, his son hated him and refused to have anything to do with him, what else was there? But you couldn't do your job twenty-four/seven; you had to have sleep, food, and like it or not there was a certain amount of downtime that you had to put up with every day. Weekends were the worst. Even weekends in L.A. Saturday he'd been able to put in a full day on the missing witness case; L.A. was a damn big place and he'd spent hours on the freeways and side streets getting from one place to another, all the way from the San Fernando Valley to Riverside. Sunday, though, had been bad. Motel room, movies and a baseball game on TV, coffee shop, and more driving, the aimless kind, to kill the rest of the time. Full workday again today, at least. And now he was home and looking at five more busy workdays before he had to face another Sunday.

Home. Just a word now, like a word in a foreign language you didn't understand.

Into the city, finally, crawling past the state university campus and on up Nineteenth Avenue. When he neared Taraval he thought about turning off—coffee shops and Asian restaurants along there—but he kept on going instead. Hungry, but not hungry enough to bother stopping. Later he'd go out to eat. A bath first, soak out some of the driving and airplane kinks, the weekend fatigue.

His apartment was in a nondescript building on Ortega, not far off Nineteenth. Four rooms that might've been rooms in a hotel or boardinghouse or the motel in L.A.; the only thing that personalized it, made it a place worth returning to, was the framed photograph of Colleen that he kept on the bedside nightstand. An eagerness to see the photo came on him as he keyed open the door, a shadow of the eagerness he'd felt when she was alive and he was coming home to her. He had another photo of her in his wallet, but it wasn't as clear and sharp a likeness as the one in the bedside frame.

The message light on the answering machine was blinking. He registered that—Tamara or Bill, probably, work-related—and kept on going into the bedroom. He picked up Colleen's photo, stood looking at it for a long time. God, she'd been beautiful. Red hair, those impish Irish green eyes, that beacon-like smile. He put the frame down. If he looked at her image too long, the pain would start again and then he'd be in for a long, bad night.

He shed his overcoat, started into the kitchen to put on water for tea—Colleen's drink, his drink now—then changed his mind and went back into the living room. Might as well find out what the office wanted first.

But it wasn't the office. The voice on the machine said, "This is Joshua. I'll probably regret this, but I need to talk to somebody . . . Call me." That was all except for his new number, the unlisted-to-avoid-his-father number.

Runyon was beyond surprise at anything, business or personal, but sometimes things happened that came close. The hostage situation just before Christmas. And now this call out of the blue. No communication between Joshua and him since their one disastrous meeting in December, the boy so poisoned by Andrea's bitter, alcohol-fueled hatred for Runyon and her imagined abandonment of them that the father-son gap seemed impossible to bridge . . . so why the sudden change of heart? *I'll probably regret this, but I need to talk to somebody.* If it was a change of heart.

Still, hope stirred in him. The kid had called. That was something; maybe it was a beginning. He played the message back, noting the day and time of the call: today, 2:27 P.M. Less than four hours ago. He wrote the unlisted number in his notebook, then picked up the receiver and tapped it out.

Joshua answered immediately, as if he'd been sitting next to the phone, waiting for it to ring. "Yes? Hello?"

"Hello, son."

Breathing sounds.

"Joshua?"

"I'm here."

Different tone of voice than on the message. The cold, distant one again.

"I'm glad you called," Runyon said.

"Don't be. It was a mistake."

"Why a mistake?"

"I can't talk to you. You wouldn't understand."

"Try me."

"No. There's nothing you can do."

"What did you want me to do?"

"Nothing. Just forget it."

"Are you in some kind of trouble?"

"No."

"Something's wrong. I can hear it in your voice."

"I said forget it. It's not important."

"No? Must've cost you a lot, that call."

"More than you'll ever know."

"Then talk to me."

"What's the use? Straight society doesn't give a shit about people like us."

"Wrong. Some of us do."

Breathing.

"Talk to me, son."

Joshua said, "I'm not your son," and broke the connection.

Runyon lowered the receiver. He stood for half a minute or so, listening to the quiet in the apartment, making a decision. All right. He went back into the bedroom for his coat and car keys.

• • •

The old house was on Hartford just off Twentieth—a steep street of one- and two-story Stick Victorians and small, plain apartment buildings. The flat Joshua shared with his roommate was in one of the two-story Sticks, on the ground level. Runyon had been there once before. A drive-by, just to see what kind of place his son had picked to live in. He'd gotten the address by checking the reverse city directory. The roommate's name was Kenneth Hitchcock, age twenty-eight—six years older than Joshua; born in Visalia in the Central Valley, graduated from Fresno State with a degree in business administration, worked as a teller in a downtown branch of B of A, had never been in trouble of any kind either as a juvenile or an adult. Curiosity had prompted the background check, nothing more. Runyon could have gotten their unlisted phone number, too, easily enough, but he hadn't bothered. It wouldn't have done any good to keep calling, invading Joshua's privacy; would've just increased the rift between them. All he cared about, once his attempts to create an understanding had been unequivocally rejected, was that his son be safe, healthy, solvent, and reasonably content.

But now there was this new contact, initiated by Joshua. A reaching out for some reason that wasn't clear yet. It had opened the door, and Runyon wasn't about to stand by and let it slam shut again without some push. Andrea's alcoholic-fueled hate and vindictiveness had prevented him from being a part of Joshua's life for the first twenty years, but he could be there for him now. And would be, whatever it took.

He hunted up a parking place, walked back to the building through a chilly night wind that had the smell of fog in it. There was a gate, and a short path that led from the street, to a narrow front stoop. He rang the bell. Before long, footsteps. A peephole was set into the door; Joshua must have looked out through it because the door came open fast. Tight-set face, eyes that snapped with anger, words that were flung more than spoken. "What're you doing here?"

"We didn't finish our conversation."

"Yes we did. I told you, I changed my mind. I don't have anything to say to you."

"You did this afternoon."

"How did you know where I live? We're not listed in the phone book. Oh, right . . . snooping's what you do for a living."

Runyon let that slide. "Something's wrong," he said. "Don't tell me different. It's in your face as well as your voice."

Joshua was a handsome kid, Andrea's kid in that respect, too—her blond hair, her smoky blue eyes, her narrow mouth and delicate features—but he wasn't so good-looking right now. Drawn, pale, puffy, as if he hadn't slept much recently. Misery as well as anger showed in the blue eyes, some kind of visceral hurt.

"Why should you care?"

"That's a stupid question and you know it."

"Why can't you just leave me alone?"

"Same category," Runyon said. "I have left you alone. If you'd wanted me to go on leaving you alone, you wouldn't have called."

Joshua met his gaze briefly, looked away.

"We're going to talk, son. Be easier on both of us if we do it inside."

He moved ahead on the last word, crowding the kid a little. No more resistance; Joshua gave ground, turned aside to let him past.

Runyon automatically catalogued details as he advanced. Foyer and a short hallway with three closed doors leading off it. The hall opened into a big living room, uncurtained windows in the south wall that framed a broken view of an overgrown yard and the backsides of neighboring houses. Neat, clean, tastefully furnished in greens and browns and dusky reds. Paintings on the walls that had an amateurish look but weren't badly done—expressionist style, all blobs and whorls of dark color on a white background, all the work of the same artist. Grouped on a folded dropcloth in front of one window were an easel, a chair, a big Tensor lamp, and a small table covered with brushes and jars of paint in symmetrical rows.

"You the painter?" he asked.

"No. Kenneth."

"He's pretty good."

"Yes, he is. I wouldn't have thought you'd like expressionist art."

"There's a lot about me you don't know. Is Kenneth here? I'd like to meet him."

"No, he's not here." A muscle spasmed in Joshua's cheek. "He's in the hospital."

"Yes? I'm sorry to hear it."

"Three days now and his condition is still critical."

"What's the matter with him?"

Hesitation. Then, in an angry, anguished rush: "He has a fractured arm, four cracked ribs, a broken cheekbone, and a punctured lung, that's what's the matter with him. Among other injuries. His face . . . God, his poor face . . ."

"What happened?"

"He was beaten up. They used some kind of club."

"They?"

"Fucking homophobes. Gay-bashers."

"So that's it. Known to him?"

"I don't think so. He's been under heavy sedation . . . confused when he's awake. He can't seem to remember much, just that there were two of them."

"When and where?"

"Last Friday night. Saturday morning. He was on his way home from work, he moonlights as a bartender three nights a week at The Dark Spot on Castro. They must've been cruising for another target, it was late and he was alone . . ."

"Another target?"

"He wasn't their first victim, the bastards."

"How many others?"

"Two in the past two weeks. I know the second man."

"Yes?"

"Gene Zalesky. He . . . used to be a friend of Kenneth's."

"How badly was he hurt?"

"Not as badly as Kenneth. He's home now."

"Was he able to provide descriptions of the attackers?"

"Young, early to mid twenties . . . the same pair."

"Driving what kind of vehicle?"

"An old pickup truck, black or dark blue." Joshua went to one of the chairs, slumped down on it. Runyon stayed where he was. "I *told* Kenneth to be careful, ask somebody to give him a ride home, take a cab if he had to. But he wasn't afraid, he didn't believe it would happen to him . . . Goddamn them! *Goddamn them!*"

"Easy, son."

"Don't tell me that. That's what they kept saying."

"Who?"

"The cops. Bullshit, that's all. They didn't care. Just another fag beating. File a report and forget about it."

Runyon said, "It doesn't work that way," but they were just words. It did work that way, much of the time. And not just in crimes against gays or other hate crimes—in nearly all low-profile street felonies. Too many crimes, too many criminals, too little time and manpower. Too many excuses and too much apathy.

Joshua said bitterly, "I thought you didn't lie. Isn't that what you told me in December?"

"All right. I'm sorry."

"Sorry. What good is sorry?" Shuddery breath. The blue eyes were moist now; shifting emotions, pain the most intense. "He could die. Kenneth could *die*."

"His condition that critical?"

"Internal bleeding. The doctors had trouble stopping it. It could start again at any time . . ."

It seemed for a few seconds that Joshua might break down. Runyon felt an impulse to sit beside him, give him a shoulder to lean on. Didn't do it because he knew the gesture would be rejected. What his son wanted from him had nothing to do with fatherly solace.

Joshua made a visible effort to pull himself together. At length he said, "I hate this," in a shaky voice. "Kenneth is the strong one. I'm no damn good in a crisis."

Runyon said, "I am."

"I just . . . I don't know what to do."

"You've already done all you can. Calling me was the right thing."

For the first time Joshua looked at him squarely. "Could you find them, stop them before they kill somebody?"

"Maybe. No guarantees."

"*Would* you? If I hired you, paid you . . ."

"No."

"But you just said—"

"I'll do what I can, but not for pay."

Silent stare.

"You're my son," Runyon said. "That's all the reason I need."

3

TAMARA

Vonda said, "Well, I met this guy."

"Uh-huh." So what else is new? Tamara thought.

"A couple of weeks ago at a club in SoMa. We danced and had some drinks and he asked me for my phone number and I gave it to him. I was a little ripped or I probably wouldn't have."

"Uh-huh."

"He kept calling me up and I gave in and I've been out with him a couple of times. A really nice guy, and gorgeous . . . I mean a real hunk. His name is Ben, Ben Sherman; he played football when he was at UC Berkeley. He has a good job, he works for a brokerage company in the financial district."

"Uh-huh."

"Saturday night we went out again, dinner and dancing, and afterward . . . well, he invited me to his place on Tel Hill, he's got a great apartment up there, terrific view and everything . . ."

"Let me guess. You ended up in bed."

"I wasn't going to, it just happened. I mean, you know me, I don't usually sleep with a guy until I get to know him first."

Oh, yeah, right. She'd been friends with Vonda since they were sophomores at Redwood City High. Shared some wild times, their gangsta period when they'd chased with some rough homies, smoked weed, done all kinds of stuff that came close to crossing the line. Vonda looked a little like a young Robin Givens, slim and sleek but with a J-Lo booty; guys had been all over her since her boobs started to show. She'd lost her cherry when she was fifteen, must've slept with fifty different guys before and after she cleaned up her act.

"How was it?" The usual girl-talk question.

"Oh, great. Wow. The best ever. I mean, Ben really knows how to treat a woman in bed. But it wasn't just sex."

"Uh-huh."

"No lie. There's a difference, you know there is. Sex is one thing, making love's another. I thought I'd made love a time or two, but with Ben . . . Lord, I think I'm in love with that man."

"Uh-huh." She'd heard that one before, too.

"Seriously, Tam. And it's mutual. He came right out and said he loves me."

Tamara covered a sigh with a sip from her glass. Mineral water. And a white wine spritzer for Vonda. Tamara Corbin and Vonda McGee, the two badass young 'ho's all cornrowed and grunge-dressed and party-ready. If those high school homies could see the two of them now, nine years later, one a partner in a private investigation agency, the other an up-and-coming sales rep at the S.F. Design Center, wearing conservative business outfits and sipping mineral water and white wine spritzers in a crowd of mostly white establishment types in the South Park Café. Whoo! Sometimes she could hardly believe it herself, all the big jumps and sharp-angle turns in her life . . .

"And I wish neither of us was," Vonda said.

"Was what?"

"In love. Ben Sherman, my God, of all the guys in the world."

"Why? What's wrong with him?"

"He's white," Vonda said.

Tamara stopped being bored. "Uh-oh."

"That's not all. He's more than just white."

"How can he be more than just white?"

"He's Jewish, too," Vonda said.

". . . Damn, girl!"

"I know, I know. That's why I wanted to get together to-night, I had to talk to somebody about this and you're the only one I can tell. I've never been with a white guy before, you know that, it's never been my thing. And you know how my people feel about the interracial thing. Alton'll go ballistic when he finds out."

"He doesn't have to find out." Alton was her brother, a head case who'd never outgrown his hatred of Whitey. "If you don't see this Ben Sherman again."

"I don't think I can do that, just blow him off. I really do love him, Tam."

"Great sex isn't love. You've only known the guy two weeks."

"It's not just physical and it doesn't matter how long I've known him. You've been there, you understand what I'm say-ing. Same feelings you had for Horace right from the first."

Horace. Let's not get started on Horace.

"What am I gonna do?" Vonda said.

"Got to be your decision, nobody else's. Yours and Ben's. What's he say about it?"

"He says it doesn't matter how other people feel, it only matters how we feel about each other."

"Yeah, well, he's right. But not a hundred percent right."

"I know it."

"Still got to do what your heart and your gut tell you to."

"What would *you* do? I mean, suppose Horace was white. *And* Jewish."

Horace again. "Well, he's not."

"Come on, Tam. Suppose he was. What would you do?"

"I don't know," Tamara said, "I don't know what I'm going to do."

Eastbound traffic on the Bay Bridge was still moderately heavy, even though it was nearly seven o'clock when Tamara drove up the ramp and joined the stream. The westbound upper deck and the bridge railings and girders created a tunnel effect that magnified car and tire sounds into a steady shushing hum. After a while it seemed almost like a whispering voice.

Saying Horace, Horace, Horace.

Get a grip, she thought. She would have turned on the radio and slipped in a CD, but there was something wrong with the volume control—you couldn't turn it up past a low hum not much different from the one outside. Damn thing had worked fine before he left. Figured. His car. Ten-year-old Ford hatchback that he'd left with her because he hadn't wanted to chance driving it all the way to Philadelphia in the middle of winter. Maybe it missed him too. Yeah, or it was just a sign of things going wrong, screwing up.

Vonda wasn't the only one with a screwed-up love life. All God's chillun got troubles and love troubles were high on the list. You could empathize with other people's, but you couldn't get too caught up in them when you had your own to deal with. Couldn't give somebody else advice when you couldn't advise yourself.

Three and a half months now since Horace had left for Philly. Got his gig with the philharmonic back there, second seat cello, doing fine. Living with one of the other black men on the orchestra, a violinist named Cedric. Settled in. Just as she was settled in: agency partnership, new offices, expanding caseload and all the details and decisions that were part of the package. She wasn't going anywhere for a long time, if ever. And neither was Horace.

They talked on the phone once a week, exchanged e-mails, said all the right things about how much they missed each other and loved each other, made tentative plans to get together here or back east. But they still hadn't done it. Something got in the way every time. And the phone calls were getting shorter because they didn't seem to have as much to say to each other, couldn't relate long distance to all the changes that made up their new, separate lives.

She'd known it would be this way. Three-thousand-mile relationships might work for a while, but without personal contact, days and nights together to pump some fresh blood into the relationship, it's bound to start withering. Sooner or later it would wither past the point of saving. Just dry up and croak, like a plant without water.

It was already happening to her. She felt it, fought it, couldn't stop it. All the lonely nights in the Outer Richmond flat they'd shared . . . she'd got so she hated going there after work. Stayed later and later at the office, started taking on after-hours field jobs like this deadbeat dad case tonight. Better that than staring at the walls or the boob tube and throwing pizza and junk food down her neck, which she'd done for about a week after Horace left. After that she'd gone the other way, started to lose her appetite. That was the main reason she'd dropped twelve pounds, not any real desire to shed the flab; she just wasn't interested in food anymore. Or much of anything else except work.

Now that's a lie, she thought as she pulled out to pass a slow-moving truck. She was still interested in sex, oh Lord yes. On her mind more and more lately. Tonight, thanks to Vonda. Three and a half months is a long time to go without it when you're used to getting it regularly. So damn horny sometimes she felt like she was ready to explode. Vonda might've gotten in over her head with a white, Jewish dude, but at least Vonda was getting *laid*.

Maybe Vonda would loan out Ben Sherman for a night. Or maybe he had a friend who wanted to change his luck. She'd never slept with a white guy herself—or a Jewish guy, for that matter. Might change *her* luck.

Stupid thoughts.

Come on, Tamara. You want to do the nasty so bad, you know you can find somebody to do it with without even try-ing. Half a fox now that the love handles were slimmed down. Sleek and sassy. Must be a few hundred guys in the city that wouldn't mind getting into her pants for a night or two, no strings. Pick a night, pick a club, pick a dick.

More stupid thoughts.

She sighed. She was off the bridge now, moving toward the

interchange and 880 south, but she could still hear that damn shushing hum.

Horace. Horace, Horace, Horace . . .

The house George DeBrissac's cousin owned in San Leandro was on Willard Street, 1122 Willard. She'd looked it up on the Netscape MapQuest site before leaving the office: Willard was in the wide trough between the 880 and 580 freeways, closest to 880 off San Pablo Avenue. Simple directions, should be pretty easy to find.

It was. Blue-collar residential neighborhood, not much different from dozens of others in the East Bay—that was apparent even on a dark night in an area without many streetlights. Old houses, mostly frame, a few stucco, on pretty good-sized lots. Probably an ethnic mix of whites, blacks, maybe a few Latinos and Asians.

Finding 1122 was a little harder. No numbers on the street signs, no reflector curbside numbers for the headlights to pick up, the houses set far enough back from the street so it wasn't easy to read the numbers on them. Tamara drove slow, with the driver's window down, until she passed a house with the porch light on: 906. Which way did the numbers run, up or down? Down—the next block was 800. She made a U-turn, came back to the 1100 block, finally pinpointed the right one.

Boxy frame house, hedges hiding most of the front porch, low-maintenance yard behind a Cyclone fence interwoven with some kind of scraggly vine. Dark, no light showing anywhere. But that didn't mean there wasn't anybody inside. The front windows looked like they had heavy coverings, and there might be lights at the back that she couldn't see from here.

She kept on going, circled the block, eased back up Willard in the same direction as before. Fifty yards or so across from 1122, a gnarly curbside tree laid out a big puddle of shadow. She parked in the puddle, darkened the car. Unobstructed diagonal view of 1122 from there, if she needed to maintain a surveillance.

Now that she was here, out on a field job, she began to feel a little stoked. Working on the computer was satisfying, she was an expert hacker, but it got boring sometimes. Fieldwork wasn't, not yet anyway. She'd worked with Bill long enough to know that night jobs could be occasionally dangerous, and dull and more boring than office work when long stakeouts were involved, but she wasn't worried about any of that. Probably lose its fascination for her before long, but right now it was all still new and pretty cool.

She remembered what the boss man had taught her. Stay alert in unfamiliar territory, use your senses. Right. Street was deserted, nobody on the sidewalks or in any of the nearby yards. She got out, locked the door. Lights in some of the houses, salsa music playing somewhere, distant traffic sounds. Cross the street, not too fast and not too slow. Don't go into a strange yard until you make sure there aren't any dogs or BE-WARE OF DOG signs. 1122 was a canine-free zone as far as she could tell. Don't try to get past locked gates unless it's absolutely necessary. Gate in the Cyclone fence wasn't locked. She opened it, walked up the path and up the steps to the door.

Nothing to hear from inside. There was a doorbell; she pushed it and it made a noise that sounded more like a long fart than a bell. She waited a minute or so, then released the fart again. Still silent inside.

Alongside the house on the left was a gravel driveway. She

quit the porch, went over there. Make sure you're alone and unobserved before you go prowling around strange property. Yeah, she thought, and that goes double for a black woman even in a mixed neighborhood after dark. Alone and unobserved as far as she could tell; the house next door on that side was as dark as this one. She moved along the driveway to a garage that was just about big enough for one car. A rear yard opened up alongside the garage, but there wasn't anything in it except a half-dead tree and some ground cover that was more weeds than lawn. The garage didn't have any windows that she could see. The lift-up door was probably locked, and even if it wasn't, she'd be asking for trouble to even try looking inside. Never take unnecessary risks. Right. No point in it anyway. If the deadbeat was hiding out here, he was somewhere else right now.

Tamara strolled back down the driveway, not too fast and not too slow. Two options now. One was to go ring a couple of doorbells, find out if any of the neighbors had seen DeBrissac. Only problem with that was, if he *was* living here, wasn't any way of knowing what his relationship was with the neighbors. He might've given them some song-and-dance, asked them to cover for him or report to him if anybody came poking around. That happened, he'd fly again and be twice as hard to find. So . . .

She crossed the street, crawled back into Horace's Toyota. Surveillance time. Prospect of that killed off the last of her little high; this was the part that could get boring. But she wouldn't stay all that long, an hour, maybe two. If nobody showed at 1122, she could always come back again tomorrow night.

She wiggled her butt into a comfortable position on the seat and settled down to wait.

4

Russ Dancer, dying. Cirrhosis and emphysema. Refused to quit drinking or smoking, refused hospitalization or treatment beyond painkillers and an oxygen bottle that he carried around with him. He'd finally collapsed five days ago in the hallway of his rooming house. Bitched and moaned about going to the hospital, wanted to die in his room, but he was too sick and too weak and the croakers wouldn't let him stay there alone. All of this courtesy of Buck Trail. And all of it typical Russ Dancer.

I felt bad about it, in a detached sort of way. The detachment—a reflection on me and on the sad, bitter life of Russell Dancer—made me feel bad, too. So did my having assumed he was already dead, that he must have drunk and smoked himself into his grave years ago. So did the fact that he still considered me enough of a friend, even though I'd made no effort to get in touch with him in more than a decade, to ask for me on his deathbed.

I confessed this to Kerry when I called her with the news.

She said, "You have no reason to feel guilty. He really didn't want you in his life, you know that. Particularly after you and I got together. Too much of a reminder of Cybil."

"I know it. Still . . ."

"Why do you suppose he wants to see you?"

"No clue. But I have to find out."

"Of course you do."

"And I wish I didn't."

"Do you want me to call Cybil? She'll want to know."

"Not yet. Better wait until after I see him."

I took 101 south to Redwood City. The 280 freeway would have been faster, even with the rush-hour clog getting across to the west side, but on this errand of mercy—if that was what it was—I was willing to put up with the commuter-crawl delay. Or so I thought when I started out. The trouble was, Dancer rode with me all the way down.

He was a writer, a damn good one back in the postwar forties when pulp magazines were still a viable form of popular entertainment. Creator of private eye Rex Hannigan, whose hard-boiled exploits had run in *Midnight Detective* until the magazine's demise in the early fifties, then been chronicled in a series of softcover mystery novels during that decade's paperback boom. The Hannigan stories, particularly those in the pulps, had had energy, flair, innovative plotting—the work of a raw talent that might have been developed through care and diligence into a voice to be reckoned with in the crime-fiction field. But Dancer had wasted his gift. Taken the easy road into fast-money hackwork to support a hard-living, hard-boozing lifestyle. As of ten years ago, he'd published upward of two hundred novels—mysteries, Gothics, bodice-ripper historicals, movie tie-ins, traditional westerns, adult westerns, softcore

porn, hardcore porn, just about anything somebody would
pay him to write.

Our paths had first crossed down the coast in Cypress Bay,
where he'd been living at the time, on a case involving one of
his paperback mysteries. The second time was at a pulp magazine convention in San Francisco where I'd met Kerry; he'd
been one of the guests—along with Kerry's mother and father,
Cybil and Ivan Wade, who'd also been pulp writers—and had
managed to get himself arrested for a murder he didn't com-
mit. He liked me because I got him off the hook: they don't let
you have booze or a typewriter in jail. The third and last time
I'd seen him had been a brief encounter in Redwood City,
when I'd looked him up to gather information about the murder of yet another former pulpster, Harmon Crane. All in all,
we'd spent an aggregate of less than twenty-four hours in each
other's company. And yet whenever I thought of him he was a
vivid presence in my memory.

I knew him and I didn't know him; he was both an open
book and a conundrum. Rowdy, sharp-tongued, bitter, self-
mocking, with a penchant for trouble and bad decisions: he
could make people dislike, even hate him without half trying.
A little of him went a long way. Yet there was something about
him, an innate vulnerability, that built a certain amount of pity
in me. In a sense he was a tragic figure; he had no luck and had
suffered a good deal of adversity, both personal and professional, that wasn't his fault. He was not easy to deal with because
it had never been easy for him to deal with himself. He knew
he'd compromised his talent, and hated the fiction whore he'd
become, and that was one of two reasons he kept dragging himself down into the depths. The other reason—and the other reason I pitied him—was his fifty-year letch for Kerry's mother.

I remembered how he'd looked that last day in Redwood City, on a stool in a sleazy neighborhood bar called Mama Luz's Pink Flamingo Tavern. Sagging jowls, heavy lines and wrinkles on his face and neck, tracery of ruptured blood vessels in his cheeks, rum-blossom nose. Dissipated, rheumy, too thin for his big frame as if the flesh were hanging on his bones like a scarecrow's tattered clothing. I'd had the thought then that he wasn't long for this world; maybe that was why I'd assumed he must be dead by now.

I remembered some of what he'd said to me that day, too. He'd just lost an assignment to write a series of adult westerns— screwed it up himself somehow, probably, though he blamed the editor. I'd asked him if he was still writing and he'd said, "Sure, always at the mill. Got a few proposals with my agent, a few irons in the fire. And I'm working up an idea for a big paperback suspense thing that might have a shot." Face-saving lies. I had stopped by his furnished room before going to Mama Luz's, had a quick look inside, and there'd been no sign of his typewriter. He must have hocked it to supplement his Social Security, buy more booze and cigarettes.

Russ Dancer, hunched on a bar stool. A little drunk, a little maudlin, a whole lot lonely, wanting me to stay and have a drink with him, begging for a few more minutes of companionship and compassion. And I'd walked out on him and never gone back. Why hadn't I bothered to look him up again, try to find out how he was doing? Inertia, lack of any real motivation . . . lousy excuses. He considered me his friend, and for a friendless man like him, that meant something. It should've meant a little something to me in return.

Ten long years. And he'd been down there all that time, living on Social Security and dying by centimeters. And now he was finally about to get what he'd been after for Christ knew how long, that kept eluding him because of an iron constitution and a perverse nature and a hair shirt as thick as they come. I felt lousy by the time I got to Redwood City. I felt, dammit, right or wrong, as though I'd betrayed a trust.

Kaiser Permanente Hospital. Bed in a ward, surrounded by a curtain on an oblong frame.

Dancer, hooked up to machines.

Not the Dancer I'd known, not even that last time at Mama Luz's. A shadow, a husk, a stick figure topped by a death's head coated with gray fuzz and age spots. Lying there motionless, eyes shut, his breathing aided by oxygen tubes but still coming in wheezes and gasps. My mouth dried out, looking down at him. I had to work some spit through it before I could speak.

"Hello, Russ."

He'd known I was there; a nurse had gone in first to tell him he had a visitor. The shrunken head turned slowly, the eyes flicked open and focused on me. A grimace that tried to be a smile moved the corners of his mouth. Words came in little bursts fragmented by wheezes, so low that I had to lean close to hear him.

"*No tengo* . . . for good this time . . . eh, *paisano?* Goddamnit . . . to hell."

It took a few seconds for that to signify. The old Spanish cowboy lament he'd been fond of quoting at one time as a metaphor for his life and career. "*No tengo tabaco, no tengo papel, no tengo dinero*—goddamnit to hell."

There was a white metal chair at the foot of the bed. I pulled

it up alongside, sat down. Better that than standing and looming over him. This was awkward and painful enough as it was.
All I could think of to say was, "I'm sorry."

"What for? We all . . . gotta go . . . sometime."

Some more easily than others. I nodded.

"You don't mean it . . . anyway. Nobody . . . gives a shit . . .
when a hack writer croaks."

"I do, or I wouldn't be here."

"Pity," he said. "Pity visit . . . no different than . . . pity
fuck."

Even on his deathbed, the Dancer tongue was as crude and
acrid as ever.

"Your friend Trail cares," I said.

"Buck? Hah, that's a . . . that's a laugh."

"Why would he call me if he didn't care?"

"Paid him, that's why. Twenty . . . twenty bucks. Bet
he's . . . over at Mama Luz's . . . drinking it up right now."

"One of the doctors or nurses would've done it for free."

"Wouldn't trust . . . any of those bastards. Nurses . . . can't
even empty bedpan . . ." A cough shook him, made him
wheeze harder. "Besides, what do I . . . care about money . . .
now . . ." More coughs, a staccato series of them that led to a
gasping struggle for breath.

"Russ? Should I call the nurse?"

". . . No. Be okay . . . not time yet . . ."

The struggle went on for another fifteen or twenty seconds.
That could be me, I thought. If I hadn't quit smoking when
I did, if I hadn't started taking better care of myself. The
thought put little ripples of cold on my neck.

"Why did you ask to see me, Russ?" I said when the wheez-
ing and gasping finally eased. "Just to say good-bye?"

"Hell, no. No damn good . . . at good-byes. Want you . . .
do something for me."

"All right. If I can."

"You can. Has to do with . . . Sweeteyes."

"Cybil? You want me to bring her to see you?"

"Christ! That's the . . . last thing . . . her see me like this."

"Give her a message, then?"

"Sweeteyes," Dancer said again. His pet name for her. "Bet
she's . . . still as . . . beautiful as ever."

"Yes, she is."

"Health good?"

"Yes."

"Still . . . sharp mentally, still . . . writing?"

"Yes."

"Tell her . . . read her novel. Damn good. She . . . can still
write rings . . . around most of us. Makes . . . everything I
churned out . . . look like the shit it is."

"I'll tell her. Anything else?"

Faint smile. "Remember D-Day."

I wasn't sure I'd heard him right. "What was that, Russ?"

"Remember D-Day."

"Just those words?"

"And . . . one more message. Tell her . . . amazing grace."

"You mean like the hymn?"

"Just tell her. Remember D-Day . . . amazing grace."

"All right."

"Rest of what I . . . have to say to her . . . in the package."

"Package?"

"Other thing I want you . . . do for me. Give Sweeteyes . . .
package."

"Where is it? Here?"

"No. Storage locker, trunk . . . my building. Keys . . . keys in drawer there . . . next to bed. Okay?"

"Okay."

"Big envelope, her name . . . on the front. Don't open . . . for Sweeteyes only."

"I won't."

"And don't give it . . . to her until after . . . you hear I'm gone."

"Whatever you say."

"Good. Knew I could . . . trust you. Only one . . . I can trust . . ."

The curtains slid open behind me, the sudden ratcheting of hooks on the frame making me jerk a little. A starchy nurse poked her head inside. "You'll have to leave now," she said to me. "It's time for the patient's medicine."

"Fucking cow," Dancer said when she was gone. "Time for . . . patient's medicine. You like that? Not . . . Mr. Dancer, not even . . . old bastard, just patient." He made a laughing sound. "Dead meat, pretty soon."

I'd had enough even before the nurse appeared. I stood up.

"Take keys," he said.

I opened the nightstand drawer. Two keys on a ring; I put them in my pocket.

"No . . . good-byes. Hate good-byes."

"So do I." But I couldn't just leave it at that. I felt even worse now; I had to put some of the guilt into words—for my sake, if not for his. "I really am sorry, Russ. I should've gotten in touch, I should've been a better friend."

No answer. He lay still, his eyes shut now, his breathing a little less raspy in repose. I thought he might have drifted off, hadn't heard what I'd said. But he was awake and he'd heard.

And he answered me as I turned away from the bed and parted the curtains.

"No tengo," he said. "Goddamnit to hell.*"*

The rooming house where Dancer had lived the past two decades was an ancient, two-story Victorian on Stambaugh Street, off Broadway and fairly close to the Southern Pacific railroad tracks. Downscale neighborhood that looked about the same as it had on my last, long-ago visit. The block-long thrift store where Dancer had gathered his reading material was still there; so was Mama Luz's Pink Flamingo Tavern a half block to the west. Not much had changed, in fact, except that there were a couple of empty storefronts and more graffiti on the building walls. The Victorian had had a coat of paint slapped on it in the interim, but it hadn't done much to dispel the seedy aspect; its turrets and gables were still in need of repair, its brick chimneys still unstable-looking. One of the two scraggly palm trees in the front yard had died and been cut down; the broken picket fence that had enclosed the yard had been replaced by an even uglier Cyclone job. How long before urban renewal caught up with this little patch of decay? A few years at the most. Its days were numbered in any case, and Dancer had been a perfect fit: old and blighted and dying a little more every day.

Even though I had Dancer's keys, I thought I'd better check with the manager. One of the mailboxes on the creaky porch identified C. Holloway as having that dubious distinction. I rang C. Holloway's bell. Ten years ago the manager had been a woman with a face like a gargoyle, but she was gone now; the new one was male, forty-five or so, with a milky cataract in one eye and the disposition of a scorpion. He wouldn't let me come in when I told him who I was and why I was there; I had to bribe him with a brace of dollar bills and show him my ID. He didn't ask how Dancer was, didn't seem to care. Inside he pointed me toward the basement stairs and said before he left me, "Don't touch none of the other lockers down there. I'll call the cops on you if I find out you did."

The basement was musty and cold and threaded with spiderwebs. The storage lockers were arranged along one wall—narrow cages made out of wood and chicken wire. The padlocks on each door were a joke; you could have torn through that thin wire with your bare hands and a minimum of effort. Room numbers were stenciled on the doors. Number 6, Dancer's room, had the fewest items of any of the occupied cages: a couple of cheap suitcases, half a dozen open cartons of mint but dust-covered paperback books, and a beat-up pasteboard trunk.

The package with Cybil's name on it was in the trunk, on top of a jumble of old clothing. Nine-by-twelve padded mailing bag, fairly thick and heavy, sealed with filament tape. I tucked it under my arm.

Before I locked up the cage again, I took a quick look through a couple of the boxes of books. Multiple copies of a variety of lurid titles—*Raw Day in Hell, Mistress of Bleak House, Gun Fury in Crucifix Canyon, Black Avenger #7: Slaughter Train.* Author's copies of some of Dancer's pseudonymous novels. On impulse I picked out half a dozen at random, tucked them into my coat pocket. Why not? They represented little pieces of the man's life, imagination, talent. Somebody ought to care about them, just a little.

Upstairs, there was no sign of C. Holloway in the lobby. So I climbed the rickety staircase to the second floor—impulse again—and used the other key on the ring to let myself into Dancer's room. It seemed no different than it had a decade ago. Bed, nightstand, dresser, writing table. Empty half-gallon jug of cheap bourbon on the floor next to the bed. Scatter of battered thrift-store paperbacks.

No typewriter or other writing tool, not even a pencil.

No copies of any of the paperbacks boxed up in the basement, nor any other book that might have been written by him.

Dancer's home for more than fifteen years, but it wasn't a home at all. Living space. Existing space for a broken, friendless, bitter, lovelorn, alcoholic ex-writer. Lonely space. Wasted-life space. Dying space.

I got out of there, quick. Thank God for Kerry and Emily and the kind of work I had, because without them, given my own loner instincts, I could have ended up occupying a space not much different from Russ Dancer's.

5

JAKE RUNYON

Gene Zalesky lived alone on Museum Way, a street high up in the Corona Heights area that dead-ended at the Fairbanks Randall Jr. Museum. The steep, rocky slopes of Corona Heights Park ran along one side of the street; along the other was a curving row of private homes and two-unit flats, all of which had wide-angle views of the Castro District, Bernal Heights, and pieces of the Bay in the distance. The views would add several hundred a month to rental prices, another six figures to a seller's asking price.

Zalesky's address was one of the private homes, a dark wood and stucco job set back a few steps from the sidewalk. An ornate security gate barred the entrance. It told Runyon going in that Zalesky's job as a systems analyst, whatever that was, for a banking outfit paid well. The interior of the house confirmed it. Antiques of one kind and another crowded the living room; the carpet on the floor was an expensive-looking wine-red oriental, the threads in an elaborate tapestry on one wall had the glitter of real gold. Velvety curtains were drawn over the expensive view.

The man himself was in his late thirties, short, dark, and cynical. The cynicism showed in his eyes, the set of his mouth, his voice. It wasn't the result of his beating; it had been a part of him for a long time, maybe ever since he'd found out that he was different from the so-called norm, an outsider and an object of lesser men's hate and scorn. His left forearm was in a cast; fading bruises discolored the left side of his face, and there was a bandage over some kind of wound on the right cheekbone. He moved slowly, stiffly—testimony to other bruises, other wounds, beneath the silk robe and pajamas he wore.

"Sorry I'm not dressed," he said when he let Runyon in. "Still hurts like hell when I try to put on my pants."

"No apology necessary."

"One of them kicked me in the ass. I've got a bruise on my left buttock the size of a cantaloupe."

"Must be painful."

"Only when I sit down. I'm going to stand, if you don't mind, but you go ahead and have a seat."

Runyon said he'd stand too. While he was declining the offer of a drink, a fluffball white cat appeared from behind one of the antiques and came over to sniff at his shoes.

"That's Snow White," Zalesky said. There was pride in his voice, as if he were introducing a relative. "Pure-blood Angora. You like cats?"

"Yes." Colleen had owned a cat when he met her. Pure black alley cat named Midnight. Lived with them for the first eight years they were married, and she'd cried for three days when it died.

The Angora decided it had had enough of him and his shoes and drifted away. Zalesky made clucking noises; it ignored him, too. "Independent little bastard," he said affectionately. Then he said, "So you're Joshua Fleming's father. I don't remember him mentioning you until his call a few minutes ago."

"We're estranged," Runyon said.

"Oh. I see."

"Not for the reason you might think. His mother and I were divorced when he was a baby. She blamed me. So does he."

"With just cause?"

"I don't think so, but he won't listen to my side of it."

"Young and stubborn. I was like that myself, once, for different reasons. I learned to be more tolerant of my folks as I got older. Maybe he will, too."

"What I'm hoping."

"Is that why you're doing this? Investigating these bashings?"

"Partly. He contacted me, opened a closed door that I'd like to keep open."

"What other reason?"

"He's hurting, he needs my help. That's one."

"There's another?"

"I've been in law enforcement most of my adult life," Runyon said. "I don't like to see innocent people hurt and I damn well hate the ones who do the hurting. This pair that beat you up, put Joshua's roommate in critical condition . . . if they're not stopped, they're liable to kill somebody. I don't want that to happen."

Zalesky said, "Commendable," and seemed to mean it. "I wish more cops felt that way."

"So do I."

"I'll do anything I can to help, of course, but you already know that. What is it you'd like to know?"

"To begin with, where were you attacked?"

"Just up the street from here, on the park side. I'd just come home from visiting a friend, just parked my car and gotten out."

"What time?"

"After one A.M. Close to one-thirty."

"They followed you?"

"No. They were parked a couple of spaces away, across from my house."

"As if they were waiting for you?"

"It seemed that way."

"But they were strangers?"

"Oh, yes," Zalesky said. "Definitely. I suppose they spotted me somewhere, some other time, and followed me then. One of those random things. It's quiet up here late at night, I must've seemed like a good target. I don't know. With men like that . . . who the hell knows?"

"They were in a pickup truck?"

"Yes. Black or dark blue, I'm not sure which."

"Could you identify the make and model?"

"I don't know anything about cars, much less pickups."

"Did it seem new or old?"

"More old than new."

"Anything distinctive about it that you can remember?"

"Distinctive . . ." Zalesky's brow furrowed, smoothed again. "Well, there was a Confederate flag in the back window. I noticed that when they came out at me."

"A real flag or some kind of decal?"

"I think it was real. My God, you don't suppose they could be Klan members? In San Francisco, of all places in this country?"

"Anything's possible," Runyon said. "So they came out and then what? Just attacked you, or did they say anything first?"

"Oh, they had a lot to say. The usual run of gay insults. One of them called me sweet thing . . . Christ. The other one said something ridiculous about teaching me not to mess with boys and then they started hitting me."

"They use weapons of any kind?"

"One of them had a pipe or club made out of metal. Aluminum, I think." Zalesky shuddered. "I can still hear the sound it made when he hit me with it."

"Little League baseball bat?"

"I suppose it could've been. The other one hit me with his fists, kept kicking me when I was on the sidewalk. They were both laughing. The whole time . . . laughing, as if they were really having a fun time."

"What can you tell me about them?"

"Not much. It was dark and I couldn't see their faces clearly. One of them wore a jacket with a hood and the other a cap."

"What kind of cap?"

"I'm not sure . . . it might've been a baseball cap."

"Was he the one with the aluminum club?"

". . . Yes, I think so."

"How old were they?"

"Early twenties, maybe twenty-five."

"Big?"

"The one in the jacket was. Over six feet and . . . what's the word I want? Not fat, but . . . burly, chunky. Pale skin, at least it seemed pale in the dark. He may have red hair."

"What makes you think that?"

"Freckles," Zalesky said. "On his forehead and cheeks."

"You're sure they were freckles, not blemishes?"

"Freckles, yes. And I remember a lock of hair hanging out from under his cap. Light-colored, but not blond . . . it didn't look blond to me."

Runyon said, "Good. That helps. What about the other one?"

"Tallish, slender. Average-looking. That's all I remember about him."

The white cat reappeared and began to wind itself around Zalesky's legs, purring, making little burbling noises in its throat. Zalesky said, "What's the matter, baby? You need a little love?" He bent, slowly and with evident pain, and scooped the cat up with his good hand and hugged it against his chest. The purring got louder. And louder still when Zalesky buried his face in the animal's thick fur.

Private moment; Runyon looked away. The cat wasn't the only one who needed a little love right now.

He was looking at the wall tapestry, trying to make out what the scene depicted on it was all about, when Zalesky put an abrupt end to the private moment. "I keep having the feeling I've seen him someplace before."

"Who?"

"The tall, slender one."

"Before that night? Where?"

"That's just it, I can't quite recall."

"Someplace around here, this neighborhood?"

"No."

"Near where you work?"

"The Transamerica Pyramid . . . no, not there."

"Try it this way," Runyon said. "Day or night?"

"I'm not . . . Night. It might've been at night."

"Where do you go nights? Public places, I mean."

"That's not an easy question to answer. I go out frequently. Concerts, plays, the cinema. Dinner with friends. The Castro scene, too, of course—bars, clubs. I'm not really into cruising, but now and then . . . well, never mind, you're not interested in that."

"Could that be where you saw him? Over in the Castro?"

"He's hardly the type to frequent gay bars, Mr. Runyon."

"Maybe not the bars themselves, but the neighborhood's a good possibility. The two of them have to know the general area well enough to go hunting for victims. That might include the sections where the bars and clubs are."

"I suppose so, but . . . it wasn't in a car or pickup that I saw him. I'm sure of that much."

"On foot, then. Walking the area alone or with his buddy."

Zalesky nuzzled the Angora again. It was still purring, but making twitchy movements now as if it had had enough attention. "I don't think so," he said, and kissed the cat on top of the head and then let it jump down.

"All right." Runyon wrote his home phone number on the back of one of his agency business cards. "If it comes back to you, give me a call, would you? Office or home."

"I will. If you think it might be important."

"The more information I have, the easier it'll be to find them."

Zalesky nodded. And then frowned again, tapping the business card against his lower lip. "Outside one of the clubs," he said abruptly.

"Say again?"

"That's it, that's where I saw him. Outside one of the clubs. He was arguing with somebody . . ."

"How long ago was this?"

"Two or three weeks, maybe a little longer."

"Do you know the person he was arguing with?"

"Well . . . uh . . . I'm not sure . . ."

"Not sure?"

"I've seen him around, but I don't know his name."

Lying, Runyon thought. Why?

"Seen him around where?"

"In the Castro. Here and there."

"Describe him."

"In his twenties, blond, an angelic face . . ." Zalesky seemed nervous now, ill at ease. "I'm not very good at describing people."

"This argument. What was it about?"

"I . . . don't know, I was just passing by."

Another lie. Falsehoods and deception weren't natural to him; his eyes slid sideways, a little flick of guilt, when he wasn't telling the truth.

"So it wasn't a violent argument."

"No. The guy was in his face, the blond's face, but not touching him."

"Doing all the talking?"

"Yes."

"Was anyone with you at the time?"

"With me? Oh . . . no, I was alone."

One more lie.

"That's all I can tell you," Zalesky said. "I'm not feeling very well . . . I'm still in a lot of pain and I took some Vicodin before you came and it's making me woozy. If you don't mind . . ."

"Sure, I understand. Just one more question. The argument was outside one of the clubs, you said. Which one?"

Hesitation. Another lie coming up? No. Zalesky held eye contact when he finally answered.

"The Dark Spot," he said.

6

TAMARA

Nine-thirty, and still nobody home at 1122 Willard.

She was terminally bored already. She had her headset on, Norah Jones's Grammy-winner, "Come Away With Me," cranked up in the Walkman; the good pop-jazz kept her awake but it didn't do much for the boredom. The enforced sitting in the small, cramped car was what was messing with her head. Messing with her rear end, too. Bill had told her stakeouts could be a pain in the ass, and now she was finding out that he'd hadn't been kidding. And she'd only been here, what, not more than a couple of hours? He'd done surveillance work that lasted four, six, as many as eight hours. Whoo. Any job like that came up in the future, she'd be quick to hand it over to Jake Runyon.

She sighed and stared at the empty street and wondered if she ought to pack it in. Natural aversion to giving up on a job, even for one night, but much more of this and she'd be listening to complaints from her ass all day tomorrow. Besides which, she had to pee. Not too bad yet, but before long it'd be a crisis. Pepsi and 7UP didn't have a thing on Slim•Fast when it came to fast trips through your plumbing. One can equaled one trip to the can.

Another fifteen minutes, max. Then she was outta here.

Thinking about Slim•Fast made her wonder if maybe there was a Slim•Fast snack bar hiding in the bottom of her purse. Not that she was hungry, but nibbling one of those bars would make the fifteen minutes go by a lot faster. Small bites, let the chocolate melt on her tongue before she swallowed . . . that was the way to do it. Her mouth began to water. She pulled her purse over, rummaged around inside.

Damn! Ate the last one at noon, forgot to put another one in there.

So now she was not only bored, but she had chocolate on her mind. Tasted chocolate, craved chocolate. How could those Slim•Fast people make snack bars that were loaded with chocolate and tasted like Snickers bars but were still good for you and helped you lose weight?

Come Away with Me had cycled through and was replaying. By feel she worked the buttons on the Walkman, ejected the CD, found another one in the case that she thought was Springsteen, and fired that one up. Oh, great, she'd grabbed the wrong one. Classical instead of rock. Beethoven, with Yo-Yo Ma on the cello.

Chocolate out, Horace back in.

No. She wasn't going to think about Horace any more tonight. Hell with Horace. Vonda was better, Vonda and her new white, Jewish boy toy. In love with him? Sure, she was. She'd been in love with every guy she went to bed with, it was her sexual MO. Couldn't do the nasty for the sake of doing the nasty, just because it felt good—no, there had to be all this emotional attachment.

Well, girl? You're not much different, check out you and Horace—

Horace again. Vonda. Vonda, dammit. The black-white thing. Yeah, that'd be a big problem, if by some miracle she actually was in love with this Ben Sherman guy. And him being Jewish made the problem twice as big. Her family was borderline racist, brother Alton not so borderline; they'd make her life miserable if they found out, a living hell if she moved in with him or went all the way and married him. Stupid. Not so much Vonda, you couldn't help who you fell in love with, it was all a matter of chemistry and hormones. Her family, the us-versus-them bullshit. She'd felt that way herself once, all the militant hardass stuff, but not anymore. Everybody had to live with everybody else, what difference did it make what color you were? Or what religion? Or who you slept with or lived with or married? If people would just—

Car coming.

There'd been cars before, a bunch of them. This one probably wouldn't belong to George DeBrissac either, but the lights were coming toward her, high and slow, and she scooted down until her butt was half off the seat. The glare filled the car, only this time they didn't slide on past. Car slowed and then stopped on the street close in front of the Ford.

Oh, man, she thought, cops. Somebody saw me sitting out here, called 911, and now I'm gonna get hassled.

But it wasn't cops, cop cars didn't have high-riding headlights. In the next second she heard gears grinding and then the lights began to retreat and swing out away from her. Backing up. Backing into one of the driveways on this side, close to where she was parked.

Tamara blew out her breath, eased up on the seat until she could squint over the dashboard. Van. No, SUV, one of those big mothers with tinted windows so you couldn't see inside, gliding up the drive of the brick-faced house directly in front of her. She sighed again. Somebody coming home, people on this block had been coming home the whole time she'd been here.

She'd probably have quit paying attention, except the SUV was right in her line of sight. So she watched it stop within a few feet of a closed garage set just back from the house. Lights went off. Driver didn't get out right away, must've been a minute or so before the door opened. It was dark over there, but the distance wasn't much more than twenty-five yards. Big dude. Black man? She had the impression he might be, but she couldn't be sure. Wore dark clothes, some kind of cap pulled down low on his forehead.

A cramp was forming in her left buttock. Terrific. She wiggled, trying to ease it. No good. She needed to sit up, but she didn't want to do that while the dude was hanging over there, maybe call his attention to her. She wiggled some more, willing him to hurry up, go inside, let her sit up—let her get out of here. Now she *really* had to pee.

He hurried, but not straight into the house. Went around to the back of the SUV instead and hauled up the hatch. Light didn't go on inside. But in he went, on hands and knees, out of sight for a few seconds. Then he backed out again to where she could see him, and when he straightened up he had something cradled against his chest with one arm. Something a couple of feet long wrapped in what looked like a blanket.

Something that moved, kicked . . . struggled.

Tamara blinked, squinting. Eyes playing tricks. No, there it was again, the kicking, the struggling, while the man hauled the hatch down and slammed it shut. He hugged whatever was in the blanket closer to his chest, using both hands and arms now. Stood for a few seconds, looking around, looking straight at the Ford for a heartbeat—gave her a chill even though she knew he couldn't see her in the dark—then he half ran across a patchy lawn and up onto the porch. More struggles while he was getting the door unlocked. Then he was gone inside with whatever it was in the blanket.

Dog, Tamara thought. Sure. Sick dog, picked it up late at the vet's. No big deal.

A light went on in the front room over there, punching a couple of saffron squares in the darkness. Both windows had shades pulled all the way down. She sat up, fidgeting, replaying in her mind what she'd just seen.

Hadn't kicked like a dog. Or any other kind of animal.

Kicked like . . . what? A kid?

Come on, Tamara. Why would he have a kid all wrapped up like that? Punishment of some kind? Bad boy, bad girl, wrap your sorry little ass in a blanket?

Lord. A kid could smother, all trussed up in the back of an SUV like a piece of baggage. Lot of bastard parents in this world, abuse their kids in all sorts of ways . . .

No. It hadn't been a kid.

Had it?

Too much imagination, girl. Got to be some simple explanation, nothing weird at all except inside your own head.

Still.

The way the guy had thrown looks around after he shut the

SUV's hatch, sort of furtive, like he was worried somebody might see him. She hadn't imagined that. Or the way he'd half run for the house, humped over, as if he were trying to shield the bundle with his body.

Just didn't seem natural, none of it.

Well, okay, then. What're you gonna do about it?

She sat chewing her lower lip. Call the cops? Oh, yeah, right. Go over to the house, ring the bell, ask the man if everything was cool? He'd say it was even if it wasn't. And it'd piss him off either way, maybe get her in the kind of trouble she wasn't equipped to handle.

Forget about it then. None of her business. Her business was George DeBrissac and 1122 across the street. Plus her full-up bladder. If she didn't get to a bathroom pretty quick . . .

She reached for the ignition key, then pulled her hand back and lifted it instead to click off the dome light. Then she was out of the car, creaking a little from all the sitting, drawing her thighs together against the pressure in her bladder. Always walk in a strange neighborhood as if you belong there, don't do anything to call attention to yourself. Right. Up onto the sidewalk, amble slow past the house. Glance at it, don't stare at it. Lights still on in the front room, shades still drawn tight. Just enough shine from the one nearest the door so that she could make out brass numbers on the brick wall between them. 1109. Pretty sure that was it.

On her way past the driveway, she risked a longer look at the SUV. Big, black—Chevy Suburban? The front license plate was shadowed. 1MO Something 6 Something Something.

Tamara kept on going, forcing herself not to hurry. At the far corner she paused for a few seconds, then turned and came back at the same measured pace. Nothing had changed at

the house. She squinted harder when she reached the driveway, still couldn't quite make out the license number. Caution
told her to give it up, go straight to the Toyota; curiosity sent
her a quick half-dozen steps up the drive, bent low, until she
could read the plate clearly.

1MQD689.

She retreated to the sidewalk, her heart hammering. Got
away with it. Nobody came out of the house, nobody chased
her, nothing happened. A minute later she had the Toyota's
engine rumbling and she was on her way.

Took her five minutes to find a service station on San Pablo
Avenue. Good thing it didn't take six or more; as it was, she
just made the rest room in time.

7

Kerry said, "Remember D-Day? Amazing grace?"

"That's what he said. Mean anything to you?"

"No."

D-Day. June 6, 1944, the day the Allied forces invaded Europe, the beginning of the end of World War II. "Cybil and Dancer were both living in New York in the summer of 'forty-four, weren't they? And the Pulpeteers were active then."

"So?"

"Just thinking it could have something to do with the group." The Pulpeteers had been a loose-knit writers' club of a dozen or so Manhattan-based professionals, Cybil and Ivan and Dancer among them, and a moderately wild bunch according to what Kerry had told me once—club-hopping, all-night parties, crazy practical jokes. "One of their pranks or escapades, maybe."

"That he'd want her to remember after fifty years? I don't think so."

"I guess not."

"Amazing grace," Kerry said. "Well, he couldn't have meant the hymn, that's for sure. Not Russ Dancer."

"I asked him about that and he said no."

"This package," she said. It was on the table between our chairs, where I'd put it when I arrived home a few minutes ago. She'd already fingered it twice; I watched her make it three times. "Paper, a lot of it. It feels like a manuscript."

"You said that before."

"Why would he give her a manuscript?"

"Oh, hell," I said, "all we're doing is asking each other rhetorical questions. Cybil will give us the answers if she wants us to know."

"Why wouldn't she want us to know?"

"I'm not saying she wouldn't. But whatever's in the envelope is obviously private, at least from Dancer's point of view. For her eyes only."

"I wasn't thinking of opening it, for heaven's sake."

"I know that."

Kerry kept staring at the envelope. "One of us should call her."

"What, you mean tonight?"

"Right now. It's only a little after nine. She'll still be up."

"Why should we?"

"To let her know about Dancer and the envelope."

"I told you, he doesn't want her to know he's dying. Doesn't want her to see him all wasted."

"She won't want to go down there."

"Probably not, but—"

"She can't stand him, you know that. All the crap he used to give her, coming on to her all the time . . . he could be a real bastard."

"No argument there."

"I can't stand him myself. I never could."

"Kerry, he's dying."

"That doesn't change how you've felt about somebody all your life."

"Granted. But it's also no reason not to respect his dying wishes. He doesn't want Cybil to open the package until after he's gone."

"She has a right to know."

"Right to know what?"

"That's he's dying. About this . . . legacy of his."

"I don't understand that. What gives her that right? And what difference does it make if she knows about it ahead of time?"

"I'd want to know," Kerry said.

"Why?"

"Wouldn't you? If it was somebody you'd known for fifty years?"

"Not if he specifically asked that I not be told until afterward. Why bother her with this now?"

"She has a right to know."

"You keep saying that," I said, and then made the mistake of trying to lighten things up. "How about a new career in media public relations? You'd be good at giving out the old 'the public has a right to know' line."

Big scowl. "Oh, so now I'm spouting crap."

"I didn't say that . . ."

"This is different and you know it."

"Why is it different?"

"Because it's personal."

"Personal to Cybil, not to you. Why're you getting so worked up?"

"I'm not worked up. I'm just trying to make you understand how I feel."

"Babe," I said gently, "how you feel isn't relevant."

"That's a lousy thing to say. I've had to deal with Russ Dancer off and on most of my life, dammit."

"But you're not involved in this last wish thing. He didn't say anything about you, the envelope isn't addressed to you."

"You think Cybil won't feel the same as I do? She will." Kerry fingered the package again, as if it had some kind of magnetic lure for her. "She'll be upset if we don't call her tonight."

I didn't say anything.

"You don't believe me," she said.

"That's not the issue—"

"Don't you suppose I know my own mother?"

"Sure, of course, and if she gets upset I'm sorry, but—"

"But you're not going to call her."

"*We're* not going to call her," I said.

"Just because you say so."

"No, because Russ Dancer said so. He put me in a position of trust, and like it or not, I won't violate it. Neither will you."

"Mr. Macho."

"Kerry, come on, be reasonable . . ."

She got up without looking at me or saying anything else and stomped off into the kitchen.

What just happened here? I thought.

We'd had one of our infrequent fights and I didn't even

know what the hell we'd been fighting about. Cut and dried issue, as far as I could see. Simple, basic. I tried to look at it from
her point of view, still couldn't find anything to get exercised
over. How had I got to be the bad guy in this business?

At ten-thirty I took a couple of Dancer's pseudonymous paperbacks to bed with me. Alone. Kerry was still shut up inside her home office. Working, she said—the only thing she'd
said to me since the living room. Avoiding me was more like
it. I hadn't seen much of Emily tonight, either—shut inside
her room, listening to music and doing her homework—and
her good-night kiss had been perfunctory. Home after a
long, hard day, cradled in the bosom of my loving family?
No, sir. Ignored, misunderstood, and consigned to bed with
Murder in Hot Pants and *Gun Fury in Crucifix Canyon* for
company.

The first title was a medium raunchy porn thing thinly
wrapped in a mystery-story plot. One cover blurb said it was
"a brand-new, uncensored, unexpurgated bombshell by Bart
Hardman"; a second blurb said, "He fought the scum of humanity to follow her on the road straight to hell!" Dancer
hadn't wasted any time getting down and dirty; the first sexual
encounter between the narrator, a tough cop named McHugh,
and a Hollywood starlet "whose epic body had starred with a
cast of thousands" started in the middle of page 6. I quit reading at the top of page 7. Russ Dancer's sexual fantasies held no
interest for me, and after the time I'd spent with the wasted
shell of him tonight, they seemed somehow repellent.

The other book was a western, about a range war in
Wyoming, loaded with stick-figure characters and enough

carnage in the first fifty pages to fill half a dozen novels. Pure hackwork, the writing slapdash; but here and there as I skimmed through I saw little blips—a simile, a descriptive passage, a brief exchange of dialogue—of the raw-talent, pulp-era Russell Dancer, of the writer he might have been. It made me sad, as evidence of waste always does.

I closed this one at page 50, put both books on the nightstand next to Dancer's legacy. I'd brought the envelope in there with me just in case Kerry had any ideas of jumping the gun on her mother. Tomorrow I would take all the books I'd appropriated and put them in Kerry's Goodwill bag. I'd had more than enough of the corrupt hack Dancer had become. If I ever had another urge to read him, I'd pick up an old issue of *Midnight Detective* and commune with Rex Hannigan for a little while. Probably not, though. Probably not.

I lay there in the dark and felt sorry for him and sorry for myself and wished to Christ he'd picked on somebody else to carry out his dying wishes.

In the morning I had some outside work that kept me out of the office until around eleven. Tamara was busy on the phone when I walked in. Runyon was there, too, neatly dressed in his usual dark suit and tie, studying the screen on his laptop.

"Morning, Jake. Busy?"

"Not very. Heading out pretty soon. The Great Western fraud claim."

"Talk to you for a minute before you go?"

"Sure." He switched off the computer, closed the lid. "Here or in your office?"

"Make it the office. More comfortable in there."

He followed me in and we got settled on either side of my

desk. He sat solid and stiff in the client's chair, the way he always did in the office, as if he were uncomfortable sitting in
the presence of someone else. Or as if he'd forgotten how to
relax. He was a boulder of a man, compact, with a slablike,
jut-jawed face that seldom smiled. When he'd first come in to
interview for the field operative's job, his clothes had hung
loosely on him and he'd looked ill—the physical effects of
six months of watching his second wife die a slow, painful
death from ovarian cancer. Since then he'd gained weight,
color; outwardly he seemed to have come to terms with his
loss. But there was still a distance, an inward-turned reticence
about him, that said differently. Inside he was still the same
sad and bitter and angry man, maybe always would be. I liked
him, Tamara liked him, and in his way it was probably re-
cipocal; after what we'd gone through together just before
Christmas, there was a professional bond among the three of
us. But that was as far as it went. We weren't friends, didn't so-
cialize, didn't talk about anything except business. Any efforts
to personalize our relationship were politely rejected. Colleen
Runyon hadn't been just his wife, she'd been his best friend,
his only real friend; now that she was gone, he had no one else
and wanted no one else. It had been that kind of marriage. He
was that kind of man. The only person who really mattered
to him now was his son, his only living relative, the main reason he'd moved to San Francisco from Seattle—and his son
hated him.

I said, easing into it, "How was L.A.?"

"Worth the trip. Beckmer's down there, all right. Holed up
with his ex-wife in Santa Ana."

"Cozy. You serve the subpoena?"

"He didn't want to take it. Tried to get tough."

"And?"

Runyon shrugged. "He took it."

"You give Fred Agajanian the good news yet?"

"Left a message with his secretary. He's in court this morning."

I said Fred would be pleased. Then I said, "I took a call for you yesterday afternoon. Didn't sound like business. He wouldn't leave his name, but . . . I had the impression it might've been your son."

Nothing changed in Runyon's expression. "Might've been. Message from him on my machine when I got home last night."

"He sounded upset about something. Everything okay with him?"

"No. His roommate's in the hospital. Three gay bashings in the Castro district over the past couple of weeks—he's the latest victim."

"Christ. Hurt bad?"

"Still critical."

"Police have any leads on who did it?"

"Other than sketchy descriptions of the two perps, no."

"Figures. This damn city. SFPD's in a shambles, the politicians keep tearing each other up over who's responsible instead of working together to fix the problems, and meanwhile even violent-crime cases get short shrift."

"Hate crimes against gays among the shortest," Runyon said. "I looked up last year's stats a while ago. Nearly five hundred reported cases, only a handful resolved."

"So much for San Francisco's reputation as a liberal mecca for homosexuals. What was it like in Seattle?"

"Pretty much the same. Cases like this, it takes a media howl for there to be much of an official effort."

"And the only way that happens is if there're more beatings and maybe one of the victims dies."

He nodded. "It won't get to that point if I can help it."

"An investigation of your own?"

"Joshua asked me to see what I can do. I'd go ahead even if he hadn't."

"So would I, in your shoes."

"Already started," Runyon said. "On my own time. I talked to the second victim last night."

"Anything?"

"Maybe. Too early to tell for sure."

"Well, the job doesn't have to be strictly on your own time," I said. "Agency facilities are yours if you need them. That includes Tamara and me. If there's anything we can do, just ask."

"No payoff in it."

"So? You think this agency's never done any pro bono work before? Or taken on any personal cases? If it was my kid who was hurting, or somebody in Tamara's family, wouldn't you offer to help out if you could?"

"In a minute."

"Okay. That's all the payoff we need."

"Sorry if I sounded cynical."

"Hell," I said, "it's not easy to be anything else these days."

I didn't have much opportunity to talk to Tamara during the day. Lunch with Pat Dixon, an assistant D.A. who'd become a friend after a revenge bomber case that involved the kidnapping of his son. Both of us busy in the office with our respective caseloads, client calls, and a drop-in visit from another client who wanted to talk over a report. It wasn't until three-thirty that we found time to say more than a few words to each other.

"How'd the deadbeat dad thing go last night?" I asked. "De-Brissac living in the cousin's San Leandro house?"

"If he is," Tamara said, "he was out later than I was. Three hours' surveillance was all the down time I could take."

"Told you stakeouts were a pain in the butt. How about the house? Did it look lived in?"

"Hard to tell. All the windows blinded so I couldn't get a look inside. Nothing in the front or back yards but weeds."

"Talk to any of the neighbors?"

"Not yet. Didn't want to risk it yet."

"Probably wise. So you're going back tonight?"

"Yeah." She hesitated, a frown working up little rows in the smooth skin of her face. "Funny thing," she said then.

"What is?"

"Something that went down last night."

"What kind of something?"

"What I saw, or thought I saw," she said. "Keeps messing around in my head. I did some checking, but . . . I don't know, it's probably nothing. Just my bad imagination, you know what I'm saying?"

"No," I said. "What is it you saw?"

"Well, while I was—"

The phone rang just then and cut her off. The call was for me, and by the time I finished with it Tamara was involved in a call of her own. I meant to pick up the conversation again, find out what she'd seen that was bothering her, but the press of other business kept getting in the way. Well, if it was anything important she'd come to me about it eventually.

Just before I left the office I called Kaiser Permanente Hospital in Redwood City. The last frayed thread of Russ Dancer's wasted life had snapped at 1:57 that afternoon.

8

JAKE RUNYON

The first victim of the gay bashings had been a printer and graphic artist named Larry Exeter. Time: a few minutes past midnight on April 4. Place: an alley off Eighteenth Street, not far from where he lived. He'd gone out for a walk around the neighborhood "to get some air." Two men had accosted him on the street, dragged him into the alley, beat him senseless with fists and an "unidentified blunt instrument." A resident in one of the flanking buildings had heard the commotion, looked out his window, yelled when he saw what was going on, and the perps ran. Neither Exeter nor the citizen had been able to supply detailed descriptions of the men or their vehicle. Exeter's injuries were serious enough to require hospital treatment, but the beating had been interrupted before any major damage was done: three cracked ribs but no broken bones or internal damage.

Runyon got all of this from the police report, through one

of the agency's contacts at the SFPD. Joshua hadn't been able to remember Exeter's name, and Gene Zalesky had professed not to know him, either. Exeter's Seventeenth Street address was given in the report, but no phone number; and there was no listing for him in the white pages. A check revealed that he shared an apartment with a David Mulford, who did have a listed number.

Runyon had a window of free time around three o'clock. He tried Mulford's number then, and the man who answered owned up, reluctantly, to being Larry Exeter. High, thin, timid voice and an attitude to match, he kept saying, "I just want to forget what happened, get on with my life." Runyon danced with him, playing it low-key and mentioning his son several times, and eventually talked him into a face-to-face meeting. "But you can't come here," Exeter said. "David . . . my partner . . . he wouldn't like it."

"Any time and place that's convenient for you."

"Does it have to be today?"

"If you can manage it. The sooner the better."

"Well . . . I should go out for groceries before David gets home. The Safeway on Market and Church, you know where that is?"

"You want to talk while you're shopping?"

"No, no. Across the street, on the first block of Church, there's a coffee shop . . . Starbucks. I could meet you for a few minutes around four-thirty."

"I'll be there."

The second thing Runyon did was to finish up a preliminary background check on Gene Zalesky that he'd started the night before. Financial status and credit rating: solid. Employment record: likewise, twelve years with Coastal Banking Systems. The only blot was an arrest fourteen years ago for soliciting— evidently one of those police stings in which he'd propositioned an undercover cop—and the charges had been dropped for insufficient evidence. Honest, law-abiding citizen, from all indications. So why had Zalesky lied last night? What had scared him enough to suddenly withhold information?

Larry Exeter was in his late twenties, slight, sandy-haired. Soft white skin, washed-out blue eyes. Colorless manner to go with his timid voice and monochrome appearance. If you had to sum him up in one word, it would be meek. One of the biblical inheritors.

Runyon was waiting when Exeter walked slow and stiff into the Starbucks, a plastic grocery sack dangling from each hand. The walk and a long, nearly healed cut along his jawline were the only outward signs of the beating he'd taken. He picked Runyon out of the dozen or so patrons as easily as Runyon had recognized him, came straight to his table.

"Sorry I'm late," Exeter said when he sat down. It was 4:31 by a clock on one of the walls. One minute late. An apologizer, too—the type of person who would always be sorry for something, eight or ten times a day, every day of his life. "The lines at Safeway at this hour . . ."

"No problem. Buy you a cup of coffee?"

"Thanks, but I don't want anything. I can't stay long."

"I won't keep you."

"I have to start dinner." He made it sound like another apology. "David doesn't like it if I don't have food on the table when he gets home."

Runyon nodded. That kind of relationship. The dominant and the submissive, each of them getting exactly what they wanted out of it.

"Just a few questions. What can you tell me about the two men who attacked you?"

"Not very much." Exeter closed his eyes, popped them open again. "In their twenties, I think. One of them heavyset, the other . . . I don't remember anything about him except that he was wearing some kind of hooded jacket. It all happened so fast. I was just walking, minding my own business, and all of a sudden there they were. Grabbing me, saying things, dragging me into that alley . . ." The memory was vivid enough to produce a visible shiver.

"What exactly did they say?"

"The usual slurs. Faggot. Queer. Boyfucker."

"Nothing else?"

"I don't remember. My God, I've never been so frightened in my life. I thought . . . I really thought they were going to kill me. And for what? Just because I was born different from them. Men like that . . ."

Runyon said, "Everybody needs someone to look down on."

"I'm sorry . . . what?"

Line from a song by Kris Kristofferson, one of Colleen's favorites. But he said instead, "They're blind haters. Different scares them, threatens them. They can't understand or accept it, so they look down on it, hate it, try to destroy it."

"Neanderthal behavior."

"Neanderthals and assholes—the world's full of them."

Exeter laughed a little, ruefully. "Amen to that."

"So you were out for a walk when it happened, is that right?"

Hesitation. Eye shift.

"That's what you told the police. Not so?"

"I . . . well . . ."

"I'm on your side, Mr. Exeter. Better be honest with me."

Another hesitation, longer this time. Then, "I was afraid David would find out where I'd been. He was out of town on business, he has a sales job with IBM and he travels a good deal. Usually, I stay home, but sometimes . . . I get so lonely I just have to go out for an evening . . ." Another apology.

"Where'd you go that night?"

"Castro Street. One of the bars."

"Which one?"

"A place called The Dark Spot."

The Dark Spot again.

"David doesn't like it much," Exeter said, "I suppose it's too tame for him. He's into . . . other things. So I only go there when he's out of town."

"Do you know Gene Zalesky?"

"Gene? Yes. Those animals beat him up too."

"How well do you know him?"

"Not very. Just casually."

"The Dark Spot one of his regular hangouts?"

"Well, I've seen him there a few times."

"Kenneth Hitchcock? Must know him too."

"Yes, I know Kenneth. He . . . well, never mind."

"What were you going to say?"

Eye shift. "It's not important."

"Suppose you let me be the judge of that."

"It's just that . . . well, you said he's your son's partner . . ."

"Whatever you tell me goes no farther than this table."

Exeter said uncomfortably, apologetically, "He's a flirt."

"Meaning what, exactly?"

"With the customers. Some more than others. He . . ."

"Comes on to them? Makes dates with them?"

"I don't know. Honestly, I don't."

"Gossip or rumors to that effect?"

Exeter avoided eye contact again. His pale face wore little beads of sweat now. "There are always rumors," he said.

"About Kenneth and Gene Zalesky?"

"No. No. Gene likes . . . well, younger guys."

"How young?"

"I didn't mean that's he a pedophile, if that's what you're thinking."

"I'm not thinking anything, just asking questions."

"I'm sorry, I . . ." Exeter shifted position, winced, and made a pained sound in his throat that evolved into a series of short panting breaths. It was several seconds before he spoke again. "My ribs . . . they're not healed yet. I still have trouble breathing sometimes."

Runyon nodded. "We were talking about Gene Zalesky's preferences."

"Young men. Late teens, early twenties. Kenneth Hitchcock must be almost thirty."

"Any young men in particular?"

"No. He's not into long-term relationships."

"Ever see him with a young blond guy with an angelic face?"

". . . Angelic?"

"Zalesky's description."

"Oh my God."

"What is it?"

All of a sudden Exeter was scared. "I have to go," he said, "David will be home, I can't . . . his dinner . . ." He started to get up.

Runyon caught his arm, held him. "Who is he, this young blond guy?"

"Please, I . . ."

"What's his name?"

Fidgety silence. Then, "Troy."

"Troy what?"

"I don't know his last name. He . . . oh, Christ!"

"What's got you so upset, Mr. Exeter?"

"I can't . . . if David ever finds out . . ."

"You and this Troy, is that it?"

"One night, that's all it was," Exeter said miserably. "A . . . one-night stand. David had been away two weeks, a business trip to Hong Kong, I was so lonely . . . it just happened . . ."

"When was this?"

"Last month, three or four weeks ago."

"Where'd you meet Troy? The Dark Spot?"

"Yes."

"Take him to your apartment?"

"My God, no. We went to his room . . . Troy's . . ."

"Room? A hotel?"

"No, an apartment house not far away."

"What apartment house? What address?"

"I don't remember."

"Sure you do. It wasn't that long ago."

"I was . . . I had a lot to drink that night. Somewhere in the neighborhood. Uphill toward Market. I swear that's all I remember."

"Is Troy a regular at The Dark Spot?"

"Recently. I saw him there two or three times before that night."

"With Gene Zalesky?"

"I'm not sure . . . maybe . . ."

"How about a redhead with freckles?"

"No, I don't think so. But he was . . . popular, you know? Different guys . . ."

"Promiscuous?"

"Yes. But safe sex, he was smart about that."

"Is he one of the customers Kenneth Hitchcock flirted with?"

"Well, he liked to sit at the bar."

"Last time you saw him was when?"

"Not since we . . . that night."

"But he does still hang out at The Dark Spot?"

"I don't know, I suppose so. I've only been there once since . . . the night I was attacked . . . and Troy wasn't there then." Exeter glanced nervously at the wall clock. "I really do have to go. If I'm not there when David comes home, he gets very angry."

"We're almost done," Runyon said. "Does Troy have a car?"

"Car?"

"Did he drive you to the house where he lives?"

"Oh. No, we walked. It wasn't far."

"So you don't know if he owns a car."

"I'm sorry, no. Why are you asking all these questions about Troy? He couldn't possibly have anything to do with the bashings."

Runyon said, "No more than The Dark Spot could," and let it go at that.

Gene Zalesky wasn't home. Or if he was, he wasn't answering his doorbell.

Next stop: The Dark Spot.

Runyon had been to the heart of the Castro, the section between Market and Twentieth Streets, a few times before. Driving and walking both, familiarizing himself with the area and with Joshua's world. He'd done some background research on the district as well, for the same reasons. Twenty-five years as a gay ghetto, beginning in the pioneering days of gay liberation in the early seventies; the days when dilapidated storefronts and bars and other rough edges were considered a righteous emblem of the oppressed homosexual cause, and almost all the businesses catered to gays and lesbians. The ravages of AIDS had nearly destroyed the Castro in the early nineties. When it began to show signs of life again, it was no longer a closed community; chain stores and upscale boutiques and fast-food outlets and other businesses catering to straights as well as gays elbowed in and slowly changed the face of the neighborhood. Yuppie families moved in, too, buying up and renovating some of the old Victorians. Now rainbow flags flew openly next to American flags, shops dispensing clothing and symbols of gay culture rubbed shoulders with others peddling urban chic and Starbucks coffee and Radio Shack computers, old-fashioned meat-market clubs like The Dark Spot and Queer Heaven stood cheek by jowl with brew pubs and sports bars.

At five-thirty on a week night, the district's jammed streets and sidewalks were a heterogeneous mix of gays and straights, whites and a variety of ethnics. Young mothers with kids in tow walking next to men in tight leather pants and open leather vests with nothing underneath. Suits and ties, motorcycle jackets bristling with studs and looped with chains. Orange spiked hair and crew cuts. Elaborate tattoos, body piercings, nose rings, nipple rings, and wedding rings. Sex, drugs, and rock 'n' roll coexisting, sometimes peacefully, sometimes violently, with family values and the conservative urban lifestyle.

But in essence it remained the seat of Gay Power. The huge rainbow flag that flew permanently at the corner of Market and Castro attested to that. So did the annual Gay Pride Parade that drew thousands from all over the West Coast. So did the big celebration that had taken place there recently, when the U.S. Supreme Court finally struck down the antiquated Texas sodomy law and proclaimed that gay Americans had a constitutional right to private sexual relationships.

None of its ambience had much impact on Runyon as he walked through it. Nor would it have in its early gay-ghetto days. A vice cop he'd known when he was on the Seattle PD had referred to the gay district up there as a "polyglot of perversion," but he'd never seen it that way. The gay scene, diluted or not, was no different from the straight singles scene—the gay clubs no different, for that matter, from women's clubs or garden clubs. A little more dangerous late at night, a little more desperate because of the threat of AIDS, but otherwise just people with common interests and outlooks gathering together for companionship, camaraderie, pleasure. Trying to make their lives a little easier, to put a little joy into them. Trying to keep their hurts at bay.

All pleasure was, when you got right down to it, a staving off of pain. The pain of living, the pain of dying. The ones who could manage it were the lucky ones. He wasn't one of them. There had been no pleasure for him since Colleen died, just the pain. Work was the only thing that dulled the ache, allowed him to go on, and then only for brief periods. Establishing some kind of connection with Joshua might help some, but in the heavy baggage between them there was no room for joy. Understanding, a father-son detente, was the best he could hope for.

So he walked here alone, a misfit among the straights, a misfit among the gays. The proverbial stranger in a strange land. Funny thing was, there was a kind of small, cold comfort in being part of Joshua's world, his misfit son's strange land, if only for a little while.

The Dark Spot turned out to be no different from fifty, a hundred other bars he'd visited, gay or straight, on business or otherwise. Blue lights and blue neon so dark it was almost black. Loud music, loud laughter. Men packed along the bar, men dancing, men with their heads together at tables and in dark corners. The few who glanced at him glanced away again immediately. Cop written on his face and the way he moved. Straight cop at that: avoid at all costs.

He stayed just long enough to scan the crowd and satisfy himself that neither Gene Zalesky nor a young, angelic-faced blond nor a redhead with freckles was among them. He spoke to no one. There was nothing for him here alone, no answers to any of his questions. The only way anybody would talk to him in The Dark Spot was if he came with a guide, a member of the fraternity.

Joshua?

Under different circumstances, he could at least ask. But after what Larry Exeter had told him, no. He'd have to find somebody else. Or some other way to get the information he needed.

9

TAMARA

Here she was, back for another fun evening in San Leandro. All set to rock 'n' roll.

Yeah. Right.

All set to abuse her tailbone again.

Nobody home at 1122 Willard.

Nobody home at 1109 Willard, either.

Almost eight o'clock and both houses were dark, driveways empty, no cars parked in front of either one. Sure, somebody might be in a lighted room at the back that she couldn't see from here. Or how about sitting in the dark like a humongous spider? There goes that imagination again, girl. Keep it up and you'll start scaring yourself, be rolling your eyes and shaking your booty like Mantan Moreland in one of those crappy Charlie Chan flicks. Feets, do your stuff.

Well? Gonna just sit here or gonna move?

She got out of the Toyota—parked in the same puddle of

tree-dark as last night, her own little reserved space—and locked the door and crossed the street to 1122. Through the gate, up on the porch, ring the bell, wait, ring the bell again, wait some more—just like last night, déjà vu all over again. De-Brissac wasn't home. Wasn't answering the farty doorbell, anyway. Dag. Wasn't anything worked out easy for her these days, seemed like.

Go round the side and up the driveway, look for a light at the rear? Not much point. She retreated to the sidewalk instead. The dark brick face of 1109 drew her gaze, held it and held her still for a few seconds. Front yard still empty, shades still pulled down tight over the front windows. So what? So nothing. Then how come the slithery sensation on her neck, like some bug had crawled under the collar of her blouse?

Back across the street again. Neighborhood seemed quieter than it had last night. Distant hum of traffic, salsa music pulsing a long ways off, no sounds close by. Lights, people in most houses on the block, all kinds of things going on behind closed doors, and yet those two dark houses somehow made it seem empty, lifeless. No, just that brick job there—1109. Kept messing with her mind, kept bringing back what she'd seen last night, the SUV with tinted windows and the big furtive dude and whatever it was kicking and struggling inside that blanket.

A gust of wind put a shiver on her as she unlocked the car. Inside, with the doors locked again, she pressed her cold hands between her thighs. And kept right on looking at 1109. Couldn't seem to stop looking at it or thinking about it.

Robert Lemoyne. Name of the registered owner of a 2002 Ford Explorer with the license plate 1MQD689; name of the man who'd leased 1109 Willard from Avenex Realty in Union City nine years ago. A half-and-half—African-American father and white mother. Age: forty-seven. Born in Stockton, lived there until high school graduation. No additional education. Carpenter and construction worker—three years, East Valley Construction, Turlock; twelve years, Hollenbeck & Son, El Cerrito; eight years, High Country Construction Co., Grass Valley; six years, Brinson Builders, Fremont. Married twice. First, to Dinah Elvers of Oakland, 1977; lasted ten years, divorce obtained by the wife on grounds of irreconcilable differences, no children. Second, to Mia Canfield of Rough and Ready, 1994; lasted seven years, divorce obtained by the wife on same standard no-fault grounds. One child, a daughter, Angela, born in 1995; sole custody awarded to the mother. Financial status: debts like everybody else, but kept most of them current. One felony arrest, in 1986 on a charge of reckless endangerment. No big deal, because the charge had been reduced to leaving the scene of an accident, a misdemeanor. No other brushes with the law, not even an unpaid parking ticket. And no record of non-payment of child support.

Didn't seem to be much in any of that. Unless sole custody of the daughter awarded to Mia Canfield Lemoyne meant something.

One other thing that might mean something: Robert Lemoyne apparently lived alone now, all alone in that big house there.

Whatever'd been in that blanket last night was alive, no doubt about that. Animal? If he had a dog, it didn't bark or make any other noise when he came home at night. And he hadn't bothered to license it with the city of San Leandro.

Child?

Well, could be he *didn't* live alone, was shacking with some single woman that had a son or daughter. Possible. But then where was she last night? Didn't come home with him, wasn't in the house before he got there unless she was waiting for him in the dark. Wasn't there now, either.

Besides . . . why bundle up a girlfriend's kid and bring it home stuffed in the back of an SUV? Why do that to anybody's kid?

One reason. One big ugly word that explained the SUV and the blanket and the struggles and the furtive looks and the run to the house.

Kidnapping.

Crazy. No damn basis for that kind of speculation. Except that kind of thing happened, more and more often these days. Kids snatched off the streets on their way to or from school, off playgrounds, in malls, from dozens of other places. Kids taken for ransom, for even more inhuman crimes. Kids that disappeared and were found dead or never found at all; faces on police reports and posters and milk cartons. And the sick fucks that preyed on them came in all shapes and sizes and races, from all kinds of backgrounds, and held all kinds of jobs and lived in all kinds neighborhoods including quiet ones just like this.

It *was* possible. Anything was possible. Working for Bill the past five years had taught her that.

Bill. She wished she'd talked to him about what she'd seen. Started to this afternoon and then both of them got distracted. Too much for her, trying to handle this kind of thing all by herself—she just didn't have enough experience. But he'd know what to do. Call him right now? Better do it. He—

Her cell went off.

The sudden rackety noise startled her enough so she banged her knee on the bottom of the steering wheel. Another ring.

She must've forgotten to switch it off. What if it'd cut loose while she was out on the street, or wandering around the property at 1122? Stupid, Tamara. Got to be more careful.

She fumbled her purse open, rummaged around, came up with the phone in the middle of a fourth ring. "Yeah, hello?"

". . . Tam? Is that you?"

Oh, great. Vonda. "Who else'd be answering my cell?"

"You sound funny. Out of breath."

"What you want?"

"Well, you don't have to jump down my throat."

"I can't talk now. I'm on a job here."

"Well, I'm sorry, but I really need to *talk* to you. I just saw Ben, and he—"

"Who? Oh, your white horndog. Listen, Vonda—"

"He's not a horndog. And he's not gonna be anybody's white man if he doesn't pay attention. Got it in his head he wants to meet my folks, tell them about us. I told him what they're like, the black-white thing, but he thinks he can handle it, he says—"

"Black, white . . . mercy! Got a half-and-half I'm trying to deal with here myself, all right?"

"What? You met someone?"

"No, and I hope I don't meet him."

"Huh?"

"What I'm saying, race doesn't always have to be an issue. Knamean?"

"It does in my family, you *know* how they are—"

"Later, okay? Are you home? I'll call you later."

"I'm home, but—"

Tamara's thumb came down hard on the disconnect button. And then just as hard on the off button.

Lord! Of all the damn times!

She jammed the cell back into her purse. Thirty seconds of back-and-forth babbling . . . Vonda probably thought she was stoned or something. Never mind, explain it to her later. Right now she was so creeped out, so twitched she couldn't sit still, thoughts running around inside her head bumping into each other like when you were on a speed rush. Don't keep trying to think it out, do something. Yeah, but what? Call the boss man, call Jake Runyon . . . no, not yet. Any more words coming out her mouth would just stumble and bump together like her thoughts, same kind of babble as her conversation with Vonda. Too wired to make sense. Too wired to keep on sitting here like this worrying about how wired she was.

Do something!

Next thing she knew, she was out of the car again and locking the door. And then up on the sidewalk, heading straight for 1109.

Oh, listen now, you better not do this, you don't know what you might be walking into . . .

Random thought, bumped away by all the others. Didn't even put a hitch in her stride. Up the front path, remember to go slow and look straight ahead like she belonged here. Climb the porch steps, step up close to the door. Quiet inside, nobody moving around that she could hear. Thumb on the bell . . . here we go.

No answer.

Again.

No answer.

Relief and disappointment in equal measures. She left the porch, hesitated at the foot of the steps to look both ways along the street. No cars, no people walking around in the dark. She sidestepped to her right, into the empty drive. Between the house and the garage was a narrow, shadowed areaway that led to the rear of the property. Her legs carried her that way, into the areaway and halfway along to where a side door opened into the garage. She paused long enough to turn the knob: locked. Relief and disappointment again, and another random thought—*Don't go any farther!*—that got bumped away. She kept on going into the backyard.

Big shade tree, heavy shadows that moved and rustled in the breeze. Shrubs, dead grass that crunched under her shoes. Crooked board fence at the back end. Lights in the house on the other side, but no lights in the one here. Her mouth felt dry as toast; she tried to work up some spit, but her saliva glands wouldn't cooperate. Man oh man.

She went a few steps to her right, across more dead grass toward a platform porch tacked onto the rear of the house. She wasn't thinking at all now, and too deep into her prowl to quit on instinct. Half a dozen warped steps led up to the back door; she stopped at the foot of them, squinting, holding her breath. Door was sure to be locked, and even if she could get inside she didn't dare do it. Breaking and entering, criminal trespass—

What was that?

Noise inside somewhere. Sounded like . . .

There. Again.

She moved away from the steps, in close to where a window made a black rectangle down low in the pale white wall, almost at ground level. Stood still again and flapped her ears, hard. And the hair went up on her neck, her scalp crawled, her pulse kicked and fluttered.

Crying.

Child crying in there.

Tamara squatted and leaned an ear against the cold glass. No mistake. And not just any kind of crying—lost, scared, maybe hurt. Little girl? Couldn't be sure. She tried to peer through the window, couldn't even see her own reflection, and realized that the blackness was more than just night-dark—it was paint, there was black paint all over the glass. Her fingers dug at the bottom of the sash; it wouldn't budge. Nailed or painted shut, might also be barred in some way.

Now what? Make some noise, try to attract the child's attention? What good would that do? Little kid left alone this way, must be locked up in a room.

Flash of herself breaking in, rescuing the kid. Oh no you don't. Who you think you are, Superwoman? Movie stuff, Hollywood bullshit. No clue what's going on, blunder in there and you're liable to make a bad situation worse. And it was bad. She could feel the bad coming out from behind that black-painted window, negative energy as heavy as pulses of heat. Her skin tingled and crawled with it.

Smart thing was to stay cool. Get off this property, fast. Then . . . talk to the next-door neighbors, use some pretext to make sure that kid in there didn't belong to a new girlfriend of Robert Lemoyne's. And then quit the neighborhood, get hold of Bill and convince him, and after that go find the nearest cop house. She'd have to talk long and hard, and downplay the trespassing thing, but with the boss man for backup she'd convince the law too. Then . . .

Yeah, then. Better be right about this, Tamara.

I am. Listen to that kid crying, remember the way things went down last night. Bad, all right. Bad as it can get.

She stood and backed off from the window, retraced her

route across the dry grass toward the garage. Full of purpose now. Hurrying some as she headed into the areaway.

Car on the street.

She was opposite the side door to the garage when she heard it. Couldn't see it or its lights yet, but it was in this block—engine sound getting louder. She pulled back against the wall of the house, where the shadows were deepest. Nothing to worry about. Early yet, cars passing by all the time. The street brightened ahead with the approaching lights. Just stand still, wait for them to pass by.

They didn't pass by. Without any slowdown they arced around fast, high and bright, into the driveway.

She went stumbling headlong back to the rear corner of the house, away from the lights. A long narrow section of dead lawn leaped into brightness ahead of her as she ducked around the corner. *He saw me!* No, stay cool, he didn't, stay cool. Hide! She looked around wildly. Nowhere to hide, fences at the back and far side too high to climb; oh, Lord, nowhere to go—

The funnel of light coming through the areaway vanished, plunging the yard into heavy shadow again.

Car door slammed.

Her breath caught in her throat. She froze, looking back over her shoulder, poised to run again. If he came back here, chased her and she couldn't get away, she'd start screaming. She could scream like a banshee, Pop always said that, scream like a banshee and bring out the whole friggin' neighborhood.

Shaky-legged, she went forward again. The crunch of the grass under her shoes seemed loud in the silence. Past the porch stairs, still looking over her shoulder, her breath hot and tight in her chest.

Another door slammed. Front door to the house?

He *didn't* see me! He went inside!

She quickened her pace to the corner, turned it slow. On that side a ten-foot-wide section of grass and dirt and straggly plants separated the house from the lot-line fence. Dark along there, but she could see the street ahead, the shape of Horace's Toyota parked under the curbside tree, part of a lighted house on the far side. She crept beneath two darkened windows, straining to listen. Nothing to hear except the thud of her heart. Light in that window up toward the front? Looked like it . . . yeah, pale and diffused, probably from a lamp in the room next to it. He'd gone inside, all right. All she had to do was keep easing along, be careful not to make any noise. Another minute or two and she'd be out on the sidewalk.

She edged forward to the window with the light showing, ducked under it to the front corner. Tall, thick jasmine shrub growing there, sweet-smelling in the darkness. Nobody on the street, nobody in sight. Okay, go—

He was waiting, hidden, along the wall behind the jasmine. He came out at her cat-fast, jammed one hand over her mouth, wrapped the other around her, and dragged her in against the solid bulk of his body.

No!

She couldn't tear loose, couldn't yell, could barely breathe. Something hard jammed against her rib cage—gun, he had a gun! Words and hot breath filled her ear.

"Don't fight me, don't make any noise. You do and I'll hurt you like you never been hurt before."

10

When I left the office, I drove out to Monterey Heights to pick up Emily. Some days after school she went straight home on the bus; most days, like this one, she spent two or three hours at the home of her best friend, Carla Simpson, and either Kerry or I fetched her after work. My turn today, and I was glad of it. Glad, too, that it was one of Kerry's late days at Bates and Carpenter. Otherwise, she'd have wanted to go with me to see her mother, and been even more annoyed at me when I refused. As it was I'd probably take additional flak for not calling and letting her know Russ Dancer was gone. Lose-lose situation no matter what I did. So I'd just go ahead and handle it the way I'd been asked to.

Still, I didn't particularly relish driving over to Marin County and facing Cybil alone. I liked Cybil, she was one of my favorite people, but delivering bad news along with Dancer's legacy was bound to be a little strained. What I needed was a buffer.

In the car I said to the buffer, "Emily, how'd you like to go visit Grandma Cybil before we go home?"

"Sure! But how come?"

"Well, I have to talk to her."

"What about?"

"Something private. It won't take long."

Emily didn't try to probe. She was as inquisitive as any eleven-year-old, but also accepting of the fact that there were adults-only issues not meant for her ears and that private meant private. One of her many sterling qualities.

So we crawled out Nineteenth Avenue to the Golden Gate Bridge, Emily chattering the whole way about her schoolwork. She was writing an essay on Firebell Lillie Coit, the woman whose fascination with firefighting had led to the construction of one of the city's landmarks, Coit Tower, and she regaled me with all sorts of obscure facts she'd dug up in her Internet and book research. Amazing how she'd blossomed psychologically and socially in the past year and a half. When I'd first met her, during the course of a case involving her now-deceased birth mother, she'd been shy, vulnerable, lonely, and deeply withdrawn. Some of the shyness remained, but she was no longer the scared little introvert. She'd learned to trust people, trust herself and her feelings. Kerry's and my doing, in part—plenty of the love and encouragement her selfish parents hadn't provided—and a source of pride to both of us.

She'd begun to blossom physically as well. Almost twelve now, and the too-slender little girl had grown three inches and filled out into an attractive young lady approaching puberty. Already in it, for all I knew. If she wasn't wearing a bra yet—I hadn't asked Kerry because I didn't want to know—it was all too obvious she'd have to start pretty soon. Her mother had been a beauty—flawless compexion, perfect features, great luminous eyes, dark silken hair, and a long-legged, high-breasted figure—and Emily looked just like her, with the additional attributes of character and intelligence. She was going to be a knockout by the time she was fifteen or sixteen. Boys were sure to swarm around her, and that worried me already. When she started dating, I was going to have a lot of sleepless nights and a lot more gray hairs. Served me right for becoming a father at my age, with my jumbled code of contemporary and neo-Victorian ethics.

Traffic wasn't too bad after we got past the toll plaza; we were in the quiet little town of Larkspur before six o'clock. Redwood Village, the seniors' complex where Cybil had lived the past few years, was tucked back against a grove of ancient redwoods—five acres of duplex cottages, plus a rec room, dining hall, swimming pool, and putting green set among rolling lawns and other greenery. Pretty nice place for those who could afford it. And Kerry's father, Ivan, who'd made a lot of money writing radio and TV scripts and books on occult and magic themes—and who'd been something of a jerk—had left her well fixed after his death a few years ago. Not even the shaky state of the economy had harmed her finances much; Ivan's stock portfolio had been extensive and conservative, built and nurtured to weather just about any economic downturn.

She'd been in a bad way for a while after his death. Depressed, lonely, obsessed with a feeling that her own life was all but over. Kerry had talked her into selling her L.A. home and moving in with her—this was before our marriage—but that hadn't worked out too well for any of us logistically, or improved Cybil's mental health. Enforced dependence for a woman who had been independent-minded for seventy-some years was not the answer. The answer was for her to take control of her life again, and the move to Redwood Village had accomplished that. In a way it was like a rebirth. She'd flourished in the new environment; she was past eighty now and still going strong.

In the forties and early fifties she'd been almost as prolific a contributor to the detective pulps as Russ Dancer; her Samuel Leatherman byline had appeared on dozens of stories, the bulk of them about a tough L.A. detective named Max Ruffe. When paperback novels and the emergence of television killed off the pulp markets, she'd decided to abandon fiction writing altogether rather than make the transition to full-length novels. Writing had been an avocation with her; Ivan's success meant she didn't need to make a living and she'd preferred to devote her time to her family and other pursuits. So Kerry and I were both amazed when Cybil announced one day, six months or so after taking up residency in Redwood Village, that she was writing again. Her first novel, no less. And she hadn't just dabbled at it; she'd worked as intensely as she had in the old days and produced a finished manuscript in seven months. Eroded skills after a forty-year layoff? Not Cybil's. The novel, *Dead Eye,* set in the fifties and embroiling Max Ruffe in the Communist witch hunts in the Hollywood film industry, was pretty good; it had sold on its fourth submission, to a small New York publisher. Strong reviews and decent sales had brought her a contract for a sequel, *Glass Eye,* which she'd finished in November and which was scheduled for publication this coming fall.

Quite a woman, Cybil Wade. She had my admiration and gratitude, not only for her accomplishments but for producing her one and only offspring. Kerry was her mother's daughter, thank Christ. If there'd been more than a hint of Ivan the Terrible in her makeup, I might've had second thoughts about marrying her.

I revised that thought a little when we reached Cybil's cottage: there was some of her father's contentiousness in Kerry after all. When Cybil opened the door she may have been surprised to see Emily, but she wasn't surprised to see me. There isn't much guile in her; she doesn't try to hide her feelings. One look into those tawny eyes of hers—beautiful eyes; Dancer's "Sweeteyes" tag was right on—and I knew Kerry had called her today after all.

Cybil fussed over Emily for a time; the two of them got along famously. Then she gave the kid a Coke and shooed her out to do her homework on the back patio, out of earshot. I got a bottle of beer, a seat on the couch, and a long somber look from Max Ruffe's creator.

"I know why you're here," she said.

"I figured. Kerry called you, even though I asked her not to."

"Don't be angry with her. She felt I'd want to know as soon as possible and she was right."

Sometimes I get the feeling there is a secret network of communication, understanding, and perspective among women that not only excludes men but that men wouldn't quite fathom even if they were privy to it. Situations like this make me sure of it. But I went ahead and beat my head against it anyway.

"Why?" I asked her. "You wouldn't have wanted to see him in the hospital, would you?"

"No."

"Then why?"

"I knew the man for more than fifty years."

"That's not an answer."

"What time did he die?" she asked.

". . . What time? Does it matter?"

"I'd like to know."

"One fifty-seven this afternoon."

She repeated it. Then, "What did he say about me when you saw him?"

"He said he'd read *Dead Eye* and it was damn good, you could still write rings around him."

"What else?"

"Remember D-Day."

No response; deadpan expression. Kerry told her about that, too, I thought.

"Amazing grace."

And about that. Same deadpan nonresponse.

"He said you'd understand. Do you?"

"If I do, it's private."

"Sure. But you can't blame Kerry and me for wondering. You didn't tell her what happened on D-Day either, I take it."

"Nothing happened on D-Day that involved Russ Dancer. I have no idea where he was that day. I happen to have been in Washington visiting my husband."

"Okay. What about amazing grace? That ring any bells?"

"If that's a pun, it's in poor taste."

"Come on, Cybil, you're being evasive. Secrets?"

She ignored the question. "You did bring the envelope?"

It was in my briefcase; I hauled it out, handed it over. She held it for a few seconds, moving it up and down slightly as if she were estimating its weight. Then she put it down on the glass-topped table in front of her.

"Manuscript of some kind," I said.

Sharp look. "You didn't open the envelope?"

"You know me better than that. Besides, you can see that it's still sealed."

"... I'm sorry, I didn't mean to ... oh, shit, I *hate* this!"

Cybil almost never cusses. She didn't even seem to realize she'd used a four-letter word. Which showed how upset she was under the calm facade she had on.

"Do you want to talk about it?"

"Talk about what? I'm not going to open the envelope in front of you, if that's what you're angling for."

"It's not."

"I may not even tell you later what's in it. You or Kerry."

"Your prerogative," I said. "Look, Cybil, I'm only trying to be helpful here, lend a sympathetic ear."

"There's no need for it. You think I'm mourning Russ Dancer?"

"I don't think anything."

"Well, I'm not," she said. "I despised the man."

"He loved you."

"Damn his brand of love! I'm not sorry he's dead, I wish our paths had never crossed. He left me in peace the past twenty years, why couldn't he keep on that way instead of trying to come at me from the grave?"

"Come at you? How?"

She shook her head almost violently. The outburst had put flame in her thin cheeks, like a boozer's flush. It made me remember that Cybil had been a hard drinker back in the forties, and that she'd taken at least one walk on the wild side with another member of the Pulpeteers—facts that were hard for me to imagine because of her grace and wholesome qualities. Her and Dancer, too? No, that couldn't be what this was all about. The idea of her taking him up on one of his crude advances, drunk or sober, was ludicrous.

I watched the flush fade as she tightened the reins on her

emotions. Pretty soon she said, "Finish your beer. It's time you took Emily home and gave the child her dinner. She doesn't eat enough as it is, she's too thin."

Emily's appetite was fine; so was her weight. But I didn't argue. Cybil had had enough of us. She wanted to be alone with that envelope and whatever was in it—alone with whatever private little demons Dancer's life and Dancer's death had stirred up inside her.

Kerry was home when Emily and I came in. The first thing she said when we were alone was, "I'm not going to apologize for calling her."

"I didn't ask you to. I don't want to fight about this anymore."

"Good. Neither do I."

"I'd just like to know what's going on here. What's got Cybil so riled up."

"She'll tell us if she wants us to know."

"Don't you want to know? Or maybe you already know, or at least have some idea."

"I don't," she said grimly, "I don't have a clue."

And that worried me, too. Cybil almost never cussed and Kerry almost never lied, and now both of them were acting out of character. Kerry knew or suspected, all right. And it must be pretty disturbing for her to hide it behind a flat-out lie.

11

JAKE RUNYON

He hated hospitals.

Six months of them while Colleen was dying, the last six months of her life. Short stays for tests and radiation treatments, longer stays when the cancer worsened, then that last terrible month when they both knew there was no more hope and she kept growing weaker and weaker, becoming a small wasted pitiful thing lying there among all that antiseptic white and gleaming metal. The medicine smells, sick smells, death smells. The pain, the rage he'd felt. The fight to keep a smile on his face and his voice upbeat, and the constant fear that he wouldn't be able to get through another visit, that he'd break down right there in front of her. At least she hadn't died in that place. The last few days at home, with him and a hospice nurse at her bedside, had been bad enough. In the hospital, the waiting and the slow slipping away would have been unbearable. He'd've broken down for sure.

As soon as he walked into San Francisco General, the sights and smells brought the hate spiraling up into his throat. Irrational, almost pathological—so be it. Before he'd let anybody shut him up in a place like this, stick tubes and needles in him, hook him up to machines, he'd do what he'd thought about doing in those first couple of days after Colleen was gone. He'd put the muzzle of his .357 Magnum between his teeth and this time there'd be no sweating hesitation, no waffling; this time he'd eat it.

He crossed the lobby fast to the elevators. Fourth floor, Joshua had said. He punched 4 on the panel, and while the elevator took him up there he finished shutting himself down inside, focusing his mind to basics—the only way he could deal with a place like this. Do what he'd come here to do. Get through it. Walk out and away as quickly as possible.

Kenneth Hitchcock was in Ward 6. The floor duty nurse told him where it was. Six beds, three on a side, each one outfitted with privacy curtains. The curtain was partially open at the one on the left, nearest the door; inside, Joshua sat in a chair drawn up close to the bed, holding the hand of the man who lay there. He clung to it even more tightly when he saw Runyon; his face shaped into one of his defiant looks. Runyon acknowledged him with a nod, shifted his gaze to Kenneth Hitchcock.

Well set up, dark, long hair, and a brushy mustache. Handsome, ordinarily, in an actorish way, but not now. Left arm in a sling, upper body swathed in bandages to hold his cracked ribs in place, right side of his face bandaged, the other side tallowish and raddled with lemon- and raspberry-hued bruises. He was awake, his eyes open and reflecting pain. Joshua had said on the phone that his condition had been upgraded to fair, that he'd be all right barring infection or a resumption of internal bleeding.

"Kenny," Joshua said, "this is Jake Runyon." Not "my fa-ther," just the name. As if he were introducing a stranger.

"Hello." Weak voice, ghost of a smile. "Pardon me if I don't shake hands."

"My son tells me you're feeling better."

"Might live. Wasn't so sure there for a while."

"You'll be fine," Joshua said. Then again, as though trying to convince himself, "You'll be fine."

Runyon said to him, "I'd like to talk to Kenneth alone."

"Alone? Why?"

"Indulge me. It won't take long."

"I don't know . . . Kenny?"

"It's okay. See if you can get me some bottled water, will you? I'm thirsty, and the tap water here tastes like piss."

"All right, love."

The term of endearment was for Runyon's benefit—looking right at him as he said it. Another attempt at defiance. Runyon ignored it. How long before Joshua learned, if he ever learned, that his sexual orientation meant nothing to his father? Family mattered, blood mattered. Gay didn't matter at all.

Joshua went away without looking at him. Runyon pulled the chair back a foot or so, sat down. Midnight-blue eyes, dull with pain, watched and measured him. What Kenneth thought of him, if anything, didn't register on his battered face.

"I can't tell you much," he said. "Don't remember much. Doctors say that's typical in trauma cases."

Runyon said, "Two men, young, in a pickup truck. One a chunky redhead with freckles, wearing some kind of cap, the other tall and slender wearing a jacket with a hood."

"That's more than I remember. Where did you—?"

"First two victims. Gene Zalesky, Larry Exeter."

"They were luckier. Those bastards almost killed me."

"You recognize either of them?"

"No. I told you, I don't—"

"Never saw either of them before? Hanging around The Dark Spot?"

"That type of breeder? No way."

"Zalesky saw one of them, the tall one, outside The Dark Spot one night. Talking to Troy."

Kenneth blinked at the name. The tip of his tongue flicked over dry, cracked lips. Belatedly, "Who?"

"Troy. Young, blond kid with an angelic face. Hangs out at The Dark Spot."

"Lots of guys hang out there. Busy every night."

"He likes to sit at the bar. Likes company, likes to flirt."

"That fits half our customers."

"So you don't know him?"

"No."

"I think you're lying, Kenneth."

"Lying? Why would I lie to you?"

"Because I'm Joshua's old man. Because you don't want him to find out that you're not as faithful as he thinks you are."

Unwavering eye contact. "Bullshit."

"What's Troy's last name? Where does he live?"

"How should I know?"

"Tell me the truth, I'll keep it to myself. Joshua doesn't have to find out."

"There's nothing to tell."

Runyon said evenly, "Lots of people slip now and then, cheat on a spouse or a lover. I can understand that—it's human nature. Forgivable. One thing I can't forgive is cover-your-ass lying. I don't like liars, Kenneth."

The tongue flicked again, but the blue eyes remained fixed on Runyon's. "Why all these questions? What does this Troy have to do with me getting bashed?"

"That's what I'm trying to find out. Troy hangs out at The Dark Spot, you work at The Dark Spot, Zalesky and Exeter are regulars at The Dark Spot. All three of you had sex with Troy—"

"Not me. How many times do I have to tell you I don't know anybody named Troy."

"—and then all three of you got beat up. That's more coincidence than I can believe."

"I don't care what you believe. It was random . . . random bashing of random victims."

"Because you want it to be?"

"And you want it to be something else—payback for imagined sins, queers getting their just desserts. Right? Homophobic bullshit. Joshua was right about you from the beginning. *You're* a homophobe. Why don't you admit it?"

All that in the same weak, calm voice as before. Maintaining eye contact. Stonewalling. Kenneth Hitchcock was the kind of man who refused to admit fault or accept responsibility for his own actions, would go to any lengths—lie his soul straight to hell—to keep his structured life and his image intact. Self-centered, shallow, small-minded.

"One more chance to be straight with me, Kenneth. Where can I find Troy?"

Faint, weary smile. "How can I be straight when I'm gay?"

Runyon stood up, turned away—

"Mr. Runyon."

—and turned back to look at the man in the bed.

"If you say anything to Joshua about this theory of yours, he won't believe you. It'll just make him hate you all the more. You don't want that and neither do I."

"What I want is the truth."

"The truth is, I care about your son and he cares about me. We're not casual lovers. I mean it, our relationship is a lot stronger than that."

Runyon said nothing.

"And I want you to know—I won't hurt him."

"No? Buddy, I think maybe you already have."

Joshua was sitting on one of the chairs in a waiting area near the elevators, elbows propped on his knees, a bottle of mineral water on the floor beside him. He'd rallied some, now that Kenneth was out of danger, but he still looked exhausted. His head came up when he heard Runyon approaching. All in one motion, then, he was on his feet with the bottle in his hand.

"You shouldn't have stayed so long. He's still weak."

"Yes he is," Runyon said. "Very weak."

"He needs his rest. What were you asking him?"

"Questions about what happened."

"Then why didn't you want me there?"

"It's easier to talk one on one."

"You didn't pry about anything personal, did you? Our relationship? My private life is none of your business."

Runyon had no intention of passing on his suspicions or his opinion of Kenneth Hitchcock. Joshua wouldn't believe it, Kenneth had been right about that, and it would add fuel to the bad feelings between them, but that wasn't the reason.

Even if he hadn't been forced out of the first twenty years of his son's life, he'd still keep this kind of thing to himself. Joshua was an adult; adults made their own decisions and their own mistakes. He'd find out what Kenneth was when this gay-bashing business was over, or eventually in some other way. Live and learn the hard way.

He said, "None of my business, that's right. You asked me to do a job, I'm trying to do it. That's all."

"All right. Did he remember anything helpful?"

"Not much."

"Well . . . I'd better take him this water, make sure he's okay."

"Be a good idea to get some rest yourself. How'd you get here? Bus?"

"Yes."

"I'll wait for you, give you a ride home."

"No, thanks. I'll stay until visiting hours are over."

"I don't mind waiting."

"I'd rather you didn't."

"Suit yourself," Runyon said. "Couple of quick questions before you go. You spend much time at The Dark Spot?"

"What does that . . . No, not a lot of time. Now and then, but Kenneth isn't comfortable with me around while he's working. It makes him nervous."

"You know a guy named Troy? Early twenties, blond, angelic face?"

"Troy? I don't think so. Why?"

"Roundabout lead I'm pursuing."

"Did you ask Kenneth? He knows all the Dark Spot regulars."

"I asked him," Runyon said. "He doesn't know Troy."

• • •

Gene Zalesky was home tonight, but not as friendly as he'd been on Monday. He left the chain on when he answered the door, said through the opening, "I have company. Can't you come back tomorrow?"

"I won't take up too much of your time."

"What is it? I told you everything I know Monday night."

"Not everything. Not about you and Troy."

Thick silence this time.

"Better let me in," Runyon said.

Reluctantly Zalesky complied. Nervous concern showed on his bruised and bandaged face, and his cynicism seemed tempered with resignation. No bluster or defiance, though, which meant he was going to be cooperative. The Gene Zaleskys of the world were usually cooperative when push came to shove: survival mechanism of the intelligent and downtrodden misfit.

They went into the antiques-strewn living room. It was empty; not even the Angora cat was in evidence. If Zalesky really did have company, the guest had been installed in another room. Zalesky preferred not to stand tonight; Runyon watched him lower his battered body onto a Victorian love seat, half turned to his left so that his weight rested on his nonbruised buttock, one leg splayed out in front of him. An awkward position that gave him a vulnerable aspect. Calculated, maybe, so Runyon wouldn't be too hard on him.

He sighed before he said, "I guess I should have expected this."

"Chickens and lies, Mr. Zalesky." Runyon sat on another piece of Victoriana facing him. "They both come home to roost."

"Homilies from a detective. I'm impressed." The sarcasm

was thin and bleak. "But I don't see what difference it makes in your investigation, my relationship with Troy."

"You lied about it."

"For personal reasons that have nothing to do with the beatings."

"I don't know that. Neither do you."

Zalesky gave him an analytical look. "You're good at your job, aren't you. The manhunter type. I don't think I'd want you coming after me."

"Then tell me why you lied about Troy."

"Isn't it obvious?"

"Not to me."

"You know about him, about us . . ."

"Not as much as I need to know."

"I was trying to protect myself, that's all. You can understand that."

"Protect yourself from what?"

"Well, my God, possible criminal charges, of course. My company is fairly conservative—they tolerate gay employees, but they take a dim view of negative publicity involving one of us. This beating I suffered is bad enough, but the other . . . if that came out and charges were filed, I'd be fired in a New York minute."

"What kind of criminal charges?"

"Troy is underage," Zalesky said. "You didn't know that?"

"No, I didn't. If The Dark Spot serves minors, that's their problem—"

"I don't mean drinking age, I mean the legal age of consent. He's seventeen."

"So that's it. A molestation charge, that's what you're afraid of."

"Wouldn't you be?"

"I don't mess around with underage kids."

"Neither do I," Zalesky said miserably. "If I'd known his real age, I wouldn't have had anything to do with him. I swear it, I wouldn't have. But he doesn't look that young, even with that sweet face he looks twenty-one and he claimed to be twenty-one." He spread his hands in a helpless gesture. "You don't ask to see someone's driver's license in a crowded bar."

"Bartenders are supposed to. Didn't Kenneth Hitchcock or one of the others card him?"

"Evidently not. I told you, Troy looks twenty-one, acts twenty-one . . . I've never seen any seventeen-year-old as outwardly mature as he is."

"How'd you find out his real age?"

"He told me. One night after we . . . he let it slip while we were talking. My God, I've never gotten out of a bed faster in my life."

"His bed or yours?"

"Mine. Of course I threw him out immediately. I may be a fool, but I'm not stupid."

"When was this?"

"Three weeks ago. A Friday night."

"Seen him since?"

"Once, at The Dark Spot. A few days later. We didn't speak."

Runyon asked, "What's his last name?"

"He said it was Scott, Troy Scott."

"But you don't think so."

"No, I don't. I can't say why . . . I just had the impression he was lying."

"And you didn't ask."

"Why should I? Not everyone in my world uses his right

name." Wry quirk of his mouth. "It's the nature of the beast."

"You know where he lives?"

"He has . . . had . . . a room in a house on Hattie Street."

"Had?"

"I heard he'd moved out. Somebody mentioned that . . . I don't remember who. And I don't know where he went."

"Where's Hattie Street?"

"Off Upper Market. A few blocks from here."

"Number of the house?"

"I'm not sure, but it's a large Victorian, three or four shades of blue, with a rainbow fanlight over the door. There's no other like it in the block."

"What kind of work does he do?"

"He said he wanted to be an engineer."

"Doesn't answer my question."

"I . . . don't think he has a regular job."

"Hustles? You give him money?"

Zalesky chewed his lip. He said, embarrassment in his voice, "I was afraid you'd ask that. Yes, I gave him money. We called it a loan but we both knew it was nothing of the kind."

"How much?"

"Two hundred dollars over a period of time."

"How much time?"

"A week or so."

Two hundred. Troy hadn't gotten anywhere near that much from Exeter, not for a one-night stand, but he'd got something, probably. How much from Kenneth? Others? Pretty good living if Troy was as promiscuous as advertised.

"What about his background?" Runyon asked. "He tell you anything about himself when you were together?"

"Not very much, no. He was reticent about that. Every time

I asked him a personal question, he said, 'I'd rather not talk about the past. Now's what I'm interested in.'"

"Any hint as to where he's from?"

"The Bay Area. He wouldn't say where, but . . . I think it might have been South San Francisco."

"Yes?"

"I mentioned South City once, in some context or other, and he made a face and said something about it being an armpit."

"Where'd you first meet him? The Dark Spot?"

"Yes."

"And he picked up others there besides you."

"Oh, yes," Zalesky said. "Variety was what Troy was after, not any kind of couples thing. God, he was a horny little bastard. Couldn't get enough—" He broke off, words and eye contact both. "Sorry. You don't want to hear the details of my sex life or his."

"Who else did he sleep with?"

"Does it matter?"

"Names, Mr. Zalesky. As many as you're sure of."

"You won't say where you got them?"

"Not if I don't have to."

"All right. Jerry Butterfield is one I'm sure of. And . . . Paul Venner. That's all I can think of at the moment."

"Kenneth Hitchcock?"

"Kenneth? No . . . no, I don't think so."

"You're not a very good liar," Runyon said. "I already know about Kenneth and Troy. And no, I haven't told my son. I'm not going to and neither are you."

"Of course not. It's none of my—" A sudden thought cut Zalesky off in midsentence; you could see it reflected on his face, like the reaction of a cartoon character when a lightbulb flashes on over his head. "My God, you don't believe the bashings are random at all. You think they have something to do with Troy . . . those two men singling out Troy's lovers. That's it, isn't it?"

Runyon said nothing.

"Jealousy? But that doesn't make sense. Those men are vicious homophobes."

"Not all homophobes are heterosexual."

"Jeffrey Dahmer types? Hate queers because they hate being queer themselves?"

"You don't buy it?"

"No," Zalesky said, "I don't. Not those two. They're breeders, straights . . . don't you think I know the difference?"

"Even though one of them was arguing with Troy one night outside The Dark Spot."

"They know him, I'll grant you that. But there's some other reason for the bashings, for their hatred of gays. There has to be."

"Jerry Butterfield and Paul Venner," Runyon said. "Where do they live, work? Where can I find them besides The Dark Spot?"

Jerry Butterfield lived in a private home over near Twenty-fourth Street and had a listed phone number; he was an executive with one of the big computer companies, but Zalesky didn't know which one. He didn't answer his doorbell or his phone.

No address or listing for Paul Venner, but he worked in a leather shop on Twentieth and Castro.

Projects for tomorrow.

• • •

The big, blue Victorian on Hattie Street was easy enough to find. Somebody's home once, long-since cut up into single rooms and turned into what passed for a boardinghouse these days. A sign on the front stoop said ROOMS FOR RENT and under that in smaller letters INQUIRE #4. Runyon rang the bell for #4, got no answer. He rang several others at random, one at a time. Three responses. None of the three would let him in or come out to talk to him, but it wouldn't have mattered if they had. One said he didn't know Troy Scott, the other two owned up to having seen him but claimed not to have had any dealings with him. He'd moved out two weeks ago, that was the extent of the information any of them could provide. Talk to Keith Morgan in #4, one suggested, he handled the rentals for the building's owner, maybe he knew where Troy had moved to.

One more project for tomorrow.

12

ROBERT LEMOYNE

He looked at her sprawled out on the couch where he'd pushed her down. Nobody he'd ever seen before. Scared and trying not to show it. Young, black—dark chocolate. Pretty enough, nice tits, good ass, but not his type. Skinny women, white or light-skinned black, had always been his thing. Like Dinah. Like Mia.

His head had stopped hurting and the anger and confusion were mostly gone now. He was starting to think again, real clear, and he didn't like any of it. He liked everything to move along in a straight line, according to plan. Unexpected things threw him off. Complications he didn't understand threw him off. What was he going to do about this one?

He said it aloud. "What am I going to do about you?"

"Better let me go, man," she said. She kept tonguing her lips, shifting her eyes from his face to the pocket of his coat where he had the Saturday night special. "This is all a big mis-understanding, you know what I'm saying?"

"You were prowling around my property. Why?"

"Stupid mistake. I got the address wrong."

"What address?"

"The one I'm supposed to be checking out. It's across the street."

"What's that mean, checking out?"

"I'm a private investigator," she said, "trying to find a guy skipped out on his child-support payments. I think he's living on this block, in a relative's house, but I got the address wrong. That's all."

He stared at her. "That's some story."

"It's the truth."

"Private investigator? You?"

"Lots of women in the profession now, black and white. No lie. Listen, if you don't believe me, call the police, have them check me out."

"No."

"Why not? You don't want to let me go, call the cops and have me arrested."

"Show me something that says you're what you say you are."

"I don't have ID on me . . ."

"Where is it? Where's your purse?"

"Purse?"

"In your car? Where's your car?"

She sat up straighter, tonguing her lips, looking at his coat pocket. Didn't want him looking in her purse. He kept watching her. Now she had her head cocked a little, as if she was listening for something. What? She'd been snooping around out back . . . what if she'd heard something? Angie. Angie hadn't stopped bawling since he brought her home, kept calling for her mother. What if Dark Chocolate had heard her?

Private investigator. Christ!

"Where's your car?" he said again.

That tongue of hers was doing double time. And she was still listening.

"Can't be far away," he said. "You think I won't find it?"

"Why bother? Why don't you just let the cops check out my ID when they get here?"

"You'd like it if I called them, wouldn't you. Tell them all about it."

"All about my stupid mistake, that's right."

"All about me."

"I don't know you."

"All about Angie."

". . . Who's Angie?"

She said it too fast. She'd heard, all right, she knew about the kid.

"Stand up," he said.

"What?"

"Stand up, give me your car keys."

She didn't do it right away, so he took the gun out and showed it to her again. Then she did it. Got up on her feet, good and scared now and not trying to hide it anymore. Fished the keys out of her coat pocket.

"Toss them over here." He caught the ring left-handed, dropped it into his own pocket. "All right, now move. Door to the kitchen over there."

"Why? That where the phone is?"

"Shut up."

"Listen, man, if you—"

"I said shut up!"

He gave her a shove through the door into the kitchen,

crowded her over to the basement door and made her stand to one side while he unlocked it one-handed. He pushed it open, switched on the staircase light.

"Go on down there," he told her.

"Why? What're you gonna do?"

"Shove you down the stairs, you don't walk down by yourself."

She walked, quick, without looking back at him following behind her. Cold and damp down there usually, even in nice spring weather, so he'd left the furnace turned up to seventy for Angie's sake. Warm now, she'd be warm. Good. But as they started across the concrete floor he could hear her crying and that took the good away and made him feel sad. He hated it when she cried. He wanted her to be happy, laughing. Crying cut into him like a knife. But not as deep as when she started yelling, screaming, making his head hurt. And when his head hurt he got mad and the pain got worse.

The former owners had built the room down there, next to the alcove where the washer and dryer were, for some relative of theirs. It had a toilet and shower, and a bed and other furniture that they'd left behind. He hadn't had to do much except close off the window, put a door and lock on the closet, reinforce the other door and add a hasp and padlock. He rattled the padlock getting his key into the slot, and the crying stopped inside. He slid the lock off, pushed the door open. Dark Chocolate went in this time without being told. He put the Saturday night special away in his pocket before he followed her, so Angie wouldn't see it.

Angie was sitting on the bed, the sheet and blanket pulled up to her neck, her pretty little face all scrunched up and wet with tears. The big round eyes stared at him, at Dark Chocolate, and he saw the fear in them. It put an ache in him. He couldn't stand to see her scared and unhappy. He loved her so much.

"Don't be scared, honey," he said. "Daddy's here now."

"You're not my daddy."

"Sure I'm your daddy. Didn't I give you a nice present?"

"I want to go home."

"You will. Pretty soon we'll go home, see your mama."

"You promised I could go home if I didn't wet the bed again and I didn't, I didn't!"

Dark Chocolate gave him a murderous glance. She hadn't been surprised to see Angie. Oh, she knew, all right—she knew too damn much.

He said to her, "The closet. Inside."

"What?"

"You heard me. Inside the closet."

She hesitated, her body tensing, her face pulling tight. He moved in on her, gave her a two-handed push that banged her into the wall next to the closet door. She let loose a hurt sound and that started Angie wailing again. He shoved Dark Chocolate into the closet, slammed the door, and snapped the lock on it. Angie was still wailing. The sound of it sawed across his nerves, started the red hurt behind his eyes.

"Stop that! Stop screaming!"

"I want to go home, I want my mama!"

"Stop it or I'll put you in the closet too. It's dark in there, you want to be shut up in the dark with that strange lady?"

"No!"

"Then be a good girl, be quiet. You hungry? Want something to eat?"

Sobs but no more shrieks. ". . . Yes."

"I'll get you something pretty soon. You just sit there nice and quiet and play with your coloring books or your pretty new doll."

"I don't like her, I want my own doll."

"What's the matter with this one? Her name's Kimberly, she's got a nice pink and white dress—"

"She's white, Mama doesn't like me to play with big white dolls."

"Your mama's full of shit. That doll cost me seventy dollars at Toys'R'Us. Seventy dollars, Angie, that's a lot of money."

"I'm not Angie, my name's Lauren."

"Be good, now. Don't make Daddy mad."

He smiled fondly at her and moved over to the closet door. "You in there, listen to me. You be quiet too. You can't break through this door and you can yell your head off and nobody'll hear you, the walls are too thick. Understand?"

No answer.

"You better understand if you know what's good for you," he said, and smiled at Angie again, and went out and set the padlock on the door.

Upstairs he looked at the woman's car keys. Wouldn't you know it: Toyota. Damn Jap car. He hated Jap cars. Sure, they were well engineered but they weren't American. GM was American, he was American, he loved this country body and soul. He just didn't see how any good American could buy foreign cars, any other kind of foreign shit, when loyal Americans were busting their asses building quality merchandise right here at home.

Didn't take him long to find the Toyota. Parked right out front, practically within pissing distance of the house. Dark Chocolate had balls, he had to give her that much. He unlocked the passenger door, found her purse right there on the floor on that side. He slipped it under his coat, took a look around after he shut the door again. Nobody in sight. Wouldn't pay any attention to him if there was, not in this neighborhood. People minded their own business on this block. Country'd be a lot better off if everybody minded their own business the way the folks here did. Except when it came to watching out for fucking Arab terrorists—you had to be vigilant about that like the president said.

He went back inside and dumped everything in the purse out on the kitchen table. Wallet first. Driver's license . . . Tamara Corbin, age twenty-six, San Francisco address. And another one issued by the State Board of Licences that proved she really was a private investigator. Young black woman like that, a private cop. Women these days, didn't matter what color they were, they had all kinds of jobs you'd think were just for men. That was all right by him. He didn't have any prejudice against women earning a living so long as they didn't take jobs away from family men. But a private cop . . . he didn't like that. Not one bit.

He rummaged around among the rest of the stuff. All women's purse junk except for a folded piece of paper. He unfolded it, saw that it was a computer printout. Then he saw what it said and his head started to throb again, that heavy throbbing ache behind his eyes. He squeezed them shut and jammed the heels of his hands against the socket bones and pressed and pressed until the pain began to ease some. He looked at the paper again, read everything that was printed there.

His name, his address, the kind of car he drove, where he worked, where he was born and the places he'd lived and who he'd been married to . . . his whole *life*! The hell she was after some deadbeat father hiding out on this block, the hell she'd made a mistake about the address. It was him she was after. Her car parked right out front, prowling around the property, listening for Angie and wasn't surprised to see her. That was why she was here, why she was after him. Take Angie away from him.

But how? How'd she find out?

Nobody'd seen him take the girl, he was sure of that. Nobody could know, but Dark Chocolate knew. How could she know?

Who else knew?

Not the police, they'd've taken Angie away from him by now if they did. Just Dark Chocolate, or somebody else at that detective agency of hers?

He'd find out. He'd get it out of her, one way or another.

No matter what, he couldn't stay here, couldn't wait until the weekend like he'd planned to head east. Not him, not Angie, not Dark Chocolate. Leave now or wait until morning? He wasn't thinking clearly anymore, couldn't make up his mind. The pain was like fire behind his eyes. He jammed his hands against the socket bones again, pinched his eyeballs. It didn't get any better, it wouldn't go away.

Oh God, the things he'd done when he couldn't make it go away . . .

13

TAMARA

Bad minute or two after he locked her in the closet and she heard him leave. Alone, trapped in the dark . . . it brought on another scare rush. Shortness of breath, cold sweat, a crazy impulse to beat on the door with her fists, bang her head against it, punish herself for being so fucking stupid. Prowling around where she had no business, letting herself get caught like this. He'd never let her go now that she'd seen the kid. Stupid, stupid, stupid!

The little girl was crying again in the room. Deep, wracking sobs. *She's more scared than I am, got more to be scared of.* The thought brought anger back, and the anger brought calm. She made herself take slow, shallow breaths until the tightness in her chest eased; last thing she needed was to start hyperventilating. All right. Better. Hot, stuffy in there; she shrugged out of her coat, used the hem to wipe sweat off her face and neck, dropped it on the floor and kicked it to one side.

What was that smell? Mold? Okay, now she was a mouth-breather.

The closet was small and tight, not much bigger than one of those portable toilets. No matter which way she stood, she couldn't lift her arms up and out more than halfway before her hands touched wood. Nothing in it except a metal clothes rod that grazed and knocked her head until she got used to where it was. She wasn't claustrophobic, but being shut up in a box like this did funny things to your head. No wonder some people had a horror of waking up in their own coffin, being buried alive. Suppose he kept her locked up in here until she suffocated or died of starvation or went batshit crazy—

She bit her lip, hard enough to hurt. None of that crap, Tamara, you quit that right now. Worrying, running your imagination just gonna make you lose it big time. Stay cool. You didn't panic last Christmas and that was a worse scene than this, that dude was an out-of-control psycho and he had more firepower than a SWAT team. This Lemoyne's not anywhere near as whacked out and all he's got is one ugly little revolver, looks like those Saturday night specials the gangbangers in the 'hood carry. You can get out of this if you stay cool, use your head.

Yeah, sure. He outweighs me by seventy-five pounds. And he's got that gun. And he's out there somewhere and I'm locked up in this closet. Man's a kidnapper, maybe worse—and crazy and dangerous no matter how near normal he looks. The way he went off on me, violence boiling up in him sudden like that. The way he kept saying he was that little girl's daddy, calling her Angie as if he really believes she's his daughter. Wasn't an act, he meant it, and that's no way sane.

Was that why he picked her, because she looks like his

daughter? What's he intend to do to her, what's he already done?

The room out there, this closet, the locks on the doors . . . all just to hold this one kid? Or had there been others? How many others?

Now that her eyes had adjusted, she could make out faint strips of light at the bottom of the door, around the edges. She tried to get her fingers into the cracks, couldn't do it; the door was tight in the jamb. Wouldn't've done her any good anyway. No knob on this side, probably bolted on the outside. She felt all the way around the walls, squatted and felt the floorboards. Solid wood. No lie when he'd said there was no way out of here.

The little girl was still crying in rackety sobs. Tamara could hear, almost feel her terror. There'd never been much of a maternal streak in her, but she felt one now—a mothering urge to protect and comfort so strong it surprised her. What'd the child say her name was? Laura? No, Lauren.

She put her mouth close to one of the cracks. "Lauren, you hear me? Come on over here, honey."

Had to say it again twice before the crying stopped. Faint squeak of bed springs, hesitant footsteps. Then, low and teary, "I don't like it here, I want to go home."

"I know you do. So do I, Lauren."

"You know my name."

"Sure I do. Mine's Tamara."

"That man calls me Angie. Why's he do that?"

"He had a little girl named Angie once. Maybe you look like her."

"Where is she now?"

"I don't know. Maybe her mama took her away somewhere, a long way away where her daddy can't find her."

"Why?"

"I don't know." *But I can sure guess.*

Sniffling sounds. Then, "Why'd he put you in the closet? It's dark in there."

"He's a bad man, that's why."

"He keeps saying he's my daddy. He's not my daddy."

"He's not anybody's daddy anymore."

"He said I could go home if I didn't throw up or wet the bed again."

"Where do you live?"

"I'm scared. Why can't I go home?"

"Where's home? Where do you live?"

"Vallejo."

"Where in Vallejo?"

"On Patterson Street. Our house is number one-sixty-three."

Went all the way up there to snatch the kid. Why?

"You know him, honey, the man who brought you here?"

"No. I was playing in the park. Mama was there but she went to the bathroom and then he was there."

"Never saw him before he took you away?"

"Uh-uh. He grabbed me and wrapped me up in a blanket and put me in a car. He said I had to be quiet or else."

"Did he hurt you?"

"I threw up in the car. All over the blanket."

"Did he hurt you, Lauren?"

"No."

"Take your clothes off? Touch you where he shouldn't?"

"Uh-uh."

Something, anyway.

"What'd he say after he brought you here?"

"He said if I was a good girl I could go home. He gave me a doll to play with, but I don't like it, it's a white doll. I wish I had Alana Michelle."

"Who's Alana Michelle?"

"My doll. She's African-American. I'm just half African-American 'cause my daddy's white. Mama helped me braid her hair just like mine. I don't think you can braid the white doll's hair."

"What else did the man say to you?"

"He said he loved me."

The words put ice on Tamara's spine.

"How can he love me?" Lauren said. "He doesn't know me and I don't know him. He's not my daddy. I don't want to go with him to the trailer."

"What trailer, honey?"

"I don't know. He said we were going to a trailer in the woods and there'd be a big surprise for me and we'd have lots of fun. But I don't want to go."

"What woods? Where?"

"I don't know. There's deer and elk around. What's a elk?"

"A big animal like a deer. Did he say what the surprise was? What kind of fun?"

"No. Can you have fun with a elk?"

"Not unless you're another elk. Lauren—"

"I have to go to the bathroom," she said.

She went away. Tamara started to straighten up, changed her mind, and sat on the floor with her back against the wall and her knees pulled up. Trailer in the woods, deer and elk around.

That could be anywhere. Someplace isolated, for sure, where he could be alone with Lauren and show her his big surprise and they'd have "fun." Warped son of a bitch.

But he'd had her more than twenty-four hours and he hadn't done anything to her yet. Maybe he wasn't a pedophile, maybe he'd snatched the kid for some other whacko reason. Maybe he really believed she was his daughter and he had no intention of hurting her. Yeah, and pigs can fly and world peace is coming next Tuesday. Gearing up to it, that was all. Or prolonging it, savoring what he planned to do.

What was *she* gonna do? What could she do? Try to reason with him, that was one thing. If he wasn't so far gone he wouldn't listen to reason. She could be pretty persuasive. Silver Tongue Tamara. Talk at him, lay on the jive, convince him to let the kid go, let both of them go, and then turn himself in so he can get some help—

More flying pigs.

Have to try, though. Must be some good in him, a side she could appeal to. Use soft rap on him, don't show fear, and make real sure not to say or do anything to push his buttons.

The toilet flushed. Another running water sound—Lauren washing her hands. Kid was well behaved and had been raised right. Pretty soon the floorboards creaked as she came back to the closet.

"Lady? Tamara?"

She leaned forward. "Yeah, honey?"

"When he comes back, that man, will you tell him to take me home?"

"Sure I will."

"Tell him I miss my mama and daddy. My real daddy."

"I'll tell him."

"Thank you." Then, "Is he gonna hurt you?"

"Not if I can help it."

"Don't let him hurt me either, okay?"

Between her teeth: "Okay. You go on back to bed now, keep warm. And try not to cry anymore."

"My mama says big girls don't cry."

"Your mama's right," she lied.

She sat in the new silence, shallow-breathing through her mouth. Working out what she'd say to Lemoyne when she saw him again—a way to occupy her mind so she wouldn't be thinking and imagining too much. She got it pretty much straight, but after a while it didn't matter much. So hot and airless in there it was like her brain was drying up, all the cells melting and oozing out with her sweat.

The little girl was quiet. Asleep now, maybe. Poor kid must be worn out. Being scared had a way of doing that to you, making you ache all over, so damn tired you could hardly keep your eyes open. Fear and quiet and not enough air and too much heat . . .

All of a sudden she was out of her doze, groggy for a few seconds and then with her senses sharply alert. Noises out there—key sounds, lock rattling. He was back.

She tried to stand up too fast. A cramp in her right calf kept her down until she twisted around and got her foot jammed up straight against the wall. The pain eased and she was able to lift up and catch hold of the clothes rod, haul herself upright. Sweat streamed on her skin; every part of her felt soggy, like she'd taken a sauna in her clothes.

He was in the room now. Lauren was awake, too, said something in a voice too low for Tamara to catch. He yelled at the child to shut up, go back to sleep, and the force of the words started her crying again.

Then he was at the closet door, rattling on the lock out there. Breathing hard, almost snorting like a bull in heat. He had trouble getting the lock open, swore at it, finally yanked it loose. Tamara pressed back against the wall as he tore the door open.

Oh, shit!

One look at him looming there against the light, all fire-eyed and smoke-dark, and the sweat on her turned to icy jelly.

14

Tamara didn't show up for work on Wednesday morning.
The offices were locked when I got there a little before nine-
thirty. My first thought was that she'd been there and had to
go out for some reason, but if that had been the case she
would've left a message on my desk and there was no message.
None on the answering machine, either. In the five years we'd
worked together, she had only missed a total of four days
without advance notice—a three-day bout with the flu and an
impacted tooth that had needed immediate attention. On both
those occasions she'd notified me right away.

Illness or emergency, I thought, sudden and serious enough
to prevent her from calling in. Either way it was cause for concern. I rang up her apartment in the Outer Sunset, counted off
a dozen rings before I disconnected. Then I tried her cell-
phone number. Out of service.

Worrisome, but nothing to get alarmed about yet. For all I
knew she was on her way in right now and the delay would
turn out to be minor after all.

I did a little work, and some time passed, and when she still didn't show up I stood again and went into her office. The paper file on George DeBrissac was on her desk. I read through it, and there was nothing there that rang any alarm bells. Simple, straightforward case of nonpayment of child support; by all indications DeBrissac seemed to be your average white-collar deadbeat dad. While I was poking around among the other files and papers on her desk—nothing unusual in them, either—I heard the outer door open. But it wasn't Tamara. Jake Runyon. I motioned to him to join me in my office.

"What's up?" he said. "Where's Tamara?"

"Good question. No sign of her this morning, and no message."

He digested that before he said, "Not like her."

"No, it isn't."

"You try her cell phone?"

"Out of service. And no answer at her apartment."

"Could be a combination of car trouble and a discharged cell."

"Could be. But I keep thinking about that deadbeat dad surveillance she's been on the past couple of nights."

"One over in the East Bay?"

"San Leandro."

"Pretty standard case, isn't it?"

"Looks to be," I said. "Subject has no criminal record and no apparent history of violence. If he had, I'd've talked her into letting you handle it. But there's something else. Yesterday she started to tell me about something that happened Monday night, something she saw or thought she saw that bothered her enough to do some checking. That was as far as she got before the phone rang and we never did get back to it. She mention any of this to you?"

"No. Connected to the surveillance?"

"She didn't say one way or the other. Could've happened while she was staked out in San Leandro, or before or afterward someplace else. There's nothing on her desk that might help explain it."

"Might be something on her computer," Runyon said.

"Could you get in there and find it?"

"Well, I could try. But she has a security code, doesn't she?"

"I don't know. Probably."

"If so, I won't be able to get in without the password. I'm no expert."

"Better not, then. She doesn't like anybody messing with her computer. Hell, we're getting ahead of ourselves here anyway. It's only a little after ten—two hours late doesn't make her a missing person."

"Sure. She'll probably show up any minute."

But she didn't show up. Not by ten-thirty, not by eleven.

Runyon came in again from the outer office. "I've got a meeting with Fred Agajanian at eleven-thirty. Shouldn't last long. Tamara still hasn't shown up by then, I could drive to her place, make sure everything's all right there."

"Good idea." I gave him the address. "If she shows or checks in meanwhile, I'll call your cell. If you don't hear from me, go ahead out there."

Too much on my mind. And too quiet in the office with Runyon gone and Tamara absent. I couldn't seem to concentrate on my work; my mind kept skipping around helter-skelter.

Dancer, Cybil. Remember D-Day. Amazing grace. That bulky envelope. Kerry's odd behavior. Cybil's reticence. Secrets. But what kind?

Dancer had made any number of passes at her and once tried to talk her into divorcing Ivan the Terrible and marrying him, back around 1950; but she'd had very little to do with him after the war, and no contact at all since the pulp convention fiasco. Kerry had disliked him for his crude ways and his open hunger for her mother. Old Ivan had actively hated him for those reasons and because he'd considered Dancer a worthless hack. During the war, while Ivan was an army liaison officer stationed in Washington, loneliness and the Pulpeteers' freewheeling lifestyle had led Cybil into an affair with Frank Colodny, editor of *Midnight Detective*. Bad choice: Colodny had been a blackmailer and a thief, among other things—sins that many years later had gotten him murdered. But neither Dancer nor Cybil had had anything to do with his death at the pulp convention, even though Dancer had been arrested for it. And when pressed, she'd been candid about the affair. She'd also told me she had had plenty of other offers and turned them all down; she loved Ivan and she wasn't promiscuous. And I believed her.

No buried secrets in any of that, as far as I could see.

But there had to be something pretty disturbing either in her past relationship with Dancer or that Dancer knew about to upset her this way. Something that Kerry also either knew about or suspected. The contents of the envelope felt like a manuscript, book length or close to it. A novel or nonfiction work he'd written for or about Cybil, and wanted her to have as a love offering—or maybe hate offering—from the grave? Dancer had had his sentimental side, and he could also be mean-spirited and cruel; he was perfectly capable of concocting one type or the other. But I couldn't imagine anything fact or fiction that would rattle her after so many years. Or what D-Day had to do with it. Or what amazing grace might signify.

I kept telling myself to quit picking at it and forget about it, it was none of my business anyway. Fat chance. It *was* my business. Cybil and Kerry were family and Dancer had put me in the middle of it and it was having a none too pleasing effect on my marriage. Besides which, I don't like secrets and I chafe at puzzles I can't solve.

One way or another, I was going to dig out some idea of what this was all about.

Noon came and went.

No Tamara.

The more time that passed without word, the more edgy and restless it made me. Every time the phone rang I jumped at it. Routine business, until Jake Runyon's voice came over the wire at a quarter to one.

"She's not at her apartment," he said. "I talked to a couple of the neighbors. Nobody's seen her in the past twenty-four hours."

"What about her car . . . her boyfriend's car? Red Toyota . . ."

"I remember. No sign of it in the neighborhood."

"I don't like this. I'm starting to get bad vibes here, Jake."

"I hear you. Want me to take a run over to San Leandro, check out that surveillance address?"

"I'll do it. You've got other business."

"Nothing that won't keep."

"What about the gay bashings? How's that going?"

"Making progress."

"Line on the perps?"

"No IDs yet, but it turns out they're not picking at random—the victims were sexually involved with a seventeen-year-old kid named Troy."

"All three victims?"

"All three."

Including his son's partner. But I didn't say it and neither did he. All I said was, "Hell of a hard row to hoe sometimes, being a father. Particularly for men like us."

"Yeah," he said.

"You have more work you can do on the investigation—now, I mean?"

"It can wait until I'm on my own time."

"The hell with that," I said. "Go ahead and get on it. I'll let you know if there's any news about Tamara."

The trip to the East Bay was a waste of nearly two hours. The San Leandro neighborhood Tamara had been staking out was lower middle class and early-afternoon quiet. There was no sign of Horace's red Toyota on the 1100 block of Willard Street, or anywhere else on Willard or within a four-block radius. I parked in front of number 1122, the house where deadbeat George DeBrissac might or might not be hiding out, and went and rang the bell and got no answer.

Start ringing other doorbells? Bad time for it. Most of the residents were away at work or out shopping; Tamara had been here after dark, so anybody who might've seen her might not be home until after dark. Better to wait until tonight, if it came down to that.

So I drove back to the city and South Park. It was just three o'clock when I got off the elevator in front of the new offices. Still no Tamara, still no word from her.

Time, past time, to start making some calls. I decided on a compromise where her family was concerned. If there was a serious problem and her family knew about it, I was pretty sure somebody would have let me know by now. And I didn't want to sound an alarm to them yet. Her father was a Redwood City cop, overprotective and none too keen about her choice of profession, even less so after that close call last Christmas; they had a prickly relationship, and he and I had never been more than civil to each other. He'd be in my face from the get-go. And if it turned out the absence had a simple explanation, I'd have Tamara's disapproval to deal with as well.

So I made my first call to her sister Claudia, a lawyer with the public defender's office. Tamara was out somewhere, I said, and I was trying to locate her. Had Claudia heard from her today? No, Claudia hadn't. Like her sister, she was a sharp young woman; there must have been something in my voice that she picked up on, because she asked immediately if anything was wrong. I gave her an evasive answer and got off the phone by pretending I had another call.

We had an office Rolodex file of names and addresses that included some personal contacts, among them Tamara's closest friends. Lucille Cranston hadn't spoken to her in several days. I couldn't get hold of Deanne Cotter. The third call, to Vonda McGee at the Design Center, produced some results.

"Well, yeah," Vonda said, "I talked to her last night."

"In person or on the phone?"

"Phone."

"She call you or you call her?"

"I did, on her cell."

"What time?"

"I think . . . around eight or so."

"Where was she? San Leandro?"

"Didn't say. We only talked for a couple of minutes. She kind of blew me off."

"Is that right? Why?"

"Said she couldn't talk, she was on a job. She sounded a little weird. Off the hook."

"Meaning what, exactly?"

"Like she was messed about something."

Young people and their slang. "Upset? Scared?"

"Not scared. Just sort of heavy-duty stoked."

"Does that mean excited?"

"Yeah. Not all there, you know? Off the hook."

"Distracted. Tensed up."

"Right."

"What was bothering her, she give you any idea?"

"No. Well, she said something about dealing with a half-and-half, same as I am."

"Half-and-half?"

"Half black, half white," Vonda said. "See, I'm dating this guy, a white guy who's also Jewish, and he's getting serious, he wants to meet my people and they're not too cool about the mixed-race thing. So I called Tam to—"

"Did she give you a name, say anything at all about this half-and-half?"

"Just that she was dealing with him."

"Him. A man."

"I guess so. That's the impression I got."

"Somebody she met and was attracted to?"

"No, not like that. Horace is her man, only man she wants."

"Some guy who hit on her, kept bugging her?"

"Uh-uh. Didn't sound like that either. She'd've said if it was a sex thing."

"What do you think she meant by 'dealing with him'?"

"No idea," Vonda said.

"Did it sound like an immediate thing—a situation she had to deal with then and there, wherever she was?"

"I'm not sure. That's all she said. Well, except that race doesn't always have to be an issue. Be nice if that was true. Then she said she'd call me later, we'd talk then, and cut me off."

"But she didn't call you back."

"Uh-uh. Not last night, not today. Funny—when Tamara says she's gonna do something, she always does it. You know?"

"I know," I said.

"How come you asking me all these questions anyway? I mean, why don't you just ask Tam?"

"She's been out of the office all day. I'm trying to find her."

". . . Nothing wrong, is there? I mean—"

I said, "I hope not, Vonda. Thanks for your help," and rang off.

I went and got the DeBrissac file again. As I remembered, he was down in there as a "male Caucasian." To make sure, I put in a call to the Ballard Agency in Portland. They verified it: George DeBrissac was Caucasian, his ex-wife was Caucasian, and that made it pretty likely the cousin who owned the San Leandro house was Caucasian.

So was this half-and-half part of the "something that went

down" on Monday night that'd bothered her enough to do some checking? What had she meant by "dealing with him"?

And the big question: Did he have anything to do with her sudden disappearance?

15

JAKE RUNYON

Paul Venner, Troy's lover who worked in the Castro leather shop, wouldn't talk to him. Venner was in his twenties, had orange spiked hair and a tattoo of a scorpion under his right ear and a muscled body encased in black leather pants and an orange T-shirt with the words QUEER POWER emblazoned on the front; he wore his hostility toward both heterosexuals and cops like another motto on the sleeve. He stonewalled every question Runyon put to him by saying aggressively, "No comment. Buy something or get out, you don't belong here" or "Hey, you'd look good in cowhide and chains" or "How about a fur-lined jock strap, they're on sale this week." Runyon didn't bite on any of it. Nothing ever showed on his face unless he wanted it to, and he showed Venner nothing but a flat stare the entire five minutes he was in there. When he said, "You'd better watch yourself, kid, or you'll end up in the hospital like the other three victims," and got another smart-ass comment in return, he walked out. The Paul Venners of the world, the hard-line haters, the self-involved screw-everybody-else jerks gay or straight, deserved whatever they got.

Another visit to Jerry Butterfield's house—a refurbished post-1906 earthquake cottage with an add-on garage—also bought him nothing. Still nobody home. On the back of one of his agency business cards he wrote his cell-phone number and a brief call-me-it's-important message, and wedged the card into the doorjamb above the lock. If he didn't hear from Butterfield by seven or eight tonight, he'd follow up again himself.

Next stop: Hattie Street.

Keith Morgan was fifty or so, heavyset, sad-eyed. Lines and wrinkles calipered a small mouth, scored his cheeks and neck; even his head beneath a sparse combing of brown hair showed faint furrows. His first-floor studio apartment in the big, blue Victorian was dominated by framed photographs of a thin bearded man alone and in candid shots with Morgan, and prints and lithographs of dogs of one kind and another. A live dog, old and shaggy, of indeterminate breed, followed its master everywhere and never left him alone; it showed no interest in Runyon. Cataracts made its eyes look like blobs of milky glass.

Morgan had no problem with Runyon being straight or a detective. He listened to a brief explanation for the visit, nodded, showed him into the apartment, turned off a TV tuned to a noisy talk show, offered him something to drink, and then sat in a creaky recliner with the blind animal at his feet. The room smelled of dog and some kind of food with a lot of curry powder in it.

"Troy," he said. "Well, I guess I'm not surprised he's the cause of trouble."

"Why is that, Mr. Morgan?"

"Wild young fool. The kind with no sense. Won't listen to anybody, think nothing bad will ever happen to them and they'll live forever."

"Promiscuous, I've been told."

"Lord, yes. He had a parade of lovers in and out." Wry mouth. "He even propositioned me right after he moved in— offered to trade sex for his rent. I refused, of course. I would have even if I owned the building."

"Yes?"

"I'm HIV positive," Morgan said.

"I see. Recent diagnosis?"

"No, I was diagnosed more than ten years ago. Amazing the disease hasn't killed me by now. My partner wasn't so lucky. He died nine years ago. Probably infected by me, though that's not certain."

Runyon said, "I'm sorry," and meant it.

"So am I. But you learn to live with it. Learn to live without sex, too. I gave that up when Dave died." His lips moved, shaped something that might have been a ghost of a smile. "I felt it was the least I could do to honor his memory."

"Did you tell Troy you were HIV positive?"

"I did, and he still offered me safe sex. See what I mean by wild young fool?"

"He moved out two weeks ago, is that right?"

"He vacated his room two weeks ago, yes."

"Why the distinction?"

"He didn't move voluntarily. I kicked him out."

"For what reason?"

Morgan sighed heavily. At the sound, the blind dog raised its head and keened the air; when the sound wasn't repeated, the shaggy head went down again on stretched-out forepaws.

"I found out he was underage," Morgan said. "Troy looks much older, but he's only seventeen."

"How did you find out?"

"From his brother."

Runyon said, "Brother?"

"That's right. You didn't know he had a family?"

"I don't know much about him at all. What's the brother's name?"

"He didn't say, but when I confronted Troy, he called him Tommy. He showed up here one day looking for Troy. He . . . well, he was belligerent and abusive."

"Homophobic?"

"Probably. No, definitely. He called my home a 'fag house.' Why did I let an underage kid live in this 'fag house,' he said."

"What'd he look like?"

"There's a resemblance to Troy, but he's darker, not as good-looking. In his early twenties."

"Tall, slender?"

"That's right." Morgan frowned, ran the tips of his fingers across his lower lip. "You seem to know him. I take it you think he's one of the men responsible for the assaults."

"Pretty good chance of it."

"I'm not surprised. Belligerent, abusive, homophobic, and not very bright—a lethal combination. His brother is underage and gay, so he's taking out his anger and hatred on Troy's lovers."

"Beginning to look that way."

"Sick, senseless."

"Most acts of violence are."

"Do you think I'm in any danger?"

The question was matter-of-fact, more one of curiosity than fear. The right answer was yes, anybody in the gay community who'd had anything to do with Troy was a potential victim. Runyon gave him the other answer, the one designed to reassure.

"I don't think so, Mr. Morgan. Tommy and his buddy aren't going to be running around loose much longer."

Morgan nodded. Maybe he believed it, maybe he didn't.

"Was Tommy by himself when he was here?" Runyon asked.

"I didn't see anyone else."

"You happen to notice what kind of vehicle he was driving?"

"I'm sorry, no, I didn't."

"Was Troy home at the time?"

"No, and a good thing he wasn't. As angry as Tommy was, there'd have been a scene."

"He just went away? Tommy, I mean."

"Not before he said he'd 'fix me' if I let Troy keep on living here. 'Tell him to get his ass back home fast or I'll come and drag it back.' His exact words. I don't like threats, but letting rooms in this building is my responsibility. I can't afford to lose my manager's position, or this apartment."

"So you gave Troy his walking papers that same day?"

"As soon as he came home. Once I verified his age, I had the legal right."

"How did you verify it?"

The blind dog, asleep now, let out a long, low groaning sound and one of its back paws began a spasmodic twitching. Morgan looked down at the animal, and his sad eyes grew even sadder. "Poor old Doc," he said. "He's sixteen, he has arthritis and half a dozen other ailments. I'm going to have to put him down soon."

"That's too bad."

"I hate the thought of it," Morgan said. "He's all I've had since Dave died. I don't know how I'm going to get along without him."

"You could get another dog."

"Yes. I could. I suppose it's better than being alone."

For him it was. For Runyon, being alone was better than trying to replace the irreplaceable. He said, "About Troy. You were going to tell me how you verified his age."

"Well . . . I probably shouldn't admit to this," Morgan said, "but after the brother left I was so upset I used my passkey to get into Troy's room. I don't make a habit of that sort of thing—I believe in everyone's right to privacy—but under the circumstances . . . well, I felt justified."

"And you found what?"

"His driver's license, believe it or not. It was in one of the nightstand drawers, just tossed in there."

Which probably meant that Troy had some sort of fake ID that he carried around with him, in case he was carded; that would explain how he was able to frequent clubs like The Dark Spot with impunity.

Runyon said, "His real last name. It's not Scott, is it?"

"No. Douglass. With two esses."

"Do you remember the address on the license?"

"I don't, no. I only glanced at it."

"Would the city have been South San Francisco?"

"That's right, it was. South San Francisco."

Troy Douglass. Tommy Douglass. All right.

"What was Troy's reaction when you told him to vacate?"

"Oh, he argued a bit at first. Until I delivered his brother's message."

"And then?"

"He went pale, said something like 'Oh no, how did he find me? Why can't he just leave me alone, let me be who I am?'"

"That sounds as though he might be afraid of Tommy."

"No question of that."

"You think he did what Tommy told him to, went back home?"

"He said he didn't know what he was going to do, but I had the feeling he wouldn't defy his brother. The fear factor. It didn't take him long to load his belongings into that old car of his and be on his way."

"What kind of old car? Make, model?"

"A Chevrolet, I think. White, sporty, at least twenty years old. And loud—a loud engine."

"And you haven't seen or heard from him since."

"Not a word." Morgan paused, reached down absently to touch the blind dog with his fingertips. "Do you think you can find Tommy before he hurts anyone else?"

"I'm sure as hell going to try."

He was just starting down Market Street, heading for the 101 freeway and South San Francisco, when his cell phone rang. He'd never much cared for people who talked while they drove unless it was absolutely necessary, so he pulled over into a loading zone to take the call.

Bill. Still no word from Tamara. No sign of her car in San Leandro. He'd just talked to a friend of hers, Vonda something, and the news he'd gotten from her wasn't encouraging.

"I think we've got a situation here, Jake," he said. His voice was flat, professional, but there was an undercurrent of tension in it.

"Beginning to look that way. How do you want to handle it?"

"It's too soon to report her missing. Up to us, at least for the time being."

"Priority." It wasn't a question.

"Yeah. Priority. Where are you?"

Runyon told him. "I can be in the office in twenty minutes."

"Come ahead. First thing is for you to take a crack at her computer. Then we'll see."

"On my way."

Runyon pulled out into traffic again. He hadn't let himself think much about Tamara while he was working on the gay bashings. Not because he wasn't concerned; he liked the woman, respected her, shared a professional bond. Because he'd learned long ago that the only way to do a job right was to concentrate on it—one thing at a time; and because Bill was calling the shots on her unexplained absence. Now that he was needed on that, he quit thinking about Troy and Tommy Douglass and focused on Tamara. Priority. When one of your own was in trouble and there was something you could do about it, you back-burnered everything else.

16

TAMARA

The interior of Lemoyne's SUV was like a prison cell.

No, not like one—it *was* a prison cell. Not much larger than the closet in his basement room, not much smaller than the room itself. He'd taken out the rear seats, fixed the hatchback door so it couldn't be opened from inside, walled off the rear compartment from the front seat with a thick sheet of tinted plastic bolted to the frame. Windows were all tinted; you could see out—everything outside had a faint grayish tinge, the way they said things did for cats—but nobody could see in.

Lauren wasn't the first little girl he'd kidnapped. For damn sure now.

The floor in there was carpeted and he'd unrolled a couple of cheap, thin futons over it. Real thoughtful. Wasn't anything else in the cell except her and Lauren and the big white-faced, pink-dressed doll he'd made Lauren take along; she still wouldn't have anything to do with it, kicked at it whenever it rolled over her way. No matter how much Tamara tried to keep herself and Lauren braced, the two of them kept sliding around like the doll on those skinny futons. She kept a tight hold on the kid so she wouldn't hurt herself banging into metal and glass whenever the SUV swerved or hit a bump.

Where were they now? Still on Highway 80, somewhere up around Sacramento. She'd been up here a few times with the folks and once with Horace, but not recently; had to keep checking road signs to pinpoint their location. City girl, San Francisco girl. Scared girl.

So far Lemoyne hadn't hurt her. Thought he was going to when he ripped open that closet door last night, but all he'd done was shake her a few times, get in her face, and yell questions at her. How'd she find out about him? Who else knew about him and Angie? That damn printout in her purse. Stupid not to've left it in the office. One more stupid thing she'd done or hadn't done.

She'd 'fessed up the truth about seeing him bring the girl home with him Monday night. No gain in lying about that. Rest of what she threw at him was pure lie: she'd told her partner all about it, if she turned up missing he'd go straight to the cops and the cops'd come straight to 1109 Willard. Lemoyne hadn't bought it. "If your partner knew about this, he wouldn't've let you come back here alone. Nobody knows but you." Sick bastard, but a smart sick bastard.

He calmed down some after that. Hadn't even shoved her back in the closet when he was done ragging on her. "You spend the night in here with Angie. Take care of her, I don't want her crying or wetting herself anymore."

"Then what?"

"We're leaving in the morning, early, the three of us."

"Where're we going?"

"You'll find out when we get there."

"Trailer in the woods?"

That almost set him off again. "How'd you find out about that? What do you know about that?"

"Lauren . . . Angie told me. Said you were taking her up there to show her a big surprise, have some fun."

"Angie and me'll have fun. Not you."

"What you gonna do to me?"

"I don't know yet. I haven't made up my mind."

This morning, when he came down to get them—six-fifteen by her watch, still dark outside—he hadn't looked in the closet. She'd shut the door, but worried the whole time she was awake that he'd think to look in there. If he had . . . But he hadn't. Just took them out at gunpoint and locked them in this rolling prison cell and headed out. Small hope anyway. One of the other small hopes she'd had was already dead: before he'd shoved them into the SUV, she had a look at the street and the Toyota wasn't there anymore, he must've moved it out of the neighborhood sometime during the night. The small hopes that were left wouldn't fit in a gnat's eye. But any hope was something to hang on to, like a lifeline.

The SUV lurched again and Lauren grabbed hold of her blouse, pressed tight against her the way she had on the bed last night. Couldn't get close enough. Funny how that little girl made her feel. She'd never thought much about kids, beyond a vague notion that if she and Horace ever got married, maybe they'd have one or two someday, like maybe after she was thirty-five. Too much ambition, too many plans, to dive into motherhood before then. But last night, today, holding Lauren, trying to comfort her . . . it'd unleashed maternal feelings she hadn't thought she owned. Now she understood how Bill felt about Emily. Really understood, for the first time, how Ma and Pop felt about her.

Amazing thing was, her mothering instincts must be true because Lauren trusted her, took strength from her even though she was a stranger. Hadn't wet the bed or thrown up or cried much in the dark hours; hadn't cried at all the whole time they were on the road. Just sat there quiet, hanging on and now and then looking up at her with those big trusting eyes. Didn't look too good now, though. Kind of sweaty and splotchy. Carsick? The way they kept bouncing around in here, it was a wonder she wasn't carsick herself.

Surrogate mama, that's me, Tamara thought, and tightened her arm around the girl, felt little shivers rippling across the thin shoulders. Anger crawled into her again, bleak and black. *He's not gonna mess with her if I can help it. Word. He'll have to kill me first.*

Freeway signs slid past, gray-green in gray-tinged sunlight. Reno. Highway 80. Downtown Sacramento. They kept riding 80. Cars whizzed by in the other lanes, people just a few feet away. Yo, in here! Help, call the cops, kidnap victims locked up in here! But there was too much traffic noise for shouting to do any good, and no other way to signal through those tinted windows.

How about when he stopped for gas? He'd have to do it sooner or later, these big-boat SUVs were gas hogs. But he'd warned her about making any noise back here. Somebody'd get hurt if she did, he said. Meant it, all right—you could see it in his hard, light-skinned half-and-half face. Like that psycho last Christmas. Not as far off the hook, pretty much in control, but capable of using that gun of his if push came to shove.

Wasn't worth the risk, not with Lauren in the line of fire. *Take care of my little girl.* Yeah, well, that was just what she would do.

The kid made a little whimpering sound. Tamara put her face down close, smoothed sweat-damp strands of hair off her forehead. "You doing okay, honey?"

"I feel sick."

"Sick to your stomach?"

"Uh-huh. I hate throwing up."

"You won't. Take deep breaths and hold on. We'll be stopping pretty soon."

A short silence. Then, "Tamara?"

"Yes, honey?"

"I'm so scared. Are you scared?"

"Some. Don't you fret. We'll be all right."

"Am I gonna see my mama and daddy again?"

"Sure you will. Sure."

"Promise?"

She said, "Promise," and bit her tongue and added a little silent prayer: *Don't you make a liar out of me.*

Miles unrolling under them. More signs: Roseville. Rocklin. Places she'd heard of but never been to. Whole lot of places she'd never been, places she wanted to go someday. Whole lot of life ahead of her, ahead of Lauren—

Pay attention to the signs.

Another one: Auburn. Highway 49, Grass Valley.

Lemoyne slowed down, swung out of the fast lane and on over into the exit lane. Auburn—Grass Valley exit. Tamara shifted position on the futon, sat up straighter. Some little town near Grass Valley was where Lemoyne's second wife was from. Did she still live there, her and his real daughter? Like maybe in a trailer in the woods? Going there to see them for some off-the-hook reason, introduce Angie to Angie? Dude was so weird, he was capable of just about anything.

Off the freeway now, onto a busy side road. And into a Chevron station. For some reason she registered the gas prices' sign: $2.39 a gallon for regular. Goddamn oil companies, still screwing Bay Area drivers left, right, and back door.

They stopped alongside a row of pumps. Lemoyne hadn't said a word since they'd left San Leandro, but now she heard his voice, the words muffled by the plastic partition, "You keep quiet back there, Dark Chocolate. You know what'll happen if you don't."

Dark Chocolate. Second or third time he'd called her that. One of those half-and-halfs that hated the fact they were mixed race, wished they were all black or all white and wound up resenting both. Your equal opportunity racist.

She said, "Angie's feeling sick to her stomach."

"That's too bad." As if he meant it.

"Let me take her to the bathroom."

"No."

"You want her to throw up on herself?"

"We don't have much farther to go. Another hour or so."

"I don't know if she can make it that long."

"You better see she does or you'll clean her up when we get there. Clean up back there, too. I hate the smell of puke."

He opened the door on the last few words, slid out quickly, and shut the door behind him.

Lauren started to cry.

Outskirts of Auburn on 49. Broad avenue lined with shopping malls and business parks and car dealerships and fast-food places. Heavy traffic, endless string of stoplights. Then the lights got farther and farther apart, and the road narrowed into two lanes and climbed steadily into the foothills.

Lauren was quiet again. Still taking deep breaths to keep her gorge down, her face scrunched up with the effort it took. Afraid to throw up, afraid of what he might do. Good little girl. Smart, sweet-tempered. What'd she ever do to have a thing like this happen to her?

What'd I ever do? What's deserving it have to do with shit happening to you?

Still climbing, still a lot of traffic. Pine woods—they were in the foothills now.

More signs: Grass Valley. Nevada City. Highway 20— Marysville.

Exit lane again. Swinging off onto Highway 20.

Pretty soon they were heading down a long, steep grade. Day was clear and warm, sunlight hitting the windows and making it muggy inside the prison cell. Air was bad, too, from the goddamn cigarettes Lemoyne kept smoking. She called to him to turn on the air conditioner, they were suffocating back here. He ignored her.

At the bottom of the grade the freeway ended at a stoplight and another sign. Left: Penn Valley. Right: Rough and Ready. Rough and Ready—that was the name of the town Lemoyne's ex-wife was from. He turned right at the intersection, onto a narrow secondary road that climbed and twisted through thick forestland.

She tried to remember exactly where Rough and Ready was, how isolated. No use. Must've looked at a California map two or three hundred times the past five years, but always for specific counties, cities, roads; you just didn't notice all the other names, the hundreds of small towns and secondary roads that covered the state. Not if you were a confirmed urbanite, you didn't.

The constant flicker of sunlight and shadow hurt her eyes. The sharp twists and turns bounced her and Lauren around even more. Seemed to go on a long time like that, but it couldn't've been much more than five minutes before Lemoyne slowed down and Tamara saw they were in Rough and Ready. Old-fashioned little place, must've been a Gold Rush town—they passed an ancient building that said Blacksmith Shop on the front of it. Then they were out of the village and Lemoyne picked up speed again.

But not for long. Less than a mile. Another slowdown, then a left turn past a country store onto a lane hemmed in by woods, then a right turn onto another lane with an uneven surface that rattled her teeth and shook a few more whimpers out of the child.

One more twist, and they were onto an unpaved surface—driveway, also hemmed in by trees—and finally, after maybe a hundred jolting yards, the SUV bucked to a stop. Tamara lifted up onto one knee so she could see better through the side window, out front through the partition.

Appalachia.

That was her first thought. Meadowlike clearing surrounded by forest, a creek or something running through on the right side. And a trailer at the far end. Junky and about half a century old, one of those silver jobs that looked like giant sow bugs—all spotted with rust and half-buried in weeds and grass, dry pine needles and cones from a tree behind it spread over its top like dead hair. Fifty or sixty yards to the left was an old barn in better shape than the trailer, the corpse of a car angled in alongside. Off to the right, sitting in more weeds, was one of those molded plastic kids' playsets, slide and teeter-totter and climbing bars; the colors on it were bright, as if it'd been repainted not too long ago. A narrow shed leaned sideways in that direction, too, ready to fall down. Or maybe it was an outhouse. Didn't have a half-moon in the door, but it sure looked like one. An outhouse!

Wasn't anybody around, not now and not for a long time. Lemoyne's ex-wife and daughter didn't live here, if they ever had. Only one who came here was that sick bastard when he was in a mood to have fun.

Her skin began to prickle and crawl, the last of her small hopes to crumble away. Middle of nowhere. Nobody was going to find them in a primitive hole like this, not soon, probably not ever. If she couldn't find a way to save Lauren and herself, they weren't gonna be saved. Not in this life.

Lemoyne was out of the SUV, unlocking the hatchback. In spite of herself she jerked when he threw the hatch up. The Saturday night special was in his hand again; he waved it at her. "All right, come out of there. You first, and be careful with my little girl."

She obeyed, scooting out on one hip and leg, lifting the child when she was on her feet. Lauren whimpered and clung to her, blinking in the sunlight. He patted the kid on the head with his free hand, smiling down at her almost tenderly.

"Here we are, Angie," he said. "Home."

Now what?

17

Waiting for Runyon, I couldn't sit still. Up and down, shuffle papers, make yet another call to Tamara's cell number, make yet another call to her apartment, hunt through her desk and paper files again, pace around all three offices, stare out the front windows at the narrow expanse of South Park. Enforced inactivity in this kind of situation is the worst kind. I needed to be doing something, and there was nothing to do yet. Dead time, wasted time, *Where was she, what happened to her?* repeating over and over like song lyrics you can't get out of your head.

When the telephone went off I was all over it like a bear on a honeypot, but it had nothing to do with Tamara. And that was almost as much a relief as a disappointment. Too often the worst news comes by phone.

"I decided there's no reason you shouldn't know what was in the envelope," Cybil's voice said without preamble.

"Yes?"

"It's the manuscript of an unpublished novel Dancer wrote a long time ago," she said. "It's about a group of New Yorkers, mostly writers and artists, and what happens in their home-front lives and relationships on a single day—June 6, 1944. The idea being that it's a kind of D-Day for them as well. He called it *Remember D-Day*. Not a very good title, but then it's not a very good novel. An interesting idea poorly developed."

"Where does amazing grace fit in? Or does it?"

"One of the female leads is named Grace Cutter. Known as Amazing Grace to the male narrator."

"Patterned after you?"

"Obviously, yes. And the narrator, Donovan—Russ himself, of course. There's an ongoing and rather steamy affair between the two, graphically described. I wasn't surprised and I don't suppose you are, either."

"No. You think that's why he wanted you to have the manuscript?"

"A tribute to me and what might have been. So he said in a long, rambling cover letter."

"You going to let anybody else read the manuscript?"

"No. I don't know what I'm going to do with it. Destroy it, most likely—it's worthless as fiction or nostalgia or memento."

"Your choice. What else did he put in the letter?"

"Nothing to concern anyone but me," Cybil said. "I've shared and discussed this matter as much as I'm going to. Russ Dancer is dead, the past is dead, from now on suppose we just let it stay that way."

". . . Okay with me."

"And with Kerry. It's settled then."

She didn't have anything more to say, which saved me the trouble of having to prod her off the line. I put the receiver down, stood, went away from my desk a couple of paces, came back and sat down and picked the receiver up again and called Bates and Carpenter. Kerry was out of her office; her secretary went to find her. I got up and took a couple of turns around the desk until I heard her voice.

"Did Cybil call you? About Dancer's manuscript?"

"Couple of minutes ago. Kerry—"

"I don't know about you, but I'm relieved. I kept imagining all sorts of nasty things he might've given her—that's why I was so bothered. You know how weird Dancer could be—"

"Kerry, listen, I don't want to talk about that right now. That's not why I called. There's a problem here and I'm not going to be able to pick up Emily. Can you do it, or make arrangements with the Simpsons?"

She caught the tension in my voice. "I can do it. What problem?"

"It's Tamara. She's gone missing."

"Missing? For heaven's sake, what—?"

"No idea yet. She hasn't come in or called in, she's not home, her cell phone's out of service, and nobody's talked to her since last night. May or may not have something to do with a surveillance she's been on in San Leandro the past couple of nights."

"Have you called the police yet?"

"Not yet. Too soon. Jake Runyon and I are on it."

"You don't think she—?"

"Trying not to think anything yet. I don't know when I'll be home. I'll call if I'm going to be late."

"Or if there's any word."

"Soon as I can."

"Find her, you and Jake," she said. "Find her safe."

• • •

Less than a minute after Runyon switched on Tamara's computer, he said, "Yeah, I was afraid of that. I can't get in. She never gave you any idea of the password?"

"No. That kind of information is wasted on me."

"Write it down anywhere that you know of?"

"I've been through her desk a couple of times. I didn't see anything that looked like a password."

"She's too security conscious to leave something like that in her desk," Runyon said. "Probably didn't write it down at all. A person her age doesn't worry about forgetting things like that."

"Or about something unexpected happening to them."

"Yeah."

He looked through her desk anyway, didn't find anything, and then we brainstormed a couple of dozen possible words, phrases, dates that she might've used for a password. None of them worked.

"Dammit," I said, "we could sit here all night and not come up with the right one. The only lead we've got, and it's a dead end."

"Not necessarily. There're other ways to get into a secured computer."

"What ways?"

"Codebreaker program, for one. Runs every possible combination of letters and numbers until it hits on the right one. But that can take a long time. A better, faster way is to link up another computer and wipe her hard drive."

"You're losing me, Jake."

"Computer forensics," Runyon said. "Wiping the hard

drive lets you access all the stored files. Also retrieve deleted material—what we need if Tamara dumped the research she told you about."

"How long does that take?"

"Not long for the wipe job. Rest of it depends on how many files and deletions need sorting through to get what you're after. Probably no more than a couple of hours."

"Can you do that kind of thing?"

"Christ, no. Takes an expert."

"Where do we find one?"

"Some of the bigger investigative agencies have computer forensics departments now. Caldwell was just putting one together in Seattle when I left them."

"McCone Investigations," I said. "They handle computer-related cases. And Sharon's nephew, Mick, is an expert hacker."

"He'll know how to do a wipe job then."

I called over there, got Ted Smalley, McCone Investigations' office manager, on the line. "Sharon's up at Touchstone with Hy," he said when I asked for her. Touchstone was a getaway home McCone and her significant other, Hy Ripinsky, owned—in Mendocino County, a couple of hundred miles from the city. "Is there anything I can do for you?"

I said, "I hope so, Ted," and explained the situation.

"Of course we'll do whatever we can to help," he said in his crisp way. "Mick has done that kind of work before. In fact, he's so good at it Sharon is thinking of establishing a computer forensics department and putting him in charge."

"Is Mick in?"

"No, but I think I can reach him. Let me make a call or two and I'll get back to you."

He called back in six minutes. "I just spoke to Mick," he said. "He's eager to help, but he's caught up on a case in San Jose. The earliest he can be back in the city is seven-thirty."

"Seven-thirty. Okay. I'd rather not wait around here that long, so how about I drop off a key to our office?"

"I have a better suggestion. Why not bring Tamara's computer here? I can have it hooked up and ready when Mick arrives. It'll save time."

"Done. Thanks, Ted. I'll bring it right over."

Runyon and I unhooked Tamara's Mac G-4, and a good thing he was there because I might've fouled up the job on my own: it was a big machine with a lot of wires and connections that didn't mean anything to me. Together we carried it downstairs and around the corner and down to the garage where the agency rented space.

"You going back to San Leandro after you drop it off?" he asked.

"Yeah. See what I can find out from the people on Willard Street. You mind hanging around here until five-thirty or so, just in case?"

"No problem. If you need me later tonight, I'll be available."

"Right. Where'll you be? Home?"

"No. Out keeping busy. My cell'll be on wherever I am."

McCone Investigations was not far away, in Pier 24-1/2 next to the SFFD fireboat station on the Embarcadero. There were several businesses inhabiting the cavernous interior; Sharon's was the largest. She'd expanded her operations considerably in the past few years, adding office space and employees—five now, with more in the offing—and her agency now occupied the entire north side of the upper level. I drove onto the pier floor, where there was tenant parking and at the moment no empty spaces, double-parked, and lugged the computer upstairs to Ted's office.

He was a slender, compact man in his forties, with a neatly trimmed goatee and a recent predilection for gaudy Hawaiian shirts. A small smile widened his mouth when he saw the machine. "A G-4. I'm trying to talk Sharon into buying me one. They're among the best on the market."

"Mick won't have any trouble with it?"

"I'm sure not. Exactly what is it he's to look for?"

"Anything pertaining to a male of mixed race—half black, half white. There may or may not be a San Leandro or other East Bay connection. And/or a connection to a split-fee case we're working for the Ballard Agency in Portland—the reason Tamara was in San Leandro the last couple of nights. The subject's name is George DeBrissac."

Ted wrote all of that down. "Anything else?"

"Not that I know of right now," I said. "Will Mick be able to tell recent from older stuff ?"

"Yes. Everything on the hard drive is dated."

"Should be from yesterday. Either a new file, or she might've printed out her research and then deleted it."

"Mick can find it either way. And I'll have him check all her entries and searches for the past week or so, just in case."

"How long do you think it'll take him?"

"When it comes to computers, he's even more efficient than I am. I'd say no more than an hour at the most. He'll call you as soon as he has anything to report. Do you have a cell number?"

I did now, thanks to Kerry; her Christmas present had been a cell phone. I read it off to him. "I really appreciate this, Ted."

"Friends as well as business associates—you'd do the same

for us. And I like Tamara, I hate the thought of anything happening to her. Not that anything has or will. I'm sure she's all right."

He wasn't sure, any more than I was. Just trying to be upbeat, reassuring. But the truth was in his eyes, in the grave set of his features. No one who deals with crime and criminals on a daily basis can fool anybody else in the business on a thing like this.

18

JAKE RUNYON

He waited at the office until 5:35. Dead time, but necessary; until close of business there was always a chance, however small, that Tamara or somebody who knew her whereabouts might call. Then he switched on the answering machine, locked up, went down to the garage for his car.

On his own time now. Ready to jump when Bill called, but until then the priority flag was down. He let himself think again about Troy and Tommy Douglass. Keep moving, keep busy, pick up where he'd left off earlier.

South San Francisco, sprawled out in a little valley under San Bruno Mountain, was an industrial city that billed itself that way in huge white letters cut into one of the flanking hillsides. Nearly half of it was given over to factories, steel mills, maintenance shops for the airlines at SFO, meat-packing plants, paint and chemical and plastics companies. The other half was largely blue-collar and lower-income, white-collar residential—housing that was crazily overpriced, like all Bay Area real estate these days, but given its proximity to San Francisco, still affordable and desirable. Runyon knew all this because he'd driven around and familiarized himself with South San Francisco, as he'd taken the time to do with all the cities and towns within a hundred-mile radius. You couldn't operate effectively in a metropolitan area as large as this one unless you built up a good working knowledge of its component parts. Besides which, it had given him a purpose during his off-duty hours.

The usual commuter snarl on 101 turned a twenty-minute trip into thirty-five. He left the freeway on Grand Avenue, the main South City exit, and then had to make three stops, two service stations, and a convenience store, before he found a phone directory that hadn't been vandalized or stolen. Phone booths and phone books—vanishing breeds in this age of cell phones and widespread disrespect for public property. Common courtesy: another vanishing breed.

There were a pair of listings for Douglass, two esses. One was residential, G. Douglass, no address to go with the number. The other was commercial: Douglass Auto Body, on Victory Avenue. In the car he tapped out the residential number on his cell. Nine rings, no answer. He located the South San Francisco map among the pile in the glove box, found Victory Avenue. It intersected with South Linden over near the Bayshore Freeway.

Douglass Auto Body turned out to be a tumbledown frame garage, its barbed-wire-fenced side yard cluttered with junker cars. Still open for business even though the time was nearly six-thirty. Railroad tracks ran a couple of blocks away; he could hear an engine whistle and the clatter of rolling stock as he drove slowly past the garage. None of the handful of older pickups parked in the vicinity had a Confederate flag in its rear window. But parked near the set of double doors facing the street was a sporty white Chevy Camaro, vintage 1980.

Runyon parked next to the Camaro, walked inside. The overhead lighting, high up on the rafters, was dim enough to create pockets of shadow along the walls. One man was working in there, fiftyish, gray-haired and gray-bearded, the upper part of his face obscured by goggles, using a hissing acetylene torch on a Jeep Ranger's rear fender. To the left, just inside the double doors, brighter lighting illuminated a glass-partitioned office cubicle. The office had one occupant shuffling papers at a desk—a young guy with curly blond hair, lean and muscular in a blue shirt.

Runyon veered over into the cubicle's doorway. The blond kid looked up, an unsmiling look that catalogued him briefly and without much interest. The eyes were blue and innocent, the face smooth and beardless. Angelic wasn't a term Runyon would've used to describe it. More apt was clean-cut All-American College Boy, circa 1960. He could pass for twenty-one, all right.

"Yessir?" he said. Deep, soft voice. "Help you?"

"Your name Troy? Troy Douglass?"

"That's right. Do I know you?"

"No. I'm looking for your brother."

"Tommy?" The name didn't seem to taste right; his mouth quirked a little when he said it. "He's not here."

"Where can I find him?"

"You a friend of his?"

"No."

"He owe you money or something?"

"Does he owe a lot of people money?"

"Well . . ."

"I'm not one of them."

"Why're you looking for him then?"

"Personal matter."

Furrows marred the flawless complexion. Troy pushed his chair back, got to his feet. "Maybe you better talk to my father. He's right out there."

"It's your brother I'm interested in. What kind of car does he drive?"

". . . Why do you want to know that?"

"Older model pickup, Confederate flag in the rear window?"

"No, that's Bix's wheels."

"Bix. Red hair, freckles? Tommy's buddy?"

"Yeah. Why're you asking all these questions?"

"The two of them are in trouble, that's why."

"Trouble? What kind of trouble?"

"They've been on a rampage the past couple of weeks, beating up gay men in the Castro district. Gene Zalesky, Larry Exeter, Kenneth Hitchcock."

Shock turned Troy's face the noncolor of Crisco. He said, "Oh, Jesus!" and sat down hard enough to make the chair squawk loudly.

"You didn't know?"

"No. I had no idea."

"Put all three of them in the hospital," Runyon said. "Hitchcock's still there, still in critical condition."

"Because of me, of what I . . . ?"

"Looks that way."

"But it's not their fault! How can he blame them?"

"Easier than blaming you, hating you, beating you up. This way, you're just a victim and he feels justified."

"I knew he was a homophobe, but a basher . . ."

"How'd he get their names? You tell him?"

"He made me tell him. Wasn't enough he had to come looking for me, force me to move back home . . . he wanted names, addresses, everything about the men I . . . but I never thought . . . Goddamn him and that speed freak Bix!"

"What's Bix's last name?"

"Sullivan."

"Does Tommy use drugs, too?"

Brief nod. "I don't, I never hurt anybody, and he thinks what I do is sick!"

"Where can I find him and Bix Sullivan?"

"Why? What're you going to do to them?"

"Stop them from attacking anybody else, maybe killing the next man they go after."

"Put them in jail? Are you a cop?"

"Don't you think they belong in jail?"

"Yes, but—" Troy's face warped again, this time showing fear. "Oh, shit!"

The kid was staring past him, out into the garage. Runyon realized that the hissing sound had stopped, and when he half turned he saw that the gray-haired man had shed the acetylene torch, removed his goggles, and was approaching the office.

"He doesn't know about me," in a tense whisper. "That's why I came home, Tommy promised not to tell him about me. Please don't say anything. Not here, not now!"

The elder Douglass wore a quizzical smile as he came into the office, but he lost it when he got a look at his son's pale, sweaty face. "What's the matter? What's going on here?"

"Nothing, Dad, nothing, this guy's just . . . he's looking for Tommy."

Douglass transferred his gaze to Runyon. "Who're you? What do you want with my son?"

"Tommy owes him money, that's all."

"Yeah? Another damn bill collector. He stays out all hours, can't manage his finances, and you run off to Christ knows where for three weeks. Some pair of kids I got."

Runyon said, "Where can I find Tommy, Mr. Douglass?"

"Well, you won't find him at home. Come back tomorrow."

"He lives with you?"

"Both my sons, one big happy family. You're a bill collector and you don't know that?"

"It's important that I locate him right away."

"Yeah, well, you're out of luck," Douglass said. "He left about five o'clock, went up to the city with a buddy of his. Spend more money he doesn't have, make another big night of it in the friggin' city."

19

TAMARA

Three minutes after they arrived in Appalachia, Lemoyne locked her and Lauren in the sow-bug trailer and drove off by himself. Didn't say where he was going. All he said was, "I'll be back pretty soon." And "You can't get out of here so don't even try." And "Everything's locked up in there—it better still be locked up when I get back."

The inside wasn't as bad as the outside, but it was still another prison cell. Stuffy, stinking of must and stale cigarettes, and not too clean—dust on all the surfaces, spiderwebs hanging in corners, probably bugs in the old worn carpeting and mismatched Goodwill furniture. Lemoyne hadn't spent much time here. And nobody'd lived here in a long time.

Lauren said in a small, thick voice, "Tamara, I don't feel so good."

The child was still in her arms, burrowed up close. Tamara tilted her body back so she could see her face. Didn't look so good, either. Sweaty, pale, moist-eyed, coughing in little dry hacks. Running a fever? Yeah—her forehead felt overwarm.

"I think I'm gonna be sick."

Damn. Bathroom in here or not?

Turned out there was, a cubicle with a toilet and a sink and a rusty shower stall so tiny Horace would've had trouble squeezing in sideways. She set Lauren on her feet, lifted the toilet lid.

Kid said miserably, "I hate to throw up," and leaned over the bowl with Tamara holding her and threw up.

When she was done, Tamara pushed the lever and the toilet flushed all right. Septic system. And a well for drinking water, judging from the mineral-brownish color of what came out of the sink tap, so that shed outside was probably a well-house. There was a towel hanging from a rack next to the sink, not clean but not filthy either. She let the cold water run until it more or less cleared, then wet the towel and used it to clean off Lauren's face.

"Better now, honey?"

"Thirsty."

"Me, too. Must be glasses here somewhere."

Not in the bathroom. She picked Lauren up again, carried her into a dinky kitchen. Dining alcove in one corner, another sink, a propane stove, one of those pocket refrigerators, three wall cabinets and a pair of drawers on either side of the sink. Two of the cabinets were padlocked. The other one was full of plastic—plates, bowls, glasses, the kind of cheap pastel-colored crap designed for picnics. She rinsed out two of the glasses, filled one for Lauren, the other for herself. The water eased the dryness in her mouth, but it sloshed in her stomach and kicked up sharp hunger pangs. No food except a Slim•Fast shake and a Slim•Fast chocolate bar in, what, almost twenty-four hours?

Last night Lemoyne had brought a sandwich and a glass of milk for Lauren, but nothing for her. Kid had tried to share the sandwich with her—what a sweetheart she was—but she'd refused. Take food out of a hungry, frightened child's mouth? No way.

Lauren drank all of her water. Tamara asked, "More?"

"No. Can I lie down now? I still feel sick."

"Sure you can."

The trailer had two bedrooms, but she couldn't bring herself to put Lauren in either of them. The smaller one had either been the real Angie's, or Lemoyne had outfitted it that way. Bedspread with little pink animals on it. Couple of dolls and a box of toys on the dresser. Small closet full of child's dresses, playsuits, other stuff—some new, some that looked as though it had been worn. Keep Lauren out of that room as long as she could.

The only other place for her to lie down was a dusty two-person couch in what passed for a living room. She set the little girl on the cushions, got her comfortable, found a blanket in the larger bedroom to cover her. On a stand nearby was a small TV that had to be older than she was. Television: the great babysitter. Was the electricity turned on? She tried a table lamp, then the TV. Not yet. So much for that idea.

But it didn't matter anyway. When she looked at Lauren again, the poor kid was asleep.

All right. Now she could prowl.

Five rooms altogether, none of them more than about ten feet square. The only door to the outside was the one they'd come through and the lock on it was a heavy dead bolt. Forget that. Each of the rooms had a window, but only three—kitchen and the two bedrooms—were of any size. Two-by-three feet, about, the kind that split into two overlapping panes, one half stationary and the other half on a track so you could slide it open. Lauren would fit easily enough through the one half, but a grown woman with chubby buns? Be a tight squeeze, if she could manage it at all.

But the big problem was, all three windows were covered by thick, metal-framed mesh screens screwed to the wall on either side, top and bottom. You could poke fingers through the mesh far enough to release the window catch and slide the one half open—Tamara did that on each one to let fresh air in—but when she tried to animal the screens loose, they wouldn't budge. Screwed tight to the wall . . . all except the lower right-hand corner of the screen in the smaller bedroom. That one corner pulled out a half inch or so before the screw bound up and held it in place. If she could find something to use as a pry bar . . .

No tools of any kind in the kitchen, not even knives and forks. Locked up in one of two padlocked cabinets, probably, along with anything like a hammer or screwdriver. Dude didn't take any chances, even if the only victims he'd brought here before were six-year-old girls.

One of the kitchen drawers yielded a saucepan and a frying pan with a fairly slender wooden handle. She took those into the smaller bedroom, went to work with the handle of the saucepan on the loose corner. Pretty soon the screw pulled a little more, widening the gap, but not enough to slip the frying pan handle between the frame and the wall. She kept at it, streaming sweat, the muscles in her arms tight and aching. Squeaking noise and the screw pulled a little more . . . but the saucepan handle had begun to bend and she couldn't get any more leverage. Another try with the wooden handle. Almost got it wedged in . . . yank on the mesh with one hand, wiggle the handle with the other . . . there, eased the tip of it in, just like Horace the first time he—

Car sound outside. Lemoyne coming back.

She yanked the handle free, used the pan to shove the screw back in so that the corner was more or less flush again. Scrapes and gouges in the metal wall, but maybe he wouldn't notice. Wouldn't matter anyway if he didn't leave her alone in here again . . .

She hurried out to the window next to the front door. Here he came, bouncing along the rutted track, the sun throwing up needle glints of light from the SUV's hood and windshield. She could see him behind the glass, and the hate that surged into her throat almost choked her. Her fingers clenched around the handles of the saucepan and frying pan.

Frying pan. Heavy. Weapon.

The thought, sweet and hot, drew her lips in flat against her teeth. She watched the SUV rattle to a stop a few yards away, Lemoyne get out and walk around to the passenger side and open that door and lift out a couple of plastic sacks. Grocery store was where he'd gone. He carried both sacks in his left hand, a ring of keys dangled from his right.

She stepped over to the door, to the far side so she'd be behind it when it opened inward. Put the saucepan down and took a two-handed grip on the wooden handle of the frying pan, holding the pan close against her chest.

He was right outside the door now. Keys jingled; one of them rattled in the lock. She raised the pan above her head.

Yo, asshole, come and get it!

Only he didn't open the door, didn't walk inside.

His voice, loud, came through it instead. "It's open, Dark Chocolate. Step out here where I can see you."

She hesitated, frustration a sudden heavier weight than the frying pan, then slowly lowered her hands. Why the hell couldn't he be stupid, careless, the way she'd been? Make one little mistake?

"Come on, hurry it up. Don't get me pissed off."

Nothing else she could do. She put both pans back where she'd found them, went on out to where Lemoyne stood waiting.

After lunch, he took Lauren away.

Not in the SUV—on foot into the woods.

He seemed to get the idea all at once. He was sitting in the only chair in the living room, a ratty recliner, not saying anything, just watching Tamara clean up in the kitchen. Slave girl: make sandwiches, cook soup, wash dishes, tend to the kid. Mammy Tammy. And all the time watching her, never letting her get closer than a couple of feet, specially when she had a bowl of hot soup in her hands. Watching Lauren, too, sometimes with that tenderness in his eyes, sometimes with a funny sort of speculative look as if he didn't have any idea who she was. Child was still pale and feverish after her nap. Thirsty, but wouldn't eat much. Lemoyne didn't like that; he kept urging her to eat her soup and scowling when she said, "No, I don't want any, I'm not hungry." A couple of times he reached out and patted her in a kind of rough paternal way; both times she shrank away from him, and that made him scowl even harder.

Then all of a sudden he was on his feet. "You, Dark Chocolate. That's enough in the kitchen. Take Angie into the bedroom, change her clothes."

"Her clothes? What for?"

"We're going for a walk."

"She's sick, man, she's running a fever. Can't you see that?"

"No. She's all right, she just needs some fresh air. It's hot in here."

"I tell you, she's sick. Feel her forehead, she's burning up."

"You have kids of your own?"

"What? No, but—"

"Then don't try to tell me about my kid. Go on, pick her up, take her in the bedroom. Put her in those pink shorts she likes. And the white top with the little rabbits on it. She looks real cute in that outfit."

Tamara felt the hair crawl on her neck. "It's not warm enough outside for shorts."

"Bullshit. Plenty warm enough."

"Listen to me, man. She's just a child, she's only six years old."

"So? You think I don't know that?"

"You don't want to hurt her . . . your own daughter."

That pissed him off. His eyes got smoky; veins bulged in his neck. "Don't say that to me, you bitch. Fucking bitch. Don't ever say that to me." The Saturday night special was shoved down in the front of his pants; he jerked it free and waved it at her. "You do what I told you, take her in there and get her dressed. And you keep your mouth shut while you're doing it or you'll be the one I hurt."

Again, no choice. One thing to vow to protect the little girl, another to stand here helpless looking down the muzzle of a gun. He'd shoot her or start beating up on her if she didn't do what he said. And what good would she be to Lauren then, dead or all busted up?

The girl moaned when Tamara picked her up, carried her into the smaller bedroom. Skin all hot, sweaty—temperature must be over a hundred now. Tight-mouthed, she shut the door behind them. It stayed that way; Lemoyne let them have that much privacy, at least.

The pink shorts and rabbit T-shirt were in one of the dresser drawers. Took some coaxing to get Lauren into them; she kept saying, "I don't want to, I don't feel good," and when she was dressed she looked down at herself and started to cry again.

Tamara wiped away the tears. "Listen to me, Lauren. You have to go with him, have to keep pretending you're Angie and he's your daddy. Do whatever he tells you, no matter what. Don't make him mad or he might hurt you bad. Okay? You understand?"

"Yes, Tamara."

"Good girl."

Hugged her, hard, then took her by the hand and opened the door and let the crazy son of a bitch have her.

She watched them from the front window, walking slow toward the barn, him pulling her along by the hand and Lauren stumbling on the uneven ground. When she couldn't see them anymore she ran into the smaller bedroom, picked them out again from that window. And watched them vanish into the woods.

Quickly she retrieved the frying pan and managed to jam the handle between the wall and the loose corner of the window screen. Pried, yanked, wedged it in farther, slanting a look out the window every now and then at the place where they'd gone into the trees. Afraid the noise she was making was loud enough to carry and he'd hear and come running out. More afraid that he'd come walking out alone.

The screw wouldn't tear loose. Her arms and shoulders

began to cramp up. She mopped off sweat, did some upper body aerobics to loosen her muscles, and went at it again. And this time . . . starting to loosen a little? She yanked harder, twisting the pan. Yeah, it was starting to pull. She managed to wedge the pan in more tightly, yanked again—

Movement outside.

She caught it out of the corner of her eye. Quit rocking the pan and stood still, staring out through the window.

Lemoyne coming out of the woods. Carrying Lauren with one arm, slung loosely up across his shoulder, head wobbling, thin arms dangling.

Dead, he killed her!

The thought brought on a surge of emotion so intense her whole body shook. But then, as Lemoyne plowed through the tall grass toward the trailer, she saw the child's head move, one arm slide upward and the small hand clutch at his shirt collar. Sweet Lord Jesus. Not dead, but . . . hurt? Couldn't tell from here—

New thought: Don't let him see you at this window.

Tamara pulled the frying pan down, backed off quick. Scrapes and gouges on the wall . . . if he came in here, he'd know right away what she'd been up to. Nothing she could do about it, except try to keep him out of here.

She ran into the kitchen, set the frying pan on the drainboard, splashed cold water on her sweaty face. There were a couple of raw scrapes on her fingers, too, she saw then. Make up an excuse if he noticed them. She washed away the dribbles of blood, used the dish towel to dry off.

Lemoyne was out front by then. Through the kitchen window she saw him come into view, still carrying Lauren in that careless slung-up way. Maybe this time he'd just unlock the door and walk right in and she could cave in his skull with the frying pan. But she knew he wouldn't, and he didn't.

She heard his key rattle in the lock. Then, "Come on out here, Dark Chocolate. Bring some mineral water with you. Two bottles."

She put the pan away in the drawer. He'd bought half a dozen plastic bottles of Crystal Geyser at the store, sucked on one all through lunch. She took two more from the fridge, opened the door, and stepped out onto the tiny porch.

He'd set Lauren down on the bottom step, was standing off a few paces with a cancer stick hanging out of his mouth. The little girl sat slumped, her face sheened with sweat, the residue of what looked like vomit around her mouth. She perked up a little when she saw Tamara, scooted over, and clutched at her pant leg.

"Kid's sick," Lemoyne said. But not as if he was concerned about it. Flat voice, no feeling in it at all. "She puked out there in the woods."

"I told you, man."

"Put the water on the step there. Then take her inside, put her to bed."

"She needs a doctor."

"No doctor. The hell with that."

"You want her to get worse, maybe catch pneumonia?"

"I don't care."

"Don't care? Your own daughter?"

"She's not Angie," he said in that same flat voice.

"What?"

"She's not my little girl. I don't know who she is."

Tamara set the bottles down, scooped Lauren into her arms. Inside the trailer, as Lemoyne locked the door again, she took a closer look at the girl. No visible marks on her, no sign that her clothes had been messed with.

"What'd you do out there in the woods, honey?"

"Nothing. He wanted to play a game."

"What kind of game?"

"Angie's game. Naming things. Trees and things."

"He didn't touch you or anything?"

"Uh-uh. But he didn't like it when I threw up. He yelled at me. I couldn't help it, Tamara. I was dizzy, I couldn't help it."

"I know you couldn't."

"He yelled at me another time too, 'cause I couldn't play Angie's game. I'm not Angie, I don't how to play her game."

Tamara carried her into the smaller bedroom, put her down on the bed, and covered her. Cool enough in there now with the window open, air coming in.

"I feel awful," Lauren said. "Awful hot."

"Try to sleep, okay? You'll feel better after you wake up."

"Can I go home then? I miss Mama and Daddy."

"I know, baby, I know."

All afternoon, Lemoyne left them alone. He spent a few minutes in the barn, the rest of the time on his ass under a shade tree on the creek bank, drinking bottled water and smoking and staring off into space. The tree was too close to the trailer, fifty yards or so, for Tamara to mount another attack on the window screen. She couldn't use the frying pan without making some noise, and in the country quiet noise carried; the one time she tried, it brought him over quick. But all he did was stand out front for a few seconds and yell at her to knock off whatever the hell she was doing. Didn't seem to be worried, or even to care much.

That was bad. Another bad was him sitting over there like that, brooding. Third and worst was him not wanting anything more to do with Lauren, saying, *She's not Angie, I don't know who she is,* in that flat voice. Long as he'd believed she was his daughter, she'd been safe enough—they both had. But she couldn't be what she wasn't, and she'd gotten sick, and now his fantasy was busted and he'd lost interest, didn't care about her anymore.

A liability, that was all she was now. Same as Tamara Corbin, the Dark Chocolate Dick, had been all along. Two liabilities on his hands, and only one thing he could do about them.

Question was, how long would it take for him to juice himself up to it?

Bigger question than that, girl: Is there any damn thing you can do to stop him?

20

The 1100 block of Willard Street had more life to it at this hour, just past dusk. Lights in most of the houses, a guy watering his front lawn, a Hispanic couple walking a dog, a kid doing tricks on a skateboard. Number 1122, the house Tamara had been staking out, still appeared deserted—windows all dark, driveway empty. I parked in front, checked again to make sure my cell phone was on and functioning, then went up and thumbed the doorbell anyway. No answer.

When I came back to the sidewalk, the Hispanic couple was standing nearby, watching their pooch take a leak on a curbside tree with all the rapt attention of a pair of scientists studying a laboratory phenomenon. I tried them first, but their English wasn't good and my Spanish even worse and I had trouble getting across what I was after. The kid on the skateboard didn't want any part of me or any adult; all I got out of him was a sneer and some slang phrases that were even less comprehensible than the Hispanic couple's English. The guy watering his lawn was on the same side of the street, a couple of houses removed from 1122. I went on down there to see if he had anything to tell me.

A little, it turned out. There were nightlights along the front walk and two more on a pair of gateposts, so when he came over I got a good look at him. In his upper seventies, lean, energetic, with a full head of wavy hair that didn't seem to have much gray in it. And the friendly, gregarious type; before I was able to start unloading my questions, I knew that we shared a first name and that his last name was Powers, he was a retired production manager for Sikorsky Aircraft in Connecticut, and that he'd moved out here some years ago to be near his married daughter.

"Oh, sure," he said when I managed to steer the conversation to Tamara, "I noticed her. Parked across the street the past couple of nights. 'Ninety-six Toyota Camry, probably red. Cars are a hobby of mine."

"Saw her as well as the car, is that right?"

"Yep. I like to take walks around the neighborhood after supper. Helps me digest. She was crossing the street when I came out, on the way to her car. Passed under the streetlight up there, so I got a pretty good look at her. Nice-looking young black woman."

"When was this?"

"Last night, around eight or so."

"And she was alone at the time?"

"All alone. Nobody else around."

"How did she seem to you? Nervous, upset, anything like that?"

"Nope," Powers said. "Just walking across the street to her car."

"Coming from where?"

"Didn't see. Someplace on this side."

"What did you think? I mean, a young black woman, a stranger, sitting in a parked car two nights in a row."

"Figured she was waiting for somebody. Which is just what she was doing, so you told me."

"Didn't make you suspicious?"

"Nope. Why should it?"

"Some people might've been."

"On account of her being black? Not me. I notice things, but I mind my own business unless there's a good reason to mind somebody else's. And I don't judge a person by what color he is or what he looks like. Ethnic diversity's one of the reasons I like living here—three black families on this block, Hispanic couple, Asian family in the next."

"Too bad more folks don't feel that way."

He showed his teeth again—good teeth to go with the engaging grin. "Won't get any argument from me on that score."

"Three black families on this block, you said. Any of them mixed race?"

"Don't think so, no."

"Could any of the men be half Caucasian?"

"Well . . . a couple are light-skinned, but a lot of African-Americans are. Why?"

"Just checking possibilities," I said. "Did you see the young woman again after eight o'clock?"

Powers shook his head. "But her car was still there when I went to bed."

"What time was that?"

"Oh, around ten-thirty. Can't stay up as late as I used to."

"And she was in it at that time?"

"Can't swear that she was, no. Pretty dark at night where she was parked."

"Which was where?"

"Under that bay tree over there, just up the block."

"The car was gone this morning?"

"Yep. No sign of it then or since."

Ten-thirty was late for Tamara to be maintaining a surveillance. As much of a Type A as she was, she'd have had trouble sitting still that long. Still, if there'd been some reason for her to continue the stakeout, she'd have done it. One thing she'd never been was a quitter.

I said, "The house she was watching is number eleven twenty-two. The white frame with hedges and Cyclone fence. Supposed to have been vacant the past three months."

"Is that right?"

"Meaning it hasn't been?"

"Well, I've seen lights inside," Powers said. "And a man there a couple of times recently, coming and going."

"Caucasian about forty, heavyset, mustache, longish brown hair?"

"Sounds like him, except for the mustache. Clean-shaven."

"Stranger to you?"

"First time I saw him he was. Unfriendly cuss—I said hello to him once and he looked right through me."

"What name is he using?"

"Never heard it. Keeps to himself, doesn't talk to anybody in the neighborhood. What're you after him for?"

"Nonpayment of child support in Oregon."

"Uh-huh," Powers said. "One of those."

"You see any sign of him last night?"

"Nope."

"Night before last?"

"Nope. Not in three or four days."

"What kind of car does he have?"

"Blue Plymouth Fury, last year's model. I don't know the license plate number, but you won't need it."

". . . I won't?"

"Your timing's perfect," Powers said. "That's him and the Fury just pulling into the driveway over there."

I turned in time to see the car roll to a stop, the headlights frozen on the garage door as it started to swing up. I made a parting gesture to Powers, headed over there at a half trot. The driver—suit and tie, carrying a briefcase—was just coming out of the garage when I reached the driveway. He pulled up sharp when he saw me. The interior of the garage was lit from a bulb on the automatic opener; he had the remote in his hand and he pressed it and the door began to whir shut. But not before I had a clear look past him at the Fury's license plate.

As I neared him, he brought the briefcase up tight against his chest, holding it with both hands. Defensive stance: tense, wary, poised against attack. That told me something about him. Man on the edge, ruled by base emotions—the kind of survivalist capable of just about anything, if he were cornered, to save himself and preserve his freedom.

"Who are you?" Fear put a thin crack in his voice. "What do you want?"

I stopped a couple of paces away, manufactured a smile, and stood relaxed so as not to provoke him. I couldn't see his face clearly, now that the garage door was all the way down, but there wasn't much doubt that he was George DeBrissac. "Just want to ask a couple of questions."

"What kind of questions?"

"I assume you live here?"

"What business is that of yours?"

"I'm trying to find a missing woman, a young black woman who was in this neighborhood last night."

No reaction to that.

"She's about twenty-five," I said, "driving a red Toyota Camry. I wonder if you might've seen her."

"I wasn't home last night."

"Well, she might've been here pretty late—"

"I haven't been home at all the past three days," he said. "Out of town on business. Can't help you. Now if you don't mind . . ."

I stayed where I was, still smiling. "I'm really worried about her," I said. "She's a very responsible young woman—"

"I told you I can't help you. I'm sorry, good night."

He sidled away from me, his body half turned and the briefcase still up like a shield between us. Didn't take his eyes off me as he crossed the yard, climbed the front steps, fumbled his key into the door lock. The defensive tension seemed not to loosen even after he got the door open; he took it inside with him.

I retreated to the sidewalk without looking back. He'd be at a window now, with a corner of the curtain pulled aside, watching me; I could almost feel his eyes. Some DeBrissac. Some little deadbeat coward.

But was that all he was? If Tamara had braced him and he'd realized somehow who she was and felt threatened enough by her, I could see him reacting with the sudden mindless viciousness of a trapped animal. And then frantically covering up to save his ass.

Only I didn't believe something like that had happened—didn't want to believe it. Too many things argued against that kind of scenario. DeBrissac's lack of reaction when I mentioned Tamara. His disinterest in who she was, who I was, and why I was looking for her. His claim that he'd been out of town the past three days—easy enough to check up on. And the fact that Tamara was seasoned enough not to have either alerted or provoked him; if she'd talked to him at all, she'd've done it with a ready excuse and only long enough to make certain of his ID.

George DeBrissac wasn't the cause of her disappearance. Somebody else, some other scenario. If I could just pin down the *where* . . .

At my car I sat inside long enough to write down the Fury's license plate number. My memory isn't what it used to be; I'd repeated the number to myself a dozen times during and after the conversation with DeBrissac, to keep it fresh in my mind, but it wouldn't stay fresh for long. Write it down or lose it: axiom for your sixties. DeBrissac had no good reason to run again if he'd had nothing to do with Tamara's disappearance; my sudden arrival and the questions I'd asked shouldn't be enough to spook him out of what must seem to be a pretty safe harbor. But if he did run, the Fury's license plate number would make it easy enough to track him down again.

I canvassed the rest of the block, starting at the far end. Three houses were dark, nobody home. Stranger-wary residents of one of the lighted houses wouldn't answer the bell, and two others who did answer refused to talk to me. The half-dozen people who listened to my questions about Tamara had none of the answers I wanted to hear.

Dead end, at least for now.

After eight by then. How much longer before I heard from Mick Savage?

Might be another hour or two. Dead end, dead time. I could either kill it hanging around the neighborhood, keeping

an eye on DeBrissac's hideout and waiting for the occupants of
the dark houses to come home, or I could drive around again
hunting for Tamara's red Toyota. Both seemed like exercises in
futility, but driving was better than sitting. At least when you
were on the move you had the illusion of time passing more
rapidly.

I'd covered a four-block radius earlier in the day, so I doubled that to eight blocks. Trying to locate one dark-colored,
common-model parked car at night is about as difficult a job as
you can undertake. License plates, even the personalized ones,
are hard to read by headlights. Makes and models resemble
each other, red colors aren't easy to differentiate. It was a
little easier on brightly lighted thoroughfares like San Pablo
Avenue, but there you couldn't go as slowly or look as carefully because of the traffic. It was an exercise in frustration as
well as futility, and it had my nerves frayed raw by the time I
swung into a Safeway parking lot on San Pablo, some seven
blocks from Willard Street.

And that was where I found the Toyota.

It happens like that sometimes. You give up on a thing, you
make a more or less unrelated move, and you get a surprise.
Chance, divine guidance—call it what you want. I turned into
the lot because the traffic was bunched up and I was ready to
head back in the opposite direction and there was a stoplight at
the entrance and I could make an easy U-turn in the lot. And
while I was making the turn down one of the short aisles of
parked cars, my lights picked out one by itself and a pole light
nearby gave it added definition.

Red Toyota Camry, Horace's MR CELLO license plate.

I hit the brakes so hard they almost locked and the tires
squealed on the pavement. Inside of ten seconds I was parked

and out and pawing at the Toyota's driver-side door. It wasn't locked. I sucked in a breath, dragged the door open, bent inside.

The keys were in it. Not in the ignition—tossed on the passenger seat. Another piece of blind luck. If the wrong person had spotted them at any time last night or today, the car wouldn't be sitting here now.

I pocketed the keys, checked the seats, floorboards, shadowed rear deck for signs of violence. None, thank God. The contents of a trash bag hanging from a radio knob told me nothing. Neither did the usual items in the glove compartment or the armrest box where she kept her CDs. But I did find one other thing when I leaned down and swept a hand underneath the seats—Tamara's purse, stuffed under the driver's bucket.

Her wallet was there, but money, credit cards, driver's license were all missing. I couldn't tell if anything else had been taken from the jumble of other stuff.

I backed out, taking the purse with me, and made sure all the doors were locked. My hands were shaking a little. Supposed to look like a robbery that had gone down right here in the lot, but not to me. Any thief will steal cash and credit cards, but none will take a photo ID out of its celluloid holder and leave the wallet behind. No, the Toyota had been driven over here and abandoned sometime during the night, the keys left in it in the hope that somebody would steal it. Driven from Willard Street, seven blocks away.

That was the *where,* all right. I had no doubt of it now.

I was on a dark side street, heading back to Willard Street, when Mick Savage finally called. The dashboard clock, more or less accurate, said it was 9:20. I veered over to the curb before I answered the call.

"Got what you wanted from Tamara's computer," he said.

"Go ahead, Mick."

"New file, untitled, made on Monday. Looks like a preliminary background check on a man named Robert Lemoyne. L-e-m-o-y-n-e. Mixed race, black father, white mother."

"Address?"

"Eleven-oh-nine Willard Street, San Leandro."

"That's it. What else?"

Mick gave me a quick rundown on Lemoyne. Age forty-seven. Construction worker. Twice married, twice divorced. One child, a daughter, custody awarded to the mother four years ago. Evidently lived alone. No criminal record of any kind. No brushes with the law except for a couple of misdemeanors. No apparent history of domestic or substance abuse.

So?

I asked Mick, "Anything in the file about why she was checking up on him?"

"No," he said. "And no mention of him anywhere else on her hard drive. You think he's responsible?"

"Somebody on Willard Street is. I just found her car—abandoned in a Safeway parking lot a few blocks away."

"Oh, man. There wasn't . . . I mean . . ."

"No indications of foul play, no."

"What do you think happened?"

"Can't say yet. But this Lemoyne's house is right near where she was staked out the past two nights."

"So maybe he spotted her and hit on her or something?"

"That's one possibility. Is there anything in his background about violence toward women?"

"Not in the file," Mick said, "but Tamara didn't go too deep into it. Just preliminary stuff. You want me to do some digging myself, see what else I can find out?"

"Would you? But you must be pretty tired by now . . ."

"Nah. I'll work all night if it'll help find Tamara. I'd rather hack than sleep."

"Thanks, Mick. Call me if you come up with anything I should know. Otherwise I'll be in touch."

I made it fast back to Willard Street. Number 1109 had been one of the dark houses; it was still dark now. I parked down the street, and with the lights off I unclipped the .38 Colt Bodyguard from under the dash, checked the loads, and slipped the piece into my pocket. Then I went up and leaned on Robert Lemoyne's doorbell.

Empty echoes, empty house.

I checked the garage, found a window in back I could see through with the aid of my penlight. Empty garage.

Lights behind curtains made saffron squares of the two front windows in Bill Powers's house down the block. I crossed over there and rang his bell. He was in pajamas and bathrobe, a book in one hand with a finger marking his place, a pair of silver-rimmed reading glasses tilted forward on his nose. He blinked at me from behind the lenses.

"Sorry to bother you again, Mr. Powers," I said, "but I need to ask a few more questions. About another of your neighbors this time."

"Sure," he said. Then he said, "You look grim. Something happen?"

I brushed the question aside. "What can you tell me about the man who lives at eleven-oh-nine, Robert Lemoyne?"

"Bob? Quiet, friendly enough, but mostly keeps to himself."

"Aggressive? Toward women especially?"

"Not that I've heard about. Doesn't seem to be that type, but then I don't know him very well. Just to say hello to."

"Trouble of any kind associated with him?"

"How do you mean, trouble?"

"Disputes with neighbors. Excessive drinking, loud parties. That sort of thing."

"Nothing like that," Powers said, "Say, you have reason to think he's mixed up in the young woman's disappearance?"

I hedged on that. "No specific reason, no. Did you happen to see Lemoyne last night?"

"Don't think so. Not last night."

"But he was home?"

Powers thought about it. "Wasn't when I went for my walk, but I seem to remember his lights being on when I looked out before I went to bed. Won't swear to it, though. My memory's not what it used to be."

"He's not home now. Any idea where he could be?"

"Not a clue."

"Bar or restaurant he frequents?"

"Like I said, I hardly know the man. Might ask one of the other neighbors, but I doubt they'd be able to tell you any more than me."

"So he's not particularly friendly with any of them? One of the black families?"

"Never saw him hanging out with anybody around here."

"He lives alone?"

"Yep. As long as I've been here."

"Girlfriends?"

"Don't remember seeing him with a woman, but that doesn't mean he hasn't had his share."

"Male friends?"

"Same answer."

Quiet, nonaggressive, nontroublesome loner. If that was a true picture of Robert Lemoyne, what had he done to make Tamara notice him, run the check on him? And if he was responsible for her disappearance, what did he or she or both of them do to cause it?

I went back to the car, sat there with the cell phone in my hand. Call the cops—that was the right thing to do. Except that it wasn't, not yet. No clear-cut motive and nothing but circumstantial evidence to link Lemoyne to Tamara's disappearance—maybe enough circumstantial evidence to convince the local law to talk to Lemoyne, but not enough to convince a judge to issue a search warrant. Without any indication of foul play, the Toyota was just another car more or less legally parked in a supermarket lot. She hadn't even been gone long enough for an official missing person's report to be filed.

Not a damn thing the law could do, not tonight, not soon enough.

There was only one other person besides me who could do something—Jake Runyon. His number was the one I called.

21

TOMMY DOUGLASS

"Hey, Tommy," Bix said, "hey, man, you sure about this, huh?"

"Sure about what?"

"Doin' this one so early, man. People on the streets, cars, lights in all the houses . . . suppose somebody sees us?"

"We been over that already, how many times? This Butterfield's not like the other fags. He don't go out much and when he does he drives."

"The one up by the park had a car."

"So what? He stayed out late couple of nights a week, that made it easy. This one don't go out much at night and when he does he comes home early and brings some other fag back with him. Troy told us that, didn't he? We checked him out, didn't we?"

"Yeah, but—"

"Yeah but, yeah but. Come on, what's the matter with you? You turning chicken on me?"

"Chicken?" Bix glared at him from under the bill of his Giants cap. "Listen, dude, I ain't afraid of nothin' or nobody. You call me chicken, I'll kick *your* ass. You know I can do it, too."

Tommy sighed. Problem with Bix wasn't that he was chicken, problem was he had two fuckin' brain cells and one of 'em was always out looking for the other. You had to explain everything to him fifty times before he got it, and then half the time he forgot and you had to explain it all over again. It was worse when he was high. He was high now, all that crystal meth he'd smoked out at Finn's crib in Daly City. High and wired, the way he had to get to give these lousy queers what they deserved. Not Tommy. One pipe, that was all he'd smoked. He didn't need speed or anything else to get his juices flowing. Just giving it to those bastards, paying 'em back for what they did to Troy, that was enough. Better than any drug he'd ever tried.

Troy. Stupid punk kid. Ten times smarter than Bix, maybe even had a few more brains than himself, but he was still stupid. Convincing himself he was gay, of all the goddamn things, then running off to the city, the Castro, Faggotville, and letting all those queers take advantage of him, stick their dicks in him . . . Christ! Made his blood boil thinking about what they'd done to an innocent seventeen-year-old kid like his little brother. Made him want to fix them real good. Not just hurt them, like the first three—put their lights out permanent so they couldn't prey on any more underage dummies. Maybe that's what he'd do with this Butterfield or the next one. Yeah, maybe. Why not? Felt so good kicking the crap out them, think how good it'd feel taking one all the way out.

"Tommy, hey, man, what time's it now?"

"Quit worrying about the time. He'll be here pretty soon, comes home from his work about this time every night."

"Unless he goes out somewhere. What if he don't show?"

"Then we'll come back tomorrow night. Or the next."

"I'm ready now, man. I'm hot to trot."

"Just take it easy. Stay cool."

"So hot I'm cool," Bix said and giggled. "So cool I'm hot."

Two fuckin' brain cells.

They were parked behind a Dumpster across the street from Butterfield's house off Twenty-fourth Street. Nice old shingled house, big, yard in front, garage built on to one side. Rich faggot, worked for some computer company, big executive or something. Screwed businesspeople during the day, screwed underage kids at night. Bastard. Lousy queer boy-fucking bastard. Well, he'd get his pretty soon, pretty soon. Wouldn't be screwing anybody for a long time after tonight. Might never screw anybody ever again after tonight.

Cars came up the street, went down the street. None of them turned into the driveway over there, but Tommy had a feeling it wouldn't be long now. Another five minutes, ten at the most. The Little League bat was on the seat between him and Bix; he pulled it over onto his lap, ran his fingers over the dented aluminum.

Bix had one of those little rubber balls that he kept squeezing in one hand or the other. He flipped it from his left to his right, made a fist and crushed it hard. Then he giggled again. Not because anything was funny, he always giggled when he was high. The more he smoked, the more he giggled. Damn irritating habit. Sounded like a girl. Sometimes he even sounded like a faggot.

Another set of headlights crawled up the street. Tommy sat

up straight. His head felt funny all of a sudden, like it'd just been pumped full of air. His ears started ringing. His pecker stirred as if a girl had just stroked it.

"That's him," he said.

"Hey, man, how can you tell that from—"

"That's him, goddamnit, get ready to move."

Tommy took a tight grip on the handle of the bat, shoved the door handle down on his side. It was Butterfield, all right—the car slowed, lights swept off into the driveway, garage door started to slide up. Tommy was out and halfway across the street by the time the door was all the way up and the car started slotting inside, Bix a couple of steps behind him. Nobody in sight, one other set of headlights but they were a block and a half away uphill. No problem.

Click, whir, and the garage door started down again just as Tommy hit the sidewalk running. Bix was right behind him as he ducked inside. The fag was half in and half out of the car—a Beamer, wouldn't you know it—and when he saw them he tried to crawl in and slam the door, lock himself in. But Tommy got there first, yanked it out of his hand, and jammed it open with his hip. Butterfield's face twisted up at him, more pissed than scared, and quick he jammed his thumb against the remote hanging from the visor. The garage door stopped halfway down. Hell with that. Wasn't gonna do him any good, he wasn't going anywhere except down for the count.

"What the hell's the idea? Get out of my garage!"

Tough-talking fruit. Bigger than the others, over six feet, all decked out in an expensive suit and tie, ugly bearded face . . . how the hell could Troy let an ugly bastard like that screw him? Tommy felt himself swelling up with heat and rage and excitement, until he felt ten feet tall. He could've taken on the biggest queer ever lived tonight, one on one. Didn't need Bix, didn't need anybody but Tommy Douglass and his little Louisville Slugger.

"You're the one getting out," he said. "Or we'll pile in there and drag you out."

"I know you. Gay bashers, breeder trash."

Bix giggled. "That's right, sweet thing. Ass-kickers R us."

"Bastards!"

Butterfield came out sudden, kicking and swinging. But they were ready for him. He slammed a foot into the car door, but Tommy danced out of the way and as soon as the faggot came up on his feet Bix had him around the neck. Jerked his head back, legs spread so the bugger couldn't back-kick his shins. Tommy shoved the greasy rag in his mouth, jabbed the head of the bat into his gut hard enough to put a hole right through him. Air went out of him in a gagging hiss. He doubled over in Bix's grasp.

"Let go of him, man, he's all mine."

Bix let go and Tommy jabbed him again, same place, then belted him in the kneecap. Line-drive single! Butterfield went down on the other knee on the concrete floor. Tommy swung again. Crack! Two-bagger down the line! Again, on the side of the head this time. Crack! Triple up the gap!

"Hey, Tommy, hey, man, not so hard, you gonna kill him—"

"Shut up!"

The faggot was all the way down now, moaning and writhing, blood all over his ugly bearded face. Tommy took his stance, home-run stance, Barry Bonds getting ready to break McGwire's record, and lifted the bat for the big blast—

All of a sudden he didn't have it anymore.

Somebody jerked it out of his hands at the top of his swing.

At first he thought it was Bix, but then he heard Bix yell and then yowl with pain, and when he came around he saw there was somebody else in the garage, big son of a bitch he'd never laid eyes on before. Bix was sprawled over the back end of the BMW, holding his arm and trying to dodge another blow from the bat. The big son of a bitch swatted Bix across the kidneys and sent him spinning off the car onto the floor. Tommy unfroze and charged the guy, some goddamn faggot neighbor, fix him like he fixed Butterfield. Head ducked, arms reaching—

Something happened, he didn't know what, but all of a sudden bright pain burst through his head and neck and his vision went cockeyed and he was stumbling off balance, then banging into something solid with his shoulder and the back of his head. Flashes of light went off behind his eyes. He blinked and pawed at his face and the light faded and he could see the big son of a bitch standing there in front of him, practically in his face.

"Had enough, Douglass?"

Knew him, knew his name!

"Who the . . . hell're you?"

"Your worst nightmare, kid."

"Bix!"

"He can't help you. He just crawled out of here on his hands and knees."

Tommy said, "Dirty bastard," and didn't know if he meant Bix or the big stranger. He pushed off the wall, blinking, trying to see straight, and took a swing at the face in front of him, but it was as if he did it in slow motion, as if his arm had lead weights tied to it—

—and there was another burst of pain in his neck and shoulder—

—and he was sitting on the floor and his head was full of

more hurt and confusion and he couldn't see anything this time, not even flashes of light. Blind. Oh God, he was blind . . .

All the fight went out of him. And all the anger and hatred and excitement and hunger for revenge, until there wasn't anything left.

"Give it up, Douglass, you're all finished."

Finished. Yeah.

He didn't move. Couldn't have moved if he'd tried. Even when the darkness went away and he could see again, there just wasn't anything left.

22

JAKE RUNYON

He backed away from where the Douglass kid sat dazed against the rear wall and went to check on Jerry Butterfield. Not as badly hurt as it'd first looked when he came in. Butterfield was up on one knee now, spitting out the residue of whatever they'd shoved in his mouth, holding the side of his head. Blood leaked through his fingers, made a glistening snake's trail through his dark brown beard, but when he looked up his eyes were clear enough.

"Thanks," he said. "Don't know who you are or where you came from, but . . . thanks. I thought . . . Jesus, I thought they were going to kill me."

They might have at that. The way Douglass had had that aluminum bat cocked—if he'd swung with all his strength, he'd have bashed Butterfield's head in. Pure luck that Runyon had got here when he did, just as the two of them were duck-ing into the lighted garage. He hadn't even had enough time to drag his .357 Magnum out of the glove box. More luck there—that he hadn't needed the weapon.

He said, "Better not talk, Mr. Butterfield. Just take it easy."

"No, I'm all right. Not disoriented, just bruised and . . . cut. Bleeding like a stuck pig."

"Head wounds always bleed like that."

"How do you know my name?"

"Long story. Time for that later."

"What's yours, your name?"

"Runyon. Jake Runyon."

"Help me up, will you, Mr. Runyon?"

"You sure you can stand?"

"Long enough to sit down."

Runyon gave him a hand up, guided him through the open car door and onto the front seat. Butterfield had the presence of mind to sit leaning forward, so that the dripping blood spattered on the concrete floor instead of the leather upholstery. He fumbled a handkerchief from his jacket pocket, pressed it to the gash in his temple.

"I just bought this suit," he said. He was staring at the crimson streaks on his jacket and trousers. "Sixteen hundred dollars at Wilkes Bashford. Ruined now. You can't get blood out of fabric like this."

Runyon said nothing.

"Ruined," Butterfield said again. He raised his head, squinting. "You sorry excuse for a human being," he said to Tommy Douglass. "Tried to kill me and ruined my new suit."

"Fuck you, faggot."

They stared at each other across the empty space.

Douglass still sat in the same position, legs splayed out, like something discarded against the wall. He hadn't moved the entire time. And the words he'd said to Butterfield had been a by-rote response, passionless, mindless. Runyon had seen dozens like him over the years, young and old, all races and colors. Big men when they had weapons in their hands and they were in control, capable of just about any act of violence. Shriveled little cowards when the tables were turned and they were on the receiving end, capable of nothing except feeling sorry for themselves. The one who'd scrambled out on his hands and knees, Bix Sullivan, was another cut from the same cheap cloth. Long gone now in that pickup of his. But he wouldn't get far, probably wouldn't even try. Just go on home and wait the way his buddy was waiting, riddled with self-pity and banked hatred and not understanding for a minute why he deserved to be punished for what he'd done.

The hell with him. The hell with Tommy Douglass. Runyon opened his cell phone and called 911.

The SFPD's response time was nineteen minutes, not bad for a week night in a city with a fairly high crime rate and a department in a state of flux. The paramedics took a little longer to get there—more emergency medical calls than felony crime reports tonight. Runyon showed his state ID to the two uniformed officers; that didn't impress them, but they showed some respect when he mentioned his time on the Seattle PD. He gave them a full accounting of the situation, and when Jerry Butterfield added his version and said damn right he wanted to press home invasion and assault charges, the uniforms Mirandized Tommy Douglass, handcuffed him, and stuffed him into the back of their patrol car. The kid didn't have much to say and offered no resistance; he was all through making trouble for anybody tonight. While the paramedics were ministering to Butterfield, one of the cops radioed in a request for a pickup order on Bix Sullivan.

Butterfield insisted he wasn't badly hurt, but the paramedics kept talking to him about the unpredictability of head wounds and convinced him to take a ride to SF General for a doctor's exam. He closed up the garage and went with them in the ambulance. One of the uniforms told Runyon to stop by the Hall of Justice within the next twenty-four hours and talk to a Robbery and Assault inspector and sign a statement; he said he would, and they took Douglass away and left him with the usual crowd of neighbors and rubberneckers. The crowd was still milling around, reluctant to let go of their little thrill, when Runyon climbed into his car and drove off.

The whole thing hadn't taken much more than an hour. Violence erupts, blood gets spilled, the cleanup crews move in, the crowds finally disperse, and it's as if none of it ever happened. Life in the city. Confirmed all over again just how pointless human behavior, human action, human existence was. People live, people die; life goes on and then it doesn't. Everything matters for a while, and then nothing matters.

Colleen had lived, Colleen had died; his life had gone on, and then someday it wouldn't. Everything had mattered for twenty years. And now it didn't.

The apartment Joshua shared with Kenneth Hitchcock was only a few blocks from here. He was on his way there, to tell Joshua the news, see if it would make a difference in their relationship, make something matter again for a little while, when the call from Bill came through.

Bill's car was parked in tree shadow just down the block from Robert Lemoyne's house—the same place Tamara had been parked during her two-night surveillance, he'd said on the phone. Nearly ten-thirty now. Two-thirds of the houses along here were dark or just showing night-lights; Lemoyne's was one of the dark ones. Runyon made a U-turn, pulled up behind Bill's car, and went to slide in on the passenger side.

"You made good time, Jake."

"Not much traffic. Still no sign of him?"

"No." Bill's voice had a thick tension in it. Finding Tamara's car had wired him up tight. "I took a turn around the property a while ago. Doors, windows . . . everything locked up tight."

"Gone since last night?"

"Or early this morning."

As much as twenty-four hours. And the first twenty-four hours in a case like this were critical. If a snatch victim survived them, the odds jumped in favor of continued survival. Problem was, the percentage of victims who didn't survive them was a hell of a lot larger.

"So how do you want to handle it?" Runyon asked.

"Keep on waiting. For now."

"Brace him if he shows?"

"Push him hard if we have to. You carrying?"

The .357 Magnum was in his belt now. He said, "Yeah. But I hope it doesn't come down to that."

"So do I."

They sat in silence. Bill kept shifting position, finding things to do with his hands. Runyon sat without moving, tuned down inside, on hold.

After a time Bill asked abruptly, making talk, "How goes the gay-bashing investigation?"

"It's finished now. Right before you called."

"Finished how?"

Runyon told him.

"Right place, right time. Good job. Why didn't you say something before?"

"This is more important."

Bill thumped the steering wheel with the heel of his hand, kept on doing it.

Runyon said, "We'll find her. She'll be all right."

"Sure. Sure she will."

Trading standard reassurances, keeping it upbeat. Believing out loud what they were both doubting inside.

More silence. A couple of cars appeared and then disappeared, another car turned into a driveway at the far end of the block. More houses went dark. The tension in Bill thickened until you could almost smell it, heavy and sour, like rancid butter.

He smacked the steering wheel again, hard enough this time to make it vibrate. "The hell with this. He's not coming."

"Still early yet. Not even eleven-thirty."

"Patience isn't one of my long suits. I can't keep sitting here like this, Jake. What if she's in his house right now, been there all along?"

Runyon didn't say anything.

"She could be. We both know it."

"So what do you want to do?"

Bill said, "How do you feel about B and E?"

"Same as you do. Last resort."

"Yeah, well, that's where I'm at. I'm going over there."

Again Runyon said nothing.

"You don't have to go along. Stay here, keep watch."

"If you go, I go."

"I don't want to risk your license, Jake—"

"The hell with that. What kind of locks on his doors?"

"Dead bolts, front and back. We'll have to break a window."

"That can be done without too much noise, but we'll need duct tape."

"There's a roll in the trunk."

"You have a window picked out?"

"There's one on the left side—areaway between the garage and the house hides it from the neighbors."

They got out. Runyon checked the street while Bill took the duct tape and a flashlight out of the trunk; then they moved as one to the Lemoyne property, up the drive, into the shadowed areaway. The window there was small, high up, the glass pebbled and opaque. Bathroom. The sill extended outward just above Runyon's head; he reached up with both hands, pushed upward on the frame. Wouldn't budge. Locked. He ran fingertips over the glass. It didn't feel too thick.

He said against Bill's ear, "Need something to stand on."

"Me. My back. You're lighter than I am."

"Okay."

Bill gave him the duct tape, got down on all fours, and braced his body against the house wall. Runyon stepped up on his back, balanced himself by leaning his shoulder against the sill, then began tearing off strips of tape and pasting them to the cold glass just above the bottom of the frame. Took him five minutes to cover an area about a foot square. Bill bore his weight the entire time without moving or making an audible sound.

Runyon paused. The street out front remained empty. A chilly breeze had kicked up; it made rustling noises in a nearby tree. A dog barked somewhere a long way off. Otherwise the night hush was unbroken.

Ready. He leaned out from the wall, raised his left arm with the elbow extended, waited until the wind gusted, then drove the elbow quick and sharp into the center of the taped square. The glass broke all right, making the kind of sound that seemed loud when all your senses were ratcheted up but that wouldn't carry far. He punched at the taped shards until he had a hole, peeled them away to widen it. A few pieces of glass fell inside, but most clung to the gummy tape. Another few seconds and he was able to reach inside. He found the window latch, wiggled it free. The frame resisted at first, finally broke loose and slid all the way up; the sounds it made likewise wouldn't carry.

Runyon swept the sill with his palm, cutting himself on a sliver, barely taking notice. Then he got both hands on the wood and levered himself up and squeezed his body through the opening, turning it until his buttocks were on the sill, keeping his head pulled down and his face averted from the hanging section of tape and broken glass. Once the upper part of his body was inside, he was able to maneuver one leg through, then the other. Sink below, toilet next to it. He lowered himself past the sink, onto the toilet seat and then down to the floor.

When he leaned back to the window, Bill was on his feet and extending the flashlight. Runyon took it, said, "Back door. I'll let you in there." Bill nodded and drifted away.

Runyon switched the flash on, keeping the beam shielded with his hand and letting just enough light leak through to guide the way. The bathroom opened into an empty bedroom, then into a hallway. He found the kitchen, went through it onto a utility porch. Three locks on the back door—dead bolt, push button, chain. When he had the door open, Bill came in walking a little bent and stiff: Runyon's weight all those minutes must've put a strain on his back.

He said, "Anything?"

"Not so far."

Runyon flicked the light around the porch. Empty. They went into the kitchen. The shielded beam revealed dirty dishes, food left out on a dinette table. And a door with a lock on it next to the refrigerator.

"Basement," he said.

"Let's see if that door's locked."

It wasn't. Bill swept a hand along the wall inside, located a light switch. "Should be safe enough to put on the lights with the door shut. I'll look down there. You check the street, then the other rooms up here."

"Right."

Bill stepped through onto the basement stairs, pulled the door shut behind him. Runyon followed the low-held beam into the front part of the house. Nothing in the living room. He made his way to one of the windows, eased an edge of the curtain aside to look out at Willard Street. Same stop-motion night scene: no cars, no people, all the lights stationary within the range of his vision.

He went back into the hallway, opened the first door he came to. Another bedroom. He stepped in there long enough to shine the flash under the bed, inside the closet. The second bedroom was the one he'd been in before—Lemoyne's bedroom, from the look of it. Unmade bed with a scattering of dust bunnies underneath, clothing tossed around, walk-in closet that contained nothing that didn't belong there.

One more room at the rear, smaller than the others. Kid's room, little girl's room: single bed with a frilly spread, frilly curtains, stuffed animals, dolls on shelves. Smelled musty in there, as if it hadn't been aired out in a long time. Dust made a pale gleam on the dresser when the light touched it. Hadn't been cleaned in a long time.

He was back in the kitchen when he heard Bill on the basement stairs. Not being quiet now, moving fast. He had the door opened before Bill reached the landing. In the weak light from a string of overhead bulbs, Bill's face wore a shadowed, masklike grimace.

"Down here, Jake. Christ."

Runyon followed him down the stairs, across the basement, into a room that might've been a granny unit except for the padlock-and-hasp on the door. Daybed with rumpled sheets and blanket, toys on the floor, the remains of a partly eaten meal on a small table. Tiny bathroom at the far end. Closet in the side wall, another padlock on its door.

Bill stopped in the middle of the room, snapped a hand at the closet. "Take a look in there."

The closet appeared empty from a distance. Was empty—nothing on the floor, shelf, clothes pole. It wasn't until Runyon stepped all the way inside that he saw what Bill wanted him to see. On the end wall, big block letters written with a red crayon.

LEMOYNE TAKING KIDNAPPED CHILD AND ME TO TRAILER IN THE WOODS. DON'T KNOW WHERE! HELP! TAMARA CORBIN

23

TAMARA

It was almost six o'clock before Lemoyne decided he'd had enough of sitting under that tree.

By then she had a plan. Wasn't much of a plan, but anything was better than just pacing around that sticky trailer; she couldn't even sit down for more than a minute or two before her nerves popped her up again. There were cheap chintz curtains on the two front windows, and she pulled those tight closed and tucked the ends in under the mesh screens. None of the bedroom or bathroom windows had curtains; she used towels and dish towels to cover those, fastening them around the screens. Hid the work she'd done on the screen in the small bedroom with an extra towel, to make sure Lemoyne wouldn't be able to tell from outside that it'd been pried partway loose. Now if he wanted to come looking he wouldn't be able to see in, tell where she was or what she was doing. Wouldn't answer next time he called her. Wouldn't go outside again no matter what he said or did. He wanted at her and Lauren, he'd have to come in and get them. And the minute he set foot across the threshold he'd get a face full of frying pan.

That was the idea anyway. Problem was, he seemed to've lost interest in them completely. Just kept sitting out there under that tree. She peeked around the kitchen curtain every few minutes, didn't once catch him looking this way. The only times she saw him move at all was when he lit another cigarette or took another swig out of a water bottle. As if he'd taken root there. Must have a bladder the size of Milpitas.

And when he finally did quit sitting and brooding or vegetating or whatever it was, he still paid no attention to the trailer. That last time, when she looked out, he was on his feet and stretching out some of the kinks, looking off toward the barn. Then he headed off that way, walking slow. Didn't even glance in this direction. Just walked straight to the barn and disappeared inside.

Dude was totally unpredictable. For all she knew, he was in there getting a can of gas or kerosene—dump it on the trailer and set a match to it. Lord, would he actually do something like that? Roast them in here like a couple of chickens in an oven?

She went to check on Lauren again. The girl had slept all afternoon except when dehydration woke her up and she cried out for water. Asleep now, moaning and thrashing around under the blanket. Flush on her face was almost scarlet; her skin felt fire-hot, clammy. Bad fever—her temp must be a degree or two over a hundred. And there was nothing to do about it except keep her warm, keep feeding her liquids. Wasn't any aspirin, no medication of any kind in the trailer. She needed a doctor, maybe an IV—

Outside, something made a sudden shrill whining, humming noise.

Tamara hurried to the kitchen window. Empty yard was all she saw; Lemoyne was still in the barn, the door closed. That was where the noise was coming from, inside the barn.

Power tool. Saw, sander, something like that.

She waited there for a time, breathless, flapping her ears. Wouldn't have surprised her to see him walk out carrying a chain saw and wearing a hockey mask like Freddy Krueger. Nothing he did would've surprised her. But it didn't happen. Nothing happened except that the noise went on, stopped for a few seconds, started up again. Grinding and buzzing now . . . sound a saw blade made cutting through wood.

Building something out there. What?

Coffins?

Wasting time, Tamara. As long as he keeps on doing it, you don't have to worry about making noise in here.

First thing she did was pick Lauren up and carry her into the larger bedroom, where it'd be quieter and cooler with the window cracked open. Then she attacked the screen in the other one again. Imagined that loose bottom screw was Lemoyne's head and she was gonna yank it right out of his neck. Whenever the yowling power tool quit, she did the same until it started up again.

Hard, tiring work. Her arms began to feel as heavy as the pan, little shoots of pain running up them into her armpits. Sweat poured off her; she could smell herself, sour and gamy, and the smell turned her stomach and made it ache. Once she had to stop and rest for a minute because she felt woozy. Too much strain, not enough food, the sticky heat in there.

Then, seemed like all at once, she heard the squeal of ripping metal, felt the screw start to pull out of the wall. Fresh strength flowed into her; she gave half a dozen violent yanks and twists . . .

Got it!

The screw popped free, leaving a jagged hole in the wall, and the corner gap widened by several inches on both sides. She dropped the pan on the bed, hooked all her fingers in the mesh, and managed to bend the frame part of the way up toward the top corner. Rip that top screw loose and she'd be able to warp the screen away from the window. Stand on one of the chairs, wedge her body up there . . . she'd get through that opening if she had to break the glass to do it.

The power tool stopped whining, and this time it didn't start up again. She stood panting, dripping sweat, straining to hear. Other, fainter sounds came to her—rhythmic thuds, hammer blows. Building something out there, all right. And it didn't matter what, as long as he kept on doing it long enough for her to get that second screw out.

Only he didn't.

Sudden silence.

Tamara played statue. The stillness stayed heavy and unbroken except for bird sounds in the trees. She'd been making a lot of noise . . . had he heard her? On his way over here to check?

Her strength ebbed again; she was aware of throbbing pain in her arms and upper back when she lowered the frying pan. On her way to the kitchen, the wooziness came back. She had to lean against the wall to steady herself before she was able to draw an edge of the curtain aside.

He wasn't out there. The barn door was shut. Still inside?

She waited, watching and listening.

Emptiness. Quiet as dust.

She stayed there a long time—what seemed like a long time anyway. Nothing changed outside. She told herself to go back to work on that screen. But she didn't know where he was and sounds carried in this kind of heavy late-afternoon hush and she was afraid to risk it.

Come on, asshole, make some more noise out there!

The hush went on unbroken.

She stood at the window for a time, frustration like acid in her mouth and throat. Went to check on the kid again, then made herself sit down and rest, then looked out the window some more. Daylight began to fade out of the sky, shadows built and lengthened among the trees and across the weedy front yard. The barn door stayed shut.

What the hell was he doing in there now?

Nightfall.

Thick-dark and moonless, the kind of country night where you couldn't distinguish one shape from another more than a few feet away. There were stars, millions of them, no light pollution up here, but they seemed dull and remote, didn't give off much light. Crickets set up a racket in the tall grass, thrumming like a pulse. Up in the tree above the trailer, something that sounded like an owl let loose with a deep-throated cry—a mournful sound that raised up gooseflesh on her arms.

But at least Lemoyne didn't come crawling out with the rest of the night creatures. Whatever he was up to in the barn, he wasn't doing it in the dark. Tamara could see streaks and spots of light around the edges of the door, through chinks in the front wall.

She kept the lights on in the trailer. Good thing he'd turned the electricity on earlier; be twice as bad waiting here in the dark. She heated the rest of the soup, made herself eat some, woke Lauren up, and fed her a few spoonfuls. Girl could barely swallow. Didn't cry or complain, just lay there with her big eyes staring dully—half comatose from the fever. The day's trapped heat was easing now; a faint breeze blowing in through the open bedroom window had some chill in it. Tamara slid the one half all the way shut. Risk of the kid getting pneumonia was high enough as it was.

An idea came to her. She'd used up all the towels, but the bed in the small bedroom had two cased pillows; she took off the cases, slipped the frying pan inside one and doubled it into the other. Then she shut off the bedside lamp, and in the faint light from the living room, went to work on the screen again. The pillowcases muffled the noise a little, but not much—not enough when she started animaling the pan under the frame. The sounds then seemed as loud as hammer blows in her ears.

She went quickly to check outside. Empty darkness except for the scraps of light from inside the barn.

Back to the screen. Slow, now, slow. Steady rocking pressure, hold the noise down to a minimum. That's it. That's it.

Time telescoped, expanded, telescoped again. Pain, stiffness, fatigue forced her to stop and rest at four- and five-minute intervals. And every time she heard a noise outside, any noise, her heart skipped a beat and she stopped again, to listen for Lemoyne.

But he didn't come.

As if he'd completely lost interest in them, forgotten they were in here. Not that she believed that for a second. No hope in that notion. He'd come for them sooner or later. And when he did they better not be here.

Slow-rocking that pan back and forth, back and forth.

And still no Lemoyne.

And still that screw wouldn't come out, that fucking stubborn little hunk of metal standing between them and freedom would not come out . . .

24

We searched the house top to bottom, a fast, professional toss. And we did it with the lights on. The only person they were liable to attract at this late hour was Robert Lemoyne, and I wanted him to walk in on us. Real bad, I wanted it.

KIDNAPPED CHILD

Had to be a young child, a little girl judging from the scatter of toys in that basement room. How young? Five, six, seven? Not as old as Emily, but it could've been Emily—any kid was vulnerable these days. Thinking that made me all the more furious.

All right. Three possibilities in this case. Lemoyne had a daughter and the second of his ex-wives had custody; it could be one of those things. But the basement room, the padlocks on the door and the closet door, argued against a family snatch. If the victim was the child of somebody he knew, it was likely a onetime thing. If the victim was unknown to him, it was likely a worst-case scenario. Serial pedophile. Maybe a serial killer. One of those subhuman monsters who preyed on children for their own sick gratification and then broke them and threw them away.

In any case, Tamara had stumbled into it. Saw something that made her suspicious enough to run the background check, and then last night made some kind of blunder that landed her in his hands. Her and the kid, locked up in the basement room, and the only thing she could do was leave a desperate message on the closet wall. And today—

TAKING US TO TRAILER IN THE WOODS

Where? Could be anyplace. Northern California, southern California, Oregon, Nevada . . . any damn place in the country. There were no unpaid bills to give us a clue, and no receipts; either Lemoyne got rid of them or stored them somewhere—not in the garage because Runyon found a key and went out there to check. No other clues around, either. And no sign of Tamara's credit cards or driver's license; he'd probably tossed them into a trash bin after abandoning the Toyota. There wasn't any child porn or sick souvenirs or anything along those lines—not that that meant much one way or another. Just those crayoned words on the closet wall. And they still weren't enough to bring in the cops yet.

In the living room, while Runyon continued to poke around, I called Mick Savage on my cell phone. "New developments," I told him. "Better you don't know the details. How deep have you gotten into Robert Lemoyne's background?"

"Pretty deep, but there's nothing so far."

"He own a second home anywhere?"

"No way," Mick said. "He doesn't even own the one in San Leandro. Long-term lease."

"What about ties or access to rural property of some kind? A hunting or fishing club he belongs to, for instance."

"Uh-uh. He's not a joiner, isn't even registered to vote."

"His ex-wife, the second one, the mother of his daughter . . . what's her name?"

"Mia Canfield."

"Didn't you tell me she's from someplace rural?"

"More or less. Little town called Rough and Ready, near Grass Valley."

"And Lemoyne lived there with her while they were married?"

"Right, he did."

"See if you can find out if she's still in Rough and Ready. If not, where she's living now. In any case, on what kind of property and if it's a house or a trailer."

"You mean a mobile home?"

"Trailer," I said. "Trailer in the woods."

"I'm on it," Mick said. "Call you back as soon as I have something."

Runyon had been listening. He said as I pocketed the cell phone, "Stay here or wait outside?"

"In here. Lights off."

We went around the place throwing switches, returned to the living room by flashlight. I checked the street outside. Quiet, sleeping. All the houses I could see were dark now. We settled down to wait on opposite ends of an old couch with squeaky springs.

Sitting there, I had a flashback to the time, years ago, when I was a kidnap victim—taken at gunpoint by a man I'd sent to prison, driven to a remote mountain cabin, chained to a wall, and left there to die. Three months I'd spent alone and shackled in that cabin, during which time I'd nearly lost both my sanity and my humanity. Time had built a wall around that period of suffering, brick by brick, and the wall had gotten thick enough so I seldom thought or dreamed about those lost months anymore. But Tamara's abduction had breached the wall, allowed the images and emotions to leak through.

Here one day, gone the next—suddenly, without warning. Family, lovers, friends, business associates left wondering, desperate for news and dreading what the news might be. So much of that kind of lunacy these days, the high-profile cases like Chandra Levy and Laci Peterson, all the low-profile tragedies that never came to the attention of the media or were ignored because they weren't sensational enough. Some disappearances never explained, others resolved after months or years and too often with grisly results. Even the high-profile cases quickly shunted aside in favor of the next one to come along; human beings forgotten except by their families and the compilers of statistics. That was what would've happened in my case, if I hadn't managed to escape from that cabin and track down the man who put me there; and at that, the media splash following my return had lasted only a short while and now the incident was remembered by only the few who had been directly affected. It hurt like hell, remembering and thinking of Tamara going through the same kind of thing I'd endured, of her becoming just one more statistic—missing and never found, victim of foul play . . .

Runyon was saying something. "What was that, Jake?"

"Thinking out loud. If Mick can't find a lead, then what?"

"No choice. We'll have to take it to the law."

"Could mean trouble for us. Tamara's message might not be enough to justify criminal trespass."

"I know it. Too many missing persons and child abductions these days, and in this goddamn litigious society everybody's afraid of a lawsuit. The law can't push as hard as it used to, or afford to give as much latitude to get the job done. They . . . ah, Christ."

Runyon said nothing, but it was plain he felt the same.

"If they do try to bust our chops," I said, "I'll take full responsibility. Right now I don't give a damn about my license, but there's no reason you should have yours suspended."

"The hell with that. Joint decision, joint responsibility."

"Mick better come up with something, and fast. I want it to keep being up to us, Jake. Until we know one way or the other about Tamara and the child."

"So do I."

One way or the other. Alive or already dead.

When the cell phone went off, I was in that shutdown, half-dozing state you can sometimes drift into in a situation like this, brought on by a combination of inertia and an overload of tension. The noise sat me bolt upright on the couch, fuzzy-headed for a couple of seconds until I realized what it was. I muttered a profanity and dragged the thing out of my pocket.

"Got something," Mick said. "Mia Canfield Lemoyne owns rural property in Rough and Ready, inherited it from her father. Looks like that's where she and Lemoyne lived when they were married."

"Still living there now?"

"I can't find any record of her whereabouts after she divorced him three years ago. Probably means she moved out of state with the daughter. If he's paying alimony or child support it's not through his checking account, so I couldn't trace her that way."

"But she does still own the property."

"That's the interesting part. It's still in her name, and the taxes are current. But her listed mailing address on the tax rolls is eleven-oh-nine Willard, San Leandro."

". . . So Lemoyne is paying the taxes?"

"Looks that way. Part of their divorce settlement, maybe. The records on that are sealed."

"Important thing is that he probably still has access to the property. What's the address?"

"That's the bad news," Mick said. "All I've been able to get off the Net is a parcel number."

"What do you mean, parcel number?"

"That's the way it's listed on the tax rolls. Parcel 1899-A6. It's in an unincorporated section near Rough and Ready, and Nevada County's small—they don't have data available online on property that hasn't changed hands within the past couple of decades. Mia Canfield's dad died in 'sixty-five, when she was seven years old. She was raised by an uncle."

"Then how the hell do we find out where it is?"

"I should've been able to get it from Dataquick or one of the other real estate databases, but there's no listing anywhere. Same reason, probably—small county, same owner for nearly forty years. Either that or a glitch. The Internet's not perfect, though if I have anything to say about it, someday it will be."

"There must be *some* way to get the address. What about when she and Lemoyne lived there—utilities, banks, credit card companies would have records of it, wouldn't they?"

"I checked," Mick said. "Their mailing address the whole time was a P.O. box in Rough and Ready."

"Dammit."

"There's a chance the P.O. would have a record of it. I could hack into their files, but that's a federal offense. Even in a case like this . . . it'd jeopardize the agency and Sharon would kill me if she found out."

"Forget it. I wouldn't let you take that kind of risk. Isn't there any other way we can get the information tonight?"

"Not without official help, through channels."

"Take too long," I said. "So the only option is to wait until morning, get it from the county recorder's office."

"Afraid so. The county seat is Nevada City, county offices open for business at nine o'clock. I checked that, too."

I held my watch up so I could read the radium dial in the darkness. Ten past one. Almost eight hours. An interminable length of time. "What's that parcel number again?"

Mick repeated it, and I followed suit to fix it in my memory. He said then, "Luck, huh?" and I said, "And a prayer," and we rang off.

Runyon, listening, had gotten the gist of the conversation. "How far away is Nevada City?" he asked.

"Maybe three hours from here."

"Wait a while longer or head out now?"

"I'm ready to move, but once we get up there the waiting'll be worse with nothing to do. Might as well stay put for the time being. There's still a slim chance Lemoyne will show."

Slim and none. It was almost four when we left the house—right out through the goddamn front door—and there hadn't been a smell of Lemoyne the whole time.

There was no gain in taking two cars, as Runyon pointed out. He wanted to drive and I let him do it; he had better nerves and not as much personal or emotional stake in this. We left my car in the Safeway parking lot on San Pablo, in a slot next to the red Toyota. It seemed like the best place, and there was a kind of protective symbolism in it too. A feeling that if we took care of her car, we could take care of her. Another thin little hope to hang on to.

It was still dark when we picked up Highway 80 and headed east, but the first faint light of dawn had begun to creep into the sky by the time we cleared the Carquinez Bridge. Runyon drove the speed limit: there was no hurry yet. I sat staring out at the highway, watching the light traffic and the landmarks and yet seeing it all as if through a filter.

Lemoyne had had Tamara and the child at least thirty-six hours now. Thirty-six hours, and another four or five before we got to Parcel Number 1899-A6 in Rough and Ready. And maybe they'd be there and maybe they wouldn't. And if they were there, maybe they'd be alive and maybe they wouldn't.

Long haul for Runyon and me, but it was nothing compared to the nightmare the two of them had been riding.

25

ROBERT LEMOYNE

It was already dawn when he woke up.

At first he didn't know where he was. He sat up, rubbed his eyes. His head felt as if it were stuffed full of cotton, but he didn't have a headache this morning—no pain at all. Then he saw the slatted bars of daylight coming in through gaps in the walls and realized he was in the barn. On the old army cot in the storeroom. Another night on the cot in the barn.

He stood up, stretched, and went outside through the rear door. Cold. Always cold up here in the mornings. Got down into the twenties sometimes in the winter, when the snow level dropped below three thousand feet. He remembered two or three times they'd been snowed in, once for three days. Never go through that again if he could help it.

Blackberry vines were heavily tangled back there—he'd have to get the weed-whacker out, not that it stopped those suckers from growing wild. Nothing stopped them. He walked over

there and took a leak on the vines. That wouldn't stop them
either.

By the time he finished he was shivering. Should've put his
jacket on. He started back into the barn, changed his mind,
and went around to the side where he could see the trailer. Mia
was up. The kitchen lights were burning; he could see them
faintly behind the drawn curtains. She'd have the base heater
on, but not a fire started in the wood stove; she didn't like to
build fires. Lazy. Be getting breakfast ready, and it wouldn't be
much because she was lazy about that too. Eggs, toast, cereal.
Hungry. He hadn't eaten in a while.

He took a few steps that way and then stopped. What if she
was in one of her bitch moods again this morning? She'd been
in one last night . . . must've been or he wouldn't have slept in
the barn. Yelling at him, calling him all kinds of names, scaring
Angie. If he went over there now, she might start yelling again
and he couldn't take any more of that. It'd wake up Angie,
scare her all over again. She was only six years old, she didn't
understand grown-ups fighting and yelling all the time.

His head hurt a little now and the cold made his teeth chat-
ter. He turned and hurried back inside the barn and found his
jacket and put it on. The first thing he saw when he put on the
lights was Angie's dollhouse. Pride swelled in him when he
looked at it. Best damn dollhouse anybody ever built for his
kid. Biggest, too. Too big for the trailer. But he just couldn't
stop adding stories, adding rooms—it was three stories now
and twenty-two rooms. When he finally finished it, got it all
smooth-sanded and trimmed and painted, Angie would be so
excited she'd probably wet her pants. She didn't know what he
was building out here in his workshop. Mia didn't know. His
secret. His big surprise for his little girl.

Put a smile on his mouth, thinking about how her face would light up and she'd throw her arms around his neck and tell him it was the best present she'd ever had. Made him want to do some more work on the dollhouse, as early as it was. He took a piece of plywood from the stack, measured it carefully, then turned on the bench saw and put on his goggles and cut four new wall sections. He added those to the stack he'd already cut—a pretty tall stack, now, but you never knew how many wall sections you might need. When he was done with that, he used the belt sander on some of the sections he'd already fitted until the grain felt smooth as glass.

The ache behind his eyes got worse and finally made him stop. He took two more Percodan—getting low, he'd have to finagle a new supply pretty soon—swallowed them with the last of the mineral water, and sat down on the cot and lit a cigarette and waited for the pain to go away. But it didn't. Dulled a little, that was all. He got up and went to the front of the barn and stepped out again into the cold morning.

Lights on in the trailer. Mia, Angie . . . only it wasn't, not anymore. That little girl in there wasn't his little girl. Looked like her, but she wasn't Angie. And the woman wasn't Mia. Black, not white—Dark Chocolate. Strangers.

He went back into the barn and sat on the cot again. Angie, gone. Mia, gone. For three long years he'd been alone.

Alone.

Except for strangers in the trailer. Two of them this time. Why had he brought them here? The little girl, yes, because for a while he'd tried to make himself believe she was Angie. But Dark Chocolate, why her? He couldn't remember, couldn't think straight. His head hurt so bad now he felt sick to his stomach.

But he knew what he had to do. He didn't have to think about that. He knew in his gut, and that made the hurt even worse because he never wanted . . . he only wanted . . . all he ever wanted . . .

He got up and found his shovel and pick and and took them out the rear door and around past the blackberry tangle and through the trees and up onto the little knoll. The grass grew tall up there—grass and ferns and milkweed. So tall he couldn't see the graves even when he was standing right in front of them.

He tore some of the grass away, pulling up huge clumps and hurling them away. Then he could see the graves. One large, one small. No markers . . . he didn't need markers to know . . . they deserved markers, didn't they? A little moan came out of his throat. Wetness leaked from his eyes.

Angie. Mia.

Alone.

For a long time he stood looking down at the grassy mounds. Cold wind dried his cheeks, started him shivering again. He listened to it in the trees, in the eaves of the barn. It made sounds like a shrieking harpy's voice. Mia's voice. Screaming at him that last night, calling him names, telling him she'd get a restraining order if he didn't leave her alone, telling him she was going to sell the property and take Angie away, back east someplace, telling him he'd never see her again never see her again never see her again until he couldn't stand it anymore and he'd stopped the shrieking harpy's voice . . . he'd lost control and he'd . . . and Angie, she'd come out of her bedroom crying and saying Don't hurt Mommy leave Mommy alone! and he'd . . . his head felt like it would burst and he'd swung out blindly and the crying stopped too and Angie . . . all the blood on her face where she'd hit the wall and she didn't move . . . both of them lying there so still . . . oh God no! . . . not Angie, his baby, she couldn't be . . . he couldn't have . . . she wasn't dead she wasn't dead!

She was dead.

And he put her in the ground, put Mia in the ground, and went away and tried to pretend none of it ever happened, Angie was still alive, none of it ever happened. And then one day he saw her playing on the street, he was so sure it was her. And he took her. And brought her up here and put the screens on the trailer windows and kept her here and tried to make her play the game in the woods, play with her toys, play on the swing set, showed her his dollhouse surprise, but she wasn't Angie and all she did was cry and cry, like the other one who wasn't Angie cried and cried, like the one in the trailer now who wasn't Angie cried and cried . . .

The first two were over on the far side of the knoll, by the trees; he didn't want strangers sleeping too close to his family. He took the pick and shovel over there and found new places and dug two more graves in the soft earth, one large and one small. Dug them deep, deep, like he had all the others, so animals would leave them alone and they could rest in peace.

When he finished he was tired and thirsty, but his head didn't hurt so much anymore. He put the tools back in the barn and made sure the gun was still in his jacket pocket and then went out again and walked slowly to the trailer.

Now that it was time, he'd do it quick like he had before. The last thing he wanted was for anybody to suffer.

26

TAMARA

She'd just woken up, flat on her back on the single bed, held there by the weight of exhaustion, when the skirling noise of the power saw cut through the early-morning stillness. Deep into the night she'd worked on that screen, until her arms and body were a mass of hurt and she was too weak to lift and maneuver the frying pan. All but collapsed on the bed and passed out for a while and then alternately jerked awake and fell back into a matrix of crazy, terrifying dreams.

She was so foggy she thought at first she was dreaming the saw noise. Then it was like getting a jolt of something, adrenaline or speed, and all at once she wasn't foggy or exhausted or lying down half dead. On her feet, the frying pan clutched in stiffened fingers, ripping at the screen and that last clinging screw with all the strength she had left. It was close to coming out, had to be almost free, this kind of hell-with-the-noise effort was all it would take. Had to be!

The shriek of metal slicing through wood stopped and pretty soon the other burring sound started up. That was even better because it stayed loud and steady instead of stop-and-go. She manipulated that pan in a frenzy, prying and twisting. Her fingers were already scratched and bloody; scabbed cuts began to bleed again and she opened another rip in her thumb when the handle slipped and snagged flesh on a sharp edge of the screen. Blowing like a horse, sweat in her eyes, her tongue like a fat lizard in a sand hole. Thinking: Keep it up out there, you son of a bitch, just give me a little more time, a little more time . . .

Breaking loose?

Yes! Squeal of ripping metal, the pan slipping again as the gap suddenly widened and the screw came flying out.

A kind of wild joy welled up in her. She threw the pan down, stepped back for leverage, slid her fingers through the mesh. Now that the one side was free, she was able to bend the screen away from the window; the other side of the frame dug into the wall, putting enough pressure on those two screws to bend them sideways. The gap widened, kept widening. Another few inches and it'd be wide enough for her to get up to the window—

The burring sound quit.

Quiet again. Dead quiet.

No, not when she was this close! Come on, come on!

Birds chattering, nothing else.

She let go of the screen, staggered into the kitchen to the window. Her stomach churned. Skin on her neck crawled.

Lemoyne was standing in front of the open barn door. Just standing there, looking at the trailer.

But he hadn't come outside because he'd heard her. Looking

was all he was doing. Ten seconds, fifteen he stood there . . . and then he turned back into the barn, shut himself inside again.

Back to the bedroom, shaky, wiping her face. There was a folding chair in there; she positioned it under the window, waited a couple of minutes, but Lemoyne didn't start using the power tools again. Couldn't afford to wait any longer. She got up on the chair, took hold of the screen.

A couple of pulls, pause to listen, check the gap. Again. Again. Again. Wide enough? She moved the chair and tried to squeeze her body up between the bent screen and the window. Almost, not quite—wedged her shoulders, scraped skin off one arm. Too goddamn fat! Get out of this, she'd lose another twenty pounds if she had to turn anorexic to do it.

Pull, pull, pause.

What was he doing in that barn now?

Pull, pull. The deadness was back in her arms and upper body. Couldn't keep this up much longer.

Pull, pull, check the gap.

There! Tight fit, but she could make it. Had to make it. Would make it.

In the other bedroom Lauren lay so still under the blanket that Tamara, coming in, was afraid she might've slipped into a coma. No, just deeply asleep. Still running a high temp, her breathing labored and wheezy, but her color seemed better than it had yesterday. Or maybe that was just imagination, wishful thinking. She lifted the child, making sure the blanket stayed tucked around her, then shook her gently, talking to her, until she was awake and more or less alert.

"We're going home now, honey. You understand? Home to your mommy and daddy."

". . . Honest?"

"Honest. But you have to do exactly what I tell you, okay?"

"I promise."

Tamara told her. Twice, slowly, to make certain the kid understood. Then she climbed up on the chair again, holding Lauren in the crook of one arm, and slid the window open.

Sounds came to her then, faint, from somewhere over past the barn. Digging? Lord . . . hurry, now, hurry!

She unwrapped the blanket, slung it over the back of the chair. Thank God Lauren was a featherweight; no problem lifting her up and through the window, hands under her thin arms. Her own shoulders jammed in the opening and she had to wiggle sideways to free them so she could lean out, lower Lauren down the outer wall. Even when she slid first one hand up to grasp the girl's, then the other, dangling her as far down as she could reach, there was still a drop of a foot or so. Lauren didn't struggle, just hung there as she'd been told. Ground looked soft enough—grass and pine needles. Tamara said a silent prayer and let go.

The child was weak from the fever; her legs collapsed as soon as she hit the ground. But she wasn't hurt. Didn't make any noise, just rolled over and then crawled back to the wall and huddled against it a couple of feet to one side.

Tamara dropped the blanket out to her, watched her wrap herself in it again. Okay, here we go. Couple of deep breaths and she was ready. She leaned up, wiggled her shoulders through the window as she had before, twisted sideways, sucked in her belly, and shoved upward, the chair skidding and toppling over behind her. The thrust got her about half out. She fumbled along the outer wall, hunting a handhold, but there wasn't anything except the window frame and she couldn't get enough purchase on that to pull herself through. Stuck.

No, dammit, she *wasn't* stuck, no way was she stuck, she'd haul herself out if she had to scrape her chubby hide raw. She twisted again, leaned forward as far as she could, got her palms flat against the cold metal, and wiggled her body and pushed with her hands. Damn big boobs kept her hung up for a little time, and then when she squeezed them through, it was her fat booty. She kept twisting, pushing, aware of stinging pain in two or three places and ignoring it. Aware, too, that she was making little grunting sounds; she locked her throat to hold them in.

Sweat greased her body, slicked her clothing. Maybe that was what finally did it. For long struggling seconds she stayed lodged there, two-thirds of the way free like a cork that wouldn't come out of a bottle. And then her hips finally scraped loose and she popped out, headfirst, tumbling down into the grass and pine needles.

She got her head turned and her arms up in time to break the fall, take most of the impact on her forearms. But her left leg got bent somehow and there was a searing burst of pain in the ankle.

She flopped over on one hip, peered at the ankle, felt it with shaky fingers. Breath hissed out of her throat. Not broken. Tender, sore . . . could she stand on it? Her gaze shifted, past the trunk of the big pine growing there toward the barn. Seemed like she'd made a lot of noise flopping down, but nothing moved over that way. Three or four seconds to catch her breath, then she pushed up one knee and managed to stand with most of her weight on the right foot. Pain erupted again when she shifted weight to the left one. Grimacing, she took a couple of experimental steps. The pain was bad—sprain, maybe a torn tendon—but at least she could hobble without falling down.

Lauren was watching her with huge, frightened eyes. Tamara forced a smile, bent and lifted her and adjusted the blanket to keep her warm.

A jay squawked loudly somewhere close by. It was the only sound in the morning hush, she realized then.

Lemoyne wasn't digging anymore.

She'd made noise falling out the window, he might've heard—

Get out of here!

The SUV was so close, the quickest means of escape, but he'd have the keys on him and even if he didn't, it was sitting right out there in the open. Only thing she could do was get Lauren and herself into the woods, fast. The dark wall of pines rose up fifty yards beyond the trailer; she went hobbling that way on a diagonal line, ignoring the pain in her ankle, using the trailer as a shield between them and the barn. Kept casting backward looks as she passed the playset, but she quit that when she stubbed against something in the tall grass and it nearly tripped her. Couldn't watch where you were going and your backside at the same time, just get the hell into those trees.

They loomed ahead, so dense daylight didn't seem to penetrate more than a few yards. She was panting and staggering when she reached them. One more quick glance behind . . . still no Lemoyne . . . and then she was into their thick clotted shadow.

Chilly, dank, smells of resin and rotting pine needles. Jutting trunks, lots of stuff growing on the ground. Hard to see. She felt an immediate fear of getting lost. She was a city girl, streets and sidewalks were her thing. What did she know about finding her way through thick woods like these?

All right, don't go in too far. Stay close enough to the clearing to keep herself oriented. She set off through the carpeting of needles, around and through the moss-hung trunks, avoiding bushes and ferns; trying to be as quiet as she could, but she couldn't help making some scuffing noise because of her bad leg. Once her foot came down on a dead twig; it made a sound like a firecracker and the skin on her back tried to crawl up her neck.

Off on her right she made sure she had glimpses of the clearing, the rutted driveway, the SUV sitting there in the sun. So far so good. Lauren didn't make any noise, just clung to her with sweaty fingers. Ahead, then, she heard the fast-running gurgle of water. When she got across the creek she could start paralleling the driveway. And once she got to the road, follow that until she found a house or somebody came along. Plan. Good plan, if her leg didn't give out, if Lemoyne would just stay in that damn barn.

She almost blundered into a half-hidden deadfall, veered away just in time. Then she was at the creek. Not much more than six feet wide, low banks, rushing water maybe a foot deep. She took a two-handed hold on Lauren, eased down to the rocky bed, picked her way across through the icy water, bent low so she could see to avoid the larger rocks. The sudden cold aggravated the pain in her ankle; it throbbed and burned so much when she put weight on it that she had to practically crawl up the far bank on one hand and one knee. She leaned hard against one of the tree trunks to rest and wait for the pain to subside.

All right, that's long enough—move.

She moved, deeper into the trees, keeping both the creek and the driveway in sight. The pines didn't grow as close together here, and ahead they thinned even more. Through the gaps between them she could see almost all the clearing—the trailer, the SUV, the barn.

And Lemoyne.

Standing near the trailer, in the shadow of the trailer—standing still the way he had in front of the barn earlier, only this time he was all tensed with his head craned forward. Staring toward where she was in the woods.

She made like one of the tree trunks, a sick, hollow feeling in the pit of her stomach. Her heart skipped a beat, stuttered, skipped another.

Lemoyne broke into a run, heading straight at her.

Saw us!

Panic spun her around, sent her plunging away from him, away from the creek and the driveway, deeper into the woods.

27

JAKE RUNYON

Five minutes in Nevada City, and you knew two certainties
about the place. The steep streets, narrow lanes, old and false-
fronted buildings, and business and street names told you it
was an old mining town dating back to the California Gold
Rush. And the bookshops, antique stores, boutiques, restaurants, saloons, and bed and breakfasts told you the rich ore being mined there nowadays was the tourist dollar. It was the
kind of place Colleen would've liked; she'd shared his interest
in history, and she'd loved to prowl bookshops and antique
stores. He didn't have an opinion one way or the other. Now
that she was gone, it was just a place like all the other places.

They pulled into the center of town a couple of minutes
past seven. Two hours to kill, so Runyon found a café that was
open on a side street off the main drag and they went in there
and crawled into a booth. He was tired, gritty-eyed, but not as
bad off as Bill. Hollow-cheeked, bags under his eyes, beard

stubble stark against a splotchy pallor. They both needed about ten hours' sleep. Caffeine and something in their stomachs would be enough for now.

"Just coffee," Bill said when the waitress brought the menus.

Runyon said, "Better eat something."

"I'm not hungry."

"Just the same. Obvious reason."

"Yeah. Guess you're right."

Runyon ate two bear claws with his tea. Bill broke a doughnut into little pieces and nibbled down about half of it. Neither of them said much; there was nothing left to say until they pinpointed the location of Parcel Number 1899-A6.

Eight o'clock. "Let's roll," Bill said. "I can't sit here anymore."

They rolled. Mick Savage had provided the location of the Nevada County Administrative Center; it was off Highway 49 on the northern edge of town, easy to find. Big, newish complex—county offices, county jail, main library. The recorder's office was in the main building, so that was where they parked, as close to the entrance as they could get.

Bill couldn't sit still there, either. He wanted to be out and moving, so they prowled the landscaped grounds—circling each of the buildings three times. On one circuit of the jail, a county sheriff's cruiser passed by and the officer inside gave them a long curious look, but he didn't stop. Just as well. As amped up as Bill was, any sort of conversation might have made the deputy suspicious and then they'd have had to waste time smoothing it over.

At a quarter of nine they waited around in front of the main entrance. "They better open on time," Bill said once. Talking mostly for his own ears. Runyon still had his engines on idle, but still he could feel the thin blade of tension himself. Getting close to it, now. No guarantees that Lemoyne had taken Tamara and the child up here, but you developed a kind of precognitive instinct when you'd been in police work a long time; he had it now and he sensed that Bill did, too. Parcel 1899-A6 in Rough and Ready was where they were, where some if not all of this business was going to finish.

A woman came into the lobby and opened the doors at nine straight up. Runyon asked her directions to the recorder's office; two minutes later they were in there and Bill was giving the clerk Mia Canfield's name and the parcel number and asking for maps to pinpoint the exact location. It took the clerk a few minutes to look it up, bring out a big book of area maps, find the one that showed 1899-A6.

Bill studied the map with Runyon looking over his shoulder. The parcel was a couple of miles outside Rough and Ready, on Old Stovepipe Road. Looked easy enough to find: follow the Rough and Ready Highway through the village, left turn on Bugeye Mine Road, left turn on Old Stovepipe and a quarter of a mile down. The parcel itself was rectangular, half again as deep as it was wide, with a creek running through it lengthwise along the south borderline; the creek and the mileage ought to be all the landmarks they'd need.

Five minutes and they were back in the car, another ten and they were taking the Highway 20 exit off 49. They still weren't talking, but only because words were unnecessary. They were a single-purpose unit, had been all along. Bill was the emotional type until push came to shove; then he was like a rock. Plenty of proof of that last Christmas, if any was needed. He sensed that you couldn't ask for a better man to partner with in a tight situation.

As they shot downhill toward the Rough and Ready turnoff, Runyon glanced over and saw that Bill had his piece out—a .38 Colt Bodyguard—and was checking the loads. In his cop days, when Colleen was still alive, he might've told him to put the gun away, it wasn't safe riding with a loaded revolver in your lap. But he wasn't a cop anymore, and Colleen was gone, and Bill knew what he was doing; he didn't say anything. If their positions had been reversed, he'd probably have been doing the same thing.

28

ROBERT LEMOYNE

When he first saw something moving in the woods, he thought it was a deer. Lots of deer up here, roaming alone or in little herds, eating up all the ground cover and crapping everywhere so you were always stepping on their turds. Rats with hooves. But then, in the next second, there was a splash of color . . . two legs, not four . . . and that brought him up short. Somebody trespassing on his property? He squinted hard, shading his eyes. And then the figure hobbled onto a patch of open ground where sunlight slanted down among the trees, and there was a ripping sensation behind his eyes that brought fragments of confusion, disbelief.

Dark Chocolate.

Couldn't be, she couldn't have gotten out of the trailer. But it was. How? Carrying something wrapped in a blanket . . . Angie? Not Angie, the stranger who wasn't Angie. Both of them trying to get away.

She wasn't moving anymore. Poised like a deer trying to blend into the background. She'd seen him, too. Deer and hunter, only he was too far away for a clear shot and he wasn't any good with a handgun anyway. All he could do was take off running. And as soon as he did, she did the same thing—wounded deer, dark chocolate deer, limping deeper into the woods.

He raced across the yard, unzipping his jacket pocket, fumbling the gun out. Another blip of sunlit color, then he couldn't see her anymore in the tree shadow. But he could hear her, even at a distance, blundering around in there. He reached the creek, trampled some ferns getting down the bank, splashed across, and then he was in the woods with her.

Where would she go? Savage pounding ache in his head now . . . he couldn't think clearly. He gritted his teeth, pinched his eyes hard with his free hand. *Think!* Where would she go? The road, across it to the thicker woods on the other side? If she made it into that stretch, there were plenty of places she could hide and he might not be able to find her. Or would she go over the boundary fence onto Brannigan's parcel? You could see the farmhouse from there, Brannigan had a big family and there was always somebody around. If they saw her . . . if he couldn't stop her . . .

Boundary fence. Wire, barbed wire. Meadow on the other side, graze for Brannigan's mangy herd of dairy cattle. No, she wouldn't go that way . . . the barbed wire, all that open ground . . . if she made as far as the fence she'd veer off . . .

The road.

He pulled up, sucking air. Pinched his eyes again, jammed the heel of his hand against one socket, then the other. The road. Couple of hundred yards of woods . . . she didn't know them, it'd take her a while to find her way through. He didn't have to chase her on foot to catch her before she ruined everything. The road, Old Stovepipe Road.

He swung around and ran back out of the trees, over the creek and across the clearing to where the Suburban waited.

TAMARA

She heard him crashing around somewhere behind her. Then she didn't hear him anymore. Must've slowed down so he wouldn't make as much noise and she wouldn't be able to tell where he was.

She forced herself to do the same thing. Would've had to anyway because her ankle was on fire and she was afraid it'd give out on her or she'd step on a rock or something hidden under the thick matting of needles and twist it even worse, maybe break it. And Lauren, small as she was, was no longer a clinging featherweight; heavy now, a constant strain on the tired muscles in her arm and shoulder.

The first rush of panic was gone. She was still plenty scared, but mad as hell and even more determined. Son of a bitch wasn't gonna get his hands on them again. Not after all they'd been through, not this close to freedom. If he got near enough to shoot her he'd better kill her with the first bullet. Otherwise she'd find a way to claw his eyes, break his balls, tear his throat out with her teeth, take that Saturday night special away from him and shove it up his ass so far the barrel be poking out one of his nostrils. Wasn't gonna hurt Lauren. Wasn't gonna stop her. Wasn't, wasn't, wasn't!

She dodged around tree trunks, hopping on her good leg, dragging the bad. How far was the road? Couldn't be too far now. She was sure she hadn't lost her sense of direction, it had to be straight ahead. Ground slanted upward here, little moss-coated humps of rock sticking out of it, thick grass and bushes and ferns and the trees close-packed again. She made it to the top of the rise, paused with her back to one of the pine boles to catch her breath and listen. At first all she heard was Lauren's breathing—raspy, liquidy, as if she might have fluid in her lungs, hot and moist in her ear.

Sudden rustling, snapping noise somewhere behind her . . . but it wasn't Lemoyne. Jay or some other bird high up in the interlacing of branches; it squawked when it flew off.

Was that a fence over there?

She focused, staring past a tangle of brush and dead limbs to a spot twenty or thirty yards away. Yo . . . fence post, wire, barbs glinting in a patch of sun. She pushed off the tree, forgetting her ankle for a second, biting down hard against the splintering pain, and hobbled that way. Once she got to the tangle she could see all the way past. Boundary fence, long stretch of it visible from there. And on the other side a wide meadow, empty except for stumps where some trees had been cut down. Above it was a section of tilled land—

And a farmhouse. Long way off, few hundred yards. Flatbed truck parked on one side, some kind of car under a carport on the other. Thin streamers of smoke coming out a tall metal chimney.

People.

Help.

Her pulse rate jumped. But the rush of relief didn't last

long. Try to climb over or through that barbed wire, she might get herself hung up and Lauren hung up . . . and she didn't know where Lemoyne was, he might be close enough to catch her before she made it onto the other property. The farmhouse was too far away for yelling to do any good; it'd just tell him exactly where she was. And even if she did get past the fence, there was all that open space over there. She couldn't outrun him with a twisted ankle. Be easy for him to catch her in the meadow, drag her and Lauren back onto his property. Or shoot them while they were out in the open, pick them off like animals on the run . . .

Her attention snagged on a long driveway that led up to the house between rows of whitewashed wooden fence. She followed it with her eyes. She couldn't see where it intersected with the road, but in the distance she could see a piece of the road itself. Cars, other farms, other people . . . all she had to do was get to the road. It had to be closer than the farmhouse. And the boundary fence paralleled the driveway, just follow the fence.

She hobbled along it, holding on to Lauren with both hands now, straining to hear over the blood-pound in her ears. Wherever Lemoyne was, it couldn't be too near . . . there were no sounds of pursuit. A berry thicket forced her away from the fence, back among and through the trees. Sharp-thorned suckers scratched her bare legs, caught at her skirt. Twigs snapped and crackled under her shoes, loud, loud. But nothing happened, she didn't see or hear Lemoyne, and when the berry thicket ended and she veered back to the fence, she was near enough to the road to see the driveway gate next door, longer pieces of the road. Empty pieces, but somebody might come along any minute. Wasn't far now, less than fifty yards.

Long, dragging seconds . . . minutes . . . she'd lost all track of time. Follow the fence, just keep picking her way along the fence.

The trees thinned again ahead. Through them she could see part of the road directly in front of her.

A little farther . . . and out of the trees finally, onto a grassy verge, onto the road itself.

Made it!

ROBERT LEMOYNE

From behind one of the pines that edged his driveway he saw her stagger into sight a hundred yards away. Watched her limp out onto Old Stovepipe Road, turn in the direction of Brannigan's place. Just what he'd figured. He ran to where he'd left the Suburban, engine idling, just far enough back on the drive so it couldn't be seen from down the road. The Saturday night special was on the seat. He put the car in gear, swung fast out of the driveway.

Dark Chocolate heard him coming, but by then it was too late for her to get away again. She took a couple of lurching steps toward the woods on the other side, stumbled back when he veered over that way to cut her off. When she tried to run, her hurt leg gave out and she fell down, almost fell on the little girl that wasn't Angie. He hit the brakes, twisted the wheel, rocked to a stop a few feet from them, and jumped out with the gun in his hand.

She looked up at him, angry and scared. The blanket had pulled away from the little girl's head; she looked scared, too.

He felt sorry for them both, but not too sorry. They were strangers. His head hurt so much and they were strangers and the only thing that mattered was taking them back and putting them where they had to be put, so he could go home and start looking for Angie again.

29

Timing.

Everything we do in this world, everything that happens good and bad, planned and unplanned, expected and unexpected, is ruled by it. Right place or wrong place, right moment or wrong moment, salvation or disaster. Runyon's intervention in last night's gay bashing and his capture of one of the perps had been a matter of timing. And now, this morning—

We went into a turn on Old Stovepipe Road, nobody around, hadn't been another car since we passed through Rough and Ready, and we started to come out of the turn and it was going down smack in front of us, less than a hundred yards away. All three of them there on the road—Tamara, the kidnapped child, a middle-aged man who had to be Robert Lemoyne. Tamara sprawled on one hip, half on and half off the pavement, clutching the blanket-wrapped little girl protectively against her body. Lemoyne hovering over them with a gun in his hand. The Chevy Suburban was there, too, slewed at an angle across two-thirds of the road surface.

The shock of it was like a blow to the eyes. I humped forward so fast I nearly cracked my head on the windshield. "Jake!"

He punched the gas, leaned hard on the horn at the same time. The blatting noise and the sudden awareness of our approach had opposite effects on Tamara and Lemoyne. She scrambled away from him, onto the grass-furred verge. He stood as if paralyzed, still in a half crouch, looking up at us out of a rictus of confusion.

Runyon braked the car to a sliding stop on the side away from where Tamara and the little girl were. Both of us were out before it quit rocking. Lemoyne straightened with his weapon pointed downward at a forty-five-degree angle to his body, and when he saw that we were both armed he stayed that way, his mouth open and his eyes bulging. I went to one knee, the .38 straight-armed out in front of me. Runyon yelled something that had no effect on Lemoyne; he kept on standing there, gawping. If he'd lifted that piece of his any higher, made any movement to cap off a round, I'd have shot him and so would Runyon. He didn't, but even so I came close to squeezing off anyway, shooting one of his legs out from under him or worse. The only thing that stopped me was the knowledge that Tamara and the child were alive and not seriously injured.

What Lemoyne did was fling the gun down clattering and skidding onto the road, the way you'd throw something that was burning your hand, and then turn and run away.

I was up and after him almost instantly. Behind me I heard Tamara calling out something, Runyon telling her to get into the car and lock the doors. Then he was running too.

Lemoyne fled straight up the road fifty yards or so, then veered off onto a rutted driveway. He had fifteen years on me and he was in better shape; he should've been able to outdistance me from the get-go. But it didn't happen. Anger and adrenaline gave me speed I wouldn't normally have had, but the main reason was the way he ran. Splay-legged, stiff-backed, both hands clamped down hard on top of his skull and elbows jutting out at right angles, as if he were trying to keep his head from flying off his shoulders. It was the weirdest gait I'd ever seen, like a comic character being chased in a Mack Sennett two-reeler. But there was nothing funny about it. It was as if he were in the throes of an uncontrollable frenzy that had thrown his motor responses out of whack.

I dogged him up the driveway, gaining with each step. He veered sideways onto a grassy clearing with an old Silver Stream trailer at the far end, and that was where I caught him, about halfway along. I grabbed a handful of his jacket and brought us both up short, jerked him around to face me. He lashed out with one hand, the other still clutching his head. I ducked away from it and slammed the flat of the .38 across the side of his face.

The blow knocked him down, flopped him over on his back grunting and moaning. I could hear Runyon coming; I didn't need the weapon anymore. I threw it to one side, threw my body down on top of Lemoyne's. He flopped again, flailing with his arms, but I got both hands on his neck and lifted his head and slammed it on the ground.

It tore a scream out of him, a high-pitched animal sound threaded with too much pain for the amount of force I'd used. His body convulsed and he bucked me off; rolled over a couple of times clenching his head again, his back arched and his legs kicking. Sweat and spittle came flying off his face, glistening in the sunlight. His eyes were rolled up so far you couldn't see the whites; something that looked like foam crawled out of one corner of his mouth.

Runyon moved into my line of sight, gave me a hand up. He said, staring at Lemoyne, "Some kind of fit."

"Looks like it. Better get him off his back before he swallows his tongue."

Together we rolled him over, pinned him facedown in the grass. I loosened his belt and stripped it off and we used it to tie his hands. When we let go of him, he twisted over on his side and lay there twitching, his irises showing again but in an unfocused stare, foam still dribbling out of his mouth.

Runyon said, "I'll get the car."

"Tamara?"

"Okay. But looks like the little girl's pretty sick."

"Call nine-eleven."

"First thing."

It took me another couple of minutes to get my breathing back under control—too much exertion for an incipient senior citizen. Lemoyne didn't need much watching, so while I waited I scanned around the property. Trailer in the woods. Yeah. The rust-flecked Silver Stream, a barn, a wellhouse, a child's playset—it all looked ordinary enough. But it wasn't ordinary. Some places give off bad vibes, and I've always been sensitive to that kind of thing. This was one. I could literally feel faint shimmers of evil, like something crawling on my skin.

Runyon's car came bouncing up the driveway. Out on Old Stovepipe Road I could see a straggle of people—neighbors, probably, drawn by the noise—but none of them ventured onto the property. The car stopped and Tamara and Runyon both got out.

He said, "County law and paramedics on the way," and I

nodded and put my arms around Tamara and held her. Normally neither of us went in for that kind of thing, but this situation was anything but normal; we clung to each other for several seconds before I broke the embrace and stood her back to get a good look at her. Scratches, abrasions, torn clothing, and the way she stood on one leg indicated a twisted ankle. Not too bad, considering.

"You've really had a hell of a time, haven't you?"

"Not as bad as that poor little kid," she said. "I couldn't believe it when you and Jake showed up when you did. I guess we're pretty lucky."

"It wasn't luck."

"No? What was it then?"

I grinned at her. "Timing," I said. "What else?"

30

TAMARA

A lot of stuff happened over the next few days.

Some of it was kind of exciting. Lauren and her being rushed to the hospital in an ambulance with the siren on full wail. All the attention while she repeated everything that'd happened to the county law, then a bunch of reporters, then a couple of honest-to-God FBI agents. More than once hearing herself called a hero for saving Lauren's life, even though she'd made a really stupid mistake there at the end that'd almost gotten both of them killed anyway.

Some of it was horrifying. The four filled graves out back of Lemoyne's barn, one adult and three children, probably his wife and the real Angie and two other little girls he'd kidnapped. And the two freshly dug graves that'd been meant for her and Lauren. And somebody telling her Lemoyne had been examined in a hospital prison ward and he had a malignant brain tumor.

Some of it she could've done without. Doctors and nurses fussing over her in the hospital ER, poking and prodding in rude ways; she'd never much cared for medical people even when she was growing up. Telling her story so many times it began to sound remote and unreal in her own ears, as if it'd happened to somebody else. Answering the same questions over and over and over. Too much attention, too many people getting in her face.

And some of it—no surprise—was same-old, same-old.

Ma: "I almost had a heart attack when I heard. That's twice in four months we almost lost you. I swear, worrying about you is going to drive your father and me into an early grave."

Pop: "Why didn't you call me that first night, tell me what you suspected? What in God's name made you go back there by yourself and prowl around that man's property? You're too reckless, you don't think before you act, you don't follow the rules."

Sister Claudia: "Of course I'm glad you saved that poor little girl's life, but you shouldn't've been in that situation in the first place. You're not a wild child anymore, you're supposed to be a responsible adult."

Horace: "It makes me crazy, thinking about what almost happened to you . . . *again*. I understand how you feel about your career, you know I do, but maybe it's time you took a leave of absence. Come back here and let me take care of you for a while. Will you at least give it some serious thought?"

Vonda: "Tam, my God, what a horrible experience. I mean, it must've been like living through a Samuel Jackson movie or something. Makes all my troubles seem pretty small, not that they *are* small. Not to me anyway. I thought Alton was gonna take Ben's head off just for walking in the front door. And you should've heard Daddy go off on him when he said he wanted us to get married in a *synagogue* . . ."

Best part, far and away, was finding out Lauren didn't have pneumonia, just needed an IV and some antiobiotics and a few days' rest, and then later on going to the hospital with Bill and Jake to see her and meet her folks. Her dad had a city government job in Vallejo and her mom was a schoolteacher—nice mixed race couple. There were a lot of hugs and a few tears; she even got a little moist herself when the mother said, "Thank you for our daughter's life."

Lauren was all smiley and happy, surrounded by stuffed animals and her Alana Michelle African-American doll. As if the kidnapping, all that'd gone down up in Nevada County, had never happened. That was the great thing about kids—they were resilient, they could get on with their lives more easily than adults because they didn't have all the grown-up baggage to carry around yet.

She got a long, clinging hug and a kiss from Lauren. And a whisper into her ear that made her blink and grin all over her face: "I love you, Tamara."

Sweet little girl. Funny, but she had a feeling she was going to miss her a little. The bonding thing. Or maybe it was more than that. In fact, she knew it was. For the first time in her life tough Tamara, independent Tamara, really wanted kids of her own . . . someday.

JAKE RUNYON

It was Saturday before he had a chance to talk to Joshua in person, at the Hartford Street flat. If he'd thought about it beforehand, he'd've known how it would be, that it couldn't be anything else. But he'd been too busy, too tired out, and so he walked into it cold.

The first thing Joshua said to him was, "I've been reading about you in the paper," with a faint sneer in his voice. "Busy week, saving lives and catching bad guys all over the place. My father, the hero."

"I'm not a hero. And I don't give a damn about all the publicity. I'm just a man doing a job—a shitty job, most of the time."

"Cops and plumbers, experts in shit."

"Why the snotty remarks? What's chewing on you?"

"Don't you know?"

"I wouldn't ask if I knew."

"You expect me to be grateful, I suppose. Forget what you did to my mother, tell you all is forgiven and now we can start being buddies."

"I don't expect anything. I did what you asked as a favor, that's all."

"Is that why you didn't tell me the truth about the bashings? Because you were doing me a favor?"

Runyon didn't answer.

"You think I don't know about Troy Douglass? Word gets around fast in the gay community. And I had to get blindsided with it from somebody else. I felt like a goddamn fool."

"I'm sorry."

"You're sorry." Voice dripping scorn. "So why didn't you tell me?"

"I wasn't sure of the real motive the last time I saw you."

"Oh, bullshit. Don't tell me you didn't know about Kenny

and Troy then. That's why you wanted to talk to him alone at the hospital."

"All right. I didn't say anything because I didn't think it was my place."

"More bullshit. Didn't think I'd believe you is more like it. Didn't think I could handle the truth."

Again Runyon was silent.

"I'm not stupid, you know," Joshua said. "Or blind. I know what Kenny is, I've known all along. Troy wasn't his first affair since we've been together. And I'm sure it won't be the last."

"Then why do you stay with him?"

"I love him, that's why."

"Enough to risk him giving you AIDS?"

"That's right. You understand what it's like to love somebody so much you can't stand the thought of losing them, no matter what." His belligerent, challenging tone. "That's how much you loved the woman you left my mother for, isn't it?"

"I didn't leave your mother for Colleen."

"But that's how much you loved her."

"Yes," Runyon said, "that's how much I loved her."

"Well, at least I still have Kenny. And I'm going to keep him. He's coming home tomorrow."

Nothing to say to that.

"You should've told me," Joshua said.

"And you're going to hold it against me that I didn't."

"Well?"

"Another reason to hate me, another excuse not to deal with me."

"I don't need excuses. I have all the reasons I need, twenty years and a dead mother worth of reasons."

No use in arguing, in any more talk; they might have been living in alternate universes, for all the connection between them. Neither of them said good-bye when Runyon left. He might see Joshua again and he might not; it wouldn't matter to their relationship either way. His son was lost to him, had been lost to him the day the Seattle court granted Andrea sole custody.

Colleen was lost to him, too, but he had his memories of her. In that respect she was still alive, he'd have her as long as he lived and breathed. She was all he'd ever needed. She was all he'd ever really had.

31

Cybil opened her door, took one long look at me standing there alone, and she knew why I'd come. I could see the knowledge in her tawny eyes, in the play of emotions across her still beautiful face.

She turned without saying anything, leaving the door open. I went in, followed her into the living room. It was warm over here in Larkspur and her air conditioner was turned on; the motor had a hitch in it that created a clunking noise every thirty seconds or so. Cybil hesitated with her back to me, then sat down in her favorite chair. I sat facing her. The air conditioner made the only sounds in the room while each of us waited for the other to speak.

"I destroyed the manuscript," she said finally. "Burned it last night."

"I figured you probably would."

"Do you think I lied to you about what it was, what was in it?"

"No. It's what you didn't say that keeps bothering me."

"I don't understand."

"Come on, Cybil. I'm not an enemy, I'm family and I'm your friend. I'm also a detective. I know when I'm not getting the whole story and the one I am getting is too pat."

"Kerry's satisfied. Why can't you be?"

"I'm not so sure she is. If this concerns her in some way—"

"It doesn't."

"If it does, she has a right to know the whole truth."

"Does she? I don't think so."

"Those messages from Dancer in the hospital—D-Day and amazing grace. They weren't just references to his unpublished novel. They were personal."

She looked away.

"References to something that happened between the two of you," I said. "D-Day. Occurred to me that could mean something other than the day of the European invasion. It could mean a special day in his life—Dancer's Day."

The words made her flinch. "Oh, God."

"Did you have an affair with him in 1944?"

"No."

"At any time during the war?"

"No."

"After the war?"

"No."

"All right, a one-night stand then."

"No."

"If you're trying to split hairs about your relationship—"

"He raped me," she said.

I stared at her.

"You're bound and determined to know the truth, all right, that's the truth. It didn't happen in June of 1944, it happened on VJ Day, 1945. Dancer's Day—Donovan's Day in his damned manuscript. The day he took what I'd never give him voluntarily."

"Jesus. What happened?"

She stared off into space for a time before she answered. And I was glad, once she started talking, that I couldn't see exactly what she was seeing inside her head. "There was a party at his apartment. An end of the war party—a lot of heavy drinking and unrestrained hilarity, all of us a little crazy with happiness and relief. Russ kept feeding me drinks and I didn't have the sense to know when to stop taking them. I remember him saying he'd take care of me, see that I got home, but in the morning when I woke up I was in his bed. Naked and alone in his bed with the worst hangover of my life. I couldn't remember a thing about what happened after the party broke up—I still can't."

"Where was he?"

"Up and dressed by then. When he came into the bedroom . . . I knew I'd been violated, a woman can tell when she's been used that way, and I screamed accusations at him. He denied it, of course. The kind of denial with a smirk wrapped up in it. He claimed that all he'd done was take my clothes—so he could get a glimpse of what I looked like without them, he said—and put me to bed."

"What did you do?"

"What could I do? It was his word against mine. Times were so different back then. Women were considered as much to blame as men, particularly in cases of acquaintance rape. And the circumstances . . . all the drinking, passing out the way I did . . . it would have made an awful scandal. I couldn't bear that, and I didn't want Ivan to know. It happened only a few days before he came home from Washington."

"You never told him?"

"Never. You know what a terrible temper he had. I was afraid of what he might do to Russ."

"Or told anyone else?"

"Not until just now. I . . . buried it. Avoided Russ as much as I could, and when I did see him I pretended nothing had happened. But inside I was a mess. Just looking at him turned my stomach."

I said slowly, "Kerry suspects, doesn't she? If not about the rape, that there was something between you and Dancer."

No response. The air conditioner made another of its stuttering noises.

"Cybil . . . straight out. Is she Dancer's child?"

"No!"

"But she could be. The timing's right."

"She's not! Ivan was her father—Ivan!"

Too much protest. She desperately wanted it to be Ivan, but she wasn't completely sure.

I said, "Dancer believed she was his. That's what the amazing grace message meant—his sly, sick little joke. And he put it all in that unpublished manuscript, didn't he? The rape, your pregnancy, his possible fatherhood."

"In graphic detail. God, he was a son of a bitch."

Yeah. A son of a bitch, a rapist, another slimy nightcrawler. It made me sorry, very sorry, that I'd saved his ass from the murder charge years ago, that I'd cut him slack and pitied him.

Cybil drew a long breath before she said, "Are you going to tell Kerry?"

"Has she ever asked you directly if she might be Dancer's daughter, or about your relationship with him?"

"No."

"Then she doesn't believe it, doesn't really want to know. No, I'm not going to tell her. Your secret's safe with me."

". . . Thank you."

"For what? I shouldn't have come here, I should've let it stay buried. In fact, I wasn't here today. We didn't have this conversation and we'll never have another one like it."

I left her and walked slowly across the landscaped grounds to the parking lot. My car had been sitting in the direct sun; it was like an oven inside. But it could've been two hundred degrees in there and it still wouldn't have been as hot as where Russ Dancer was right then.